THE DUKE AND LADY SCANDAL

"*Alexandra.*" THE word slid over his tongue like rich whiskey. He loved speaking it aloud, and that she allowed him to.

"Yes." Her thick lashes flicked up, and she looked at him with what seemed like yearning. She drew the edge of her lower lip between her teeth, then reached out to lay her hand against his shirtfront.

"I know I should go," she whispered, "but nothing in me wants to." She studied his shirtfront, teasing her fingertips along the line of buttons. When she looked up at him again, he couldn't stop himself.

He traced the backs of his fingers along her cheek, then bent to kiss the skin he'd touched. Tracing his lips up to the delicate shell of her ear, he told her the rawest truth.

"I don't want you to go."

The words seemed to set something loose in her. She reached up, threaded her fingers through his hair, and arched against him, letting her body fall into his. She closed her eyes again, and her lush mouth trembled slightly.

He'd never been hungrier for a woman in his life. But if he kissed h protect her. To protect

By Christy Carlyle

THE DUKE AND LADY SCANDAL

A Princes of London Romance

CHRISTY CARLYLE

AVON

An Imprint of HarperCollinsPublishers

THE DUKE AND LADY SCANDAL. Copyright © 2025 by Christy Carlyle. All rights reserved. Printed in the United States of America. No part of this book may be used or reproduced in any manner whatsoever without written permission except in the case of brief quotations embodied in critical articles and reviews. For information, address HarperCollins Publishers, 195 Broadway, New York, NY 10007.

First Avon Books mass market printing: March 2025

Print Edition ISBN: 978-0-06-334734-2
Digital Edition ISBN: 978-0-06-334732-8

Cover design by Amy Halperin
Cover illustration by Judy York

Avon, Avon & logo, and Avon Books & logo are registered trademarks of HarperCollins Publishers in the United States of America and other countries.

HarperCollins is a registered trademark of HarperCollins Publishers in the United States of America and other countries.

FIRST EDITION

25 26 27 28 29 BVGM 10 9 8 7 6 5 4 3 2 1

To the friends who've seen me through the last few years. Jim, Monica, Darcy, Charis, Maire, Rae, Erica. Thank you. Your kindness, encouragement, willingness to listen, and advice have helped me in more ways than you know.

THE DUKE AND
LADY SCANDAL

PROLOGUE

Bedford Square, London
September 29, 1896

DETECTIVE INSPECTOR Benedict Drake crossed his arms to fight off a shiver. A thick fog had settled over the city and put a vicious bite in the air. He'd asked the cabbie to let him out a block away, and now he'd taken up his watch, waiting in the midnight darkness for movement in the townhouse across the square.

His heartbeat roared in his ears, and he fought the urge to run across the street, rip open the front door, and finally lay his hands on the man he'd been hunting for weeks.

But this criminal was wily and unpredictable.

Drake understood that patience would serve him best, but it was bloody hard to remain still.

The man who'd entered the townhouse ten minutes ago was a petty thief, but his connection to the master criminal was clear. It was why Drake had become Amos Howe's shadow, trailing the man to gambling dens, brothels, and loathsome pits where animals fought for the pleasure of drunken men. On a few occasions, he'd considered following other leads, despairing that this particular conspirator would ever take him to the one who mattered most.

But while he might struggle with patience, tenacity was his bedrock. He never lost the scent once he'd found a trail, and intuition paired with cold, hard logic rarely failed him.

And logic told him that Howe had just led him to the heart of this criminal enterprise. The fashionable townhouse the thug had slipped into a quarter of an hour ago wasn't his. Howe had made his name in the darkest alleys of the East End, and all the haunts he frequented were in those streets.

The mastermind of the blackmail scheme resided here. Drake knew it in his bones.

He slipped his revolver from his pocket. Violence was never his preference, but he suspected the blackmailer, known only as M, would have firearms at the ready.

He couldn't be certain how many might await him inside, but he would face them alone.

This case had been classified at the highest level of security, requiring the greatest discretion, and he'd been handpicked by his mentor because of his reputation for succeeding where others failed.

Tonight would be no different.

The townhouse wasn't located in the most fashionable of London squares, but it was elegant and well lit. Someone of consequence resided here at the edge of Bedford Square.

But was that someone bold enough to blackmail the heir to the British throne?

The letters had come in red-stained envelopes, the words on them cobbled together from newspaper clippings or scrawled in a spidery hand that was barely legible. The blackmailer claimed to have letters and photographs of Prince Edward VII that, if made public, would spell scandal for the Crown.

Drake didn't much care how the prince spent his leisure hours, but the royal family cared a great deal about avoiding scandal.

And so he waited until waiting seemed fruitless.

After half an hour had passed, Drake stepped out of the concealing trees and bushes of the square and made his way into the mews behind the row of townhouses. As he approached the gate of the house Howe had disappeared into, he was met by growls and then the rapid, panicked barks of a guard dog he'd somehow failed to spot. As the creature strained forward on the chain that tethered him, Drake could see he was a poorly looking fellow—matted hair, scrawny body, and eyes that telegraphed fear rather than ferocity.

"You've nothing to fear from me," he whispered to the canine, trying for the same gentle tone his sister used with the strays she was addicted to bringing home.

The dog barked once more and then cocked an ear.

"That's right, boy. Nothing to be afraid of." But as soon as he took a step forward, the dog growled low in his throat. The creature knew what was expected of him, even if whoever owned this townhouse mistreated him.

"You're doing a good job," Drake admitted, and then noticed a light flick on beyond the house's back door. He retreated into the shadows as the dog's barks flattened to a whine.

The back door swung open, and a man's silhouette filled the space.

"What the bloody 'ell you barking at?" The man in the doorway—Howe, judging by his stocky build and battered stovepipe hat—scanned the mews and darkened back garden.

Drake ducked his head further into his high collar and willed Howe's gaze to pass him over.

Howe stepped forward. "Bleeding fool mutt."

The dog drew back, letting out a mournful yelp.

Don't you bloody dare. Drake moved quickly, darting closer while Howe's back was turned as he shouted invectives at the canine.

He was making such a ruckus that a servant poked his head out from the back door of a townhouse abutting M's. Drake shooed the man back inside with the wave of his hand.

Then he seized the moment to sprint toward Howe, who finally heard his approach and turned to face him. The thief fumbled with his pocket, but Drake had his own revolver up and pointed at the man's face.

"I wouldn't if I were you," he told the thief quietly.

In the light spilling from the open door, Howe's face turned ashen.

They'd met before, but Howe had somehow never noticed Drake's shadowing presence over the last weeks. He'd been too busy finding marks and emptying pockets.

"How many are inside?" Drake held the revolver steady.

Howe's gaze had locked on it, and fear seemed to freeze him in place.

The dozen or so crimes Drake had witnessed while following Howe would justify hauling him off to jail, but the thief was smart enough to know that the blackmail scheme was the worst of it because it involved the royal family. Few threatened the power of the Crown and walked away unscathed.

"Only me," he finally mumbled.

"Try again. How many are inside?"

"'E'll kill me," he whispered. The man seemed to reduce in front of Drake's eyes. His shoulders slumped, and he bent his chin down as if to protect his neck. "One word and 'e'll slit me throat."

"Perhaps you should choose your friends more carefully, Amos." Drake had always suspected that M chose a man as rough-edged as Howe to do the dirtiest work. To threaten and perhaps take fists to whoever menaced their plot, but Howe was proving to be a rather flimsy thug.

"We'll go in together, shall we?" He flicked his weapon toward the back door, glancing up to make sure there were no weapons pointed at him from the windows at the back of the house. Most were curtain-covered and not a wink of light could be seen. Any watcher worth his salt would know darkness gave him a better view.

Howe approached the door, pressed a hand to the frame, and then seemed to recover a bit of his confidence. He pivoted to face Drake and then took a wide-legged stance, his sizable arms crossed. "You want in, you'll 'ave to go through me."

A little bravado had entered his tone, and the man would be a formidable opponent if it came to fisticuffs. But one of them was armed.

Drake lowered his gun a few inches, pointing it at the thief's chest. "A bullet will go through you a lot quicker than I could. Care to risk that?"

Cowering near the step, the guard dog let out a low, ominous whine.

Howe glanced behind him as if he'd heard something that Drake couldn't.

"Move aside." Drake took two steps closer. "Now."

The dog stood and emitted one brave bark as Drake approached.

Howe gave a stubborn shake of his head. "I let you in, I'm as good as dead in the grave."

He was stalling.

Then Drake heard why.

A man's voice rang out at the front of the house. Then the rustle of traces and the clatter of horse hooves.

Drake rushed Howe so fast, the man barely had time to uncross his arms before Drake shoved him bodily and opened the back door. He registered a bare kitchen, then found a short staircase up to the ground floor. There were no furnishings in the house, and the light he'd seen out front had been doused.

He took it all in as he reached the main hall, but he could hear the carriage departing even as he wrenched the front door open.

Black and unmarked, the enclosed carriage with a single, dark-coated driver departed at breakneck speed, careening out of the square into the main thoroughfare.

He didn't know if it was the elusive M or another conspirator who'd flown, but he had one of them at hand, and he meant to get all he could out of Amos Howe.

Stomping back to the kitchen, he found Howe heading toward the mews.

"Don't make me chase you," Drake shouted. Then he lifted his revolver, pulled back the hammer, and hoped Howe heard the click.

The thief turned back to him. "I 'ad nothing to do with those letters."

Drake approached, keeping his eyes on the man's hands. Howe looked defeated again.

"Tired of all of it, if you must know," he mumbled as Drake clapped shackles around his wrists.

The thief was making this so easy that a shiver of warning trickled down Drake's back.

He led Howe back inside. This time, he noticed the button Howe must have pushed. A black button in a gold-plated case attached to the frame of the kitchen threshold. A white-painted wire ran along the door frame and disappeared behind kitchen furnishings.

"You alerted him." Drake shoved the man into the kitchen and used his belt to lash Howe's handcuffs to the kitchen's grand enamel-glazed iron stove.

"Stay put." Drake met Howe's gaze as he finished the knot. "This is your last chance to tell me how many men I'll face upstairs."

Howe shook his head. "Not a one, Inspector. Came for a delivery, then you appeared, and it all went tits up."

"A delivery?"

"When 'e wants me to deliver something, I meet 'im." Howe shrugged. "Then take it where it needs to go."

"Like a letter threatening the Prince of Wales?"

Howe swallowed and ducked his head again. "Wanted nothing to do with that, I tell ya."

Drake didn't believe him. Not a single bloody word.

But even if he'd believed Howe was telling the truth, he had to know for sure.

So he searched every room. Each empty, unfurnished room. The townhouse was as clean as if it was set for sale or had just been leased. Where there were built-in cupboards, drawers had been left open. Closet doors stood ajar. And the clatter of his own footsteps was the only sound he heard as he checked every inch of the structure. He even released the ladder hidden in an upstairs hallway ceiling to access the attic, but it contained only dust and a skeletal framework of wooden beams.

He slammed a fist against one of those solid beams.

Hell and damnation to false leads. There'd been far too many in this case.

Perhaps Howe *had* known he was being followed, and his surprise in the back garden had all been feigned. And if Howe had been aware, then the menace known as M had too.

And led him to an empty townhouse.

He let out a weary sigh, and fatigue washed over him. But he sucked in a breath to fill his lungs and fire his brain. There was still much to do this evening.

First, he found a cab. Then he hauled Howe into it. Just as he was about to climb inside himself, he heard a mournful howl from the back of M's empty townhouse.

"What's his name?"

Howe grumbled and gave one firm shake of his head.

"The dog, man. What's the dog's name?"

"How the bleedin' 'ell should I know?"

The debate in Drake's mind took only a moment. As soon as he considered Helen's opinion on the matter, there was no question.

He turned and sprinted through the house and out the back again. The dog snapped its head up and looked shocked to see him.

"I may not have solved the case tonight, but I can get you a decent meal."

He used a rock to bash the lock that kept the dog tethered to the townhouse's wall and then walked him through the townhouse by the broken chain. The hound hunched low as he walked, as if trying to be furtive, fearful of whatever lurked within the pristine walls.

"You won't ever see him again," Drake told the dog. "I can promise you that much."

CHAPTER ONE

The Prince family's townhouse near Mayfair, London
October 6, 1896

"I'M SORRY, little sister."

The words came while Alexandra Prince was in the midst of packing. Or rather the tornado of it. Never having ventured much further than the city, she'd had no idea what to bring and most of the clothes she owned lay strewn across her bed.

But it was all for nothing. There'd be no journey.

Her brother sounded genuinely forlorn, but it didn't dull the sting. Didn't make her chest feel any less hollow.

"Mr. Van Arsdale only wants Eve and me, and his letter didn't arrive until today."

Allie kept quiet, pressing her lips together. Her heart ached—a real searing pain in the center of her chest—and she knew that the moment she said anything, she'd cry. Then Dom would feel worse and try to comfort her. And she couldn't think of anything she wanted less than pity.

"You know how long it takes for post from America." Dominic flicked the letter against his palm as if annoyed with the single sheet of thick linen stationery. "Why the hell couldn't he have sent a telegram?"

"It's all right, Dom." She forced the four words out and a tear immediately slipped down her cheek, warm and unwanted. She swiped it away quickly.

"Eve and I wanted you to join us. Do not doubt that." The edges of his mouth curled in a grimace and his jaw tensed the way it always did when frustration bore down on him. He cast his gaze over her clothing-strewn bed, and she thought she caught a glassy look in his eyes.

Allie turned her back on him because her own tears wouldn't stop now that they'd started.

"I'll see you in the morning, and we can talk about the other matter," he finally said softly. "Please know how sorry we both are."

"I know."

Once he'd gone, Allie slumped onto her bed, not caring if she crushed her new traveling dress. Pressing a fist to her mouth, she tried to hold in the frustration welling up, but it did nothing to stem the tears. A good cry and she could move past this. It wasn't as if it was a great surprise.

They were going, and she was staying behind. That was how it had always been.

She'd been foolish to believe it could be otherwise, even if Eveline and Dominic had been eager to bring her on this expedition. Mr. Van Arsdale, the American collector financing their venture, had no reason to include her. She had no expertise in Viking antiquities. Or Anglo-Saxon ones for that matter.

He'd hired the two Princes best suited to the expedition.

And once again, Allie didn't quite fit, and that was familiar at least. She'd long felt that she didn't fit in her famous family.

Oh, she had no doubt of her siblings' love. Nor her mother and father's while they were alive. Her mother had been quite doting. And in the long line of their history, the Princes were known for the solidity of their familial bonds.

But they were also known for their exploits, and that's where Allie came up short.

The Princes weren't titled and they were only comfortably wealthy, but they *were* a family of eminent individuals.

Whatever a Prince set their mind to, they would achieve.

Allie's father most of all.

Octavius Prince had been trained in history at Oxford, but his fame had come from his archaeological finds, his nose for discovering buried treasure, and his relationship with Queen Victoria, who'd once called upon him to retrieve a gem that had been *misplaced* from the royal holdings.

The renown he'd gained from that undertaking had won him the hand of a viscount's daughter. And Allie's mother had earned her own quieter kind of fame by detailing, via vivid drawings and eloquent writing, the expeditions they'd undertaken together.

Dom and Eve had accompanied Papa on adventures as soon as they were old enough.

And Allie?

She'd been raised to be Mama's companion. Sickness had plagued her in childhood, so she'd learned to love quiet endeavors—reading, writing, knitting, and, eventually, bicycling in London's parks.

She rarely got into the sort of mischief her siblings had, but she'd yearned to claim the confidence that came with being a Prince. And yet, regardless of how she aspired to, she didn't seem to possess the Prince propensity for notable accomplishments. She did love research, especially genealogical investigations or tracing the histories of lady pirates. In fact, she'd begun writing a book about lady pirates as a child—a mostly fanciful fiction then that had now become a more serious endeavor.

But she wasn't interested in finding buried pirates' treasure.

Allie was much more interested in *doing* something of value than finding valuables.

Unfortunately, her own nature held her back. She was awkward, often saying the wrong thing or talking too much altogether. As a result, she had a tendency to offend when she was only trying to be of help.

Mama thought finishing school would tame her with all its rules of etiquette. But so much of it had been nonsense about giving gentlemen precedence or the place ladies should occupy in Society and those they should not. Still, at five and twenty, Allie understood that diplomacy and delicacy should be considered before blurting one's thoughts.

The difficulty was that her tongue didn't always comply.

Recently, there'd been an *incident* with a long-standing customer of the family antique shop, Princes of London, and the nobleman had complained. As head of the family, her brother took it as his purview to smooth over such matters, and he had, but he'd yet to deliver the admonishing talk that inevitably followed such incidents.

In the morning, as he'd said, they would have that discussion.

So Allie fell into bed—once she'd cleared it off—still nursing disappointment and dreading whatever lecture Dom would deliver in the morning.

After a fitful sleep, Allie woke early, washed and dressed, and then made her way to the family antique shop on Moulton Street just as the first hints of the dawn lit up the brick building.

She'd considered going in later, after Dom and Eve had departed, to avoid goodbyes and apologies and whatever admonitions Dom felt compelled to deliver. But she wasn't a coward, and opening the shop was her responsibility.

Though Dom had taken to sleeping in the living quarters that had once been the family's home above the shop, he still took little interest in the everyday running of Princes. Eve and Allie suspected the only reason he resided upstairs was to shield them from his dalliances.

Allie hadn't gotten three steps past the front

door before she heard her siblings whispering in
the back room.

"Let me speak to her," Eve said softly.

She was the most even-tempered of them all. Allie
preferred to deal with Eve when trouble was afoot.

"No, I shall." Dom's insistent tone did not bode
well.

Allie took a deep breath to steel herself. His lectures weren't nearly as strident as their late father's
had been, but he did have a terrible habit of believing himself right about very nearly everything.

"*Don't* mention Aunt Jocasta," Eve put in a bit
more loudly.

At hearing the lady's name, Allie felt a mix of tenderness and sadness. Though she adored her aunt,
Allie had long feared they were two of a kind. The
odd ducklings of the Prince clan. The awkward
ones who never quite fit into a family of fame and
accomplishments. The ladies who would eventually be relegated to the countryside.

Perhaps they were plotting such a fate for Allie,
but she would fight it with everything in her.

She might not be a typical Prince, daring and
dashing and devil-may-care, but she would not for-
feit the autonomy her parents had allowed. There'd
never been pressure to marry or enter into "ac-
ceptable roles for a lady," and they'd bequeathed
each of their children an equal share of the family's
wealth and of ownership in their business affairs.

No, she would not be sent off to the countryside as her aunt had been.

"What is it that you have to say to me?" she

said in as bold and unaffected a tone as she could manage.

Dom stood in the doorway between the front of the shop and its cozy back room. He turned as soon as her question was out. "Morning, Allie."

"Morning," she told him brightly.

She was prepared for this. When necessary, she *could* be diplomatic. And she certainly wasn't a child in need of lectures. If they were going to leave her to run the shop while they were away, then they needed to trust her to do so.

And in this case, she'd done nothing wrong. Lord Corning might not have liked her "too forthright manner," but Allie had only intended to help. To do what was right. And that, unfortunately, often involved telling people what they didn't wish to hear and subsequently landing her in a muddle.

Dom paced the back room as he searched for something. She suspected it was his favorite notebook and pen, which he was forever misplacing.

"I'm still sorry about the trip," he said in a distracted tone. "Both of us are, but as to the matter with Lord Corning, you can't simply keep . . ." He shrugged as if at a loss to explain. "Rushing in to *help*, particularly when it's not wanted."

"Rushing in?" Allie repeated. "I did not rush."

That earned her an extremely older-brother look. "You know what I mean." His tone remained gentle. "You're impulsive, little sister. You get a thought in your head, and you speak it. You get a notion in your head, and off you go."

Wasn't that true of anyone? A person decided

on what to say and spoke. They pondered an action and then took the action. She longed to say so but forced herself to keep mum.

"A little pause. A good deal of contemplation. Some hesitancy would do you a world of good," he called over his shoulder as he trod the polished wooden floor, still searching.

"On the shelf over there," Allie told him, and pointed to the items he'd deposited and forgotten.

"Ah." He scooped up the notebook and pen and tucked both into the pocket of his coat. "Yes, there they are."

A simple *thank you* wouldn't have gone amiss, but he was in that single-minded Dominic Prince mode that seemed to cause much of his usual thoughtfulness to evaporate.

"All I'm saying is have a care how you speak to customers while we're gone."

She understood her brother's worry about offending a longtime customer of the shop. And she also understood that as the eldest, Dom felt responsible for maintaining the reputation and success of the family's business.

He stopped and patted his pocket as if to reassure himself that the journal he'd placed there was in fact still tucked away. Then he sighed. A bit of the tension in his expression ebbed, and he gave her one of those charming tip-tilted smiles that made other ladies swoon.

"I wish you were coming, but do take care while we're gone." The genuine tenderness in his tone had the desired effect.

Allie nodded and grinned, doing her best to re-assure him. "Please don't worry, Dom. I can take care of myself."

That seemed to be the wrong thing to say. His chiseled jaw tightened and one dark brow arched in the condescending way that, unfortunately, caused Allie and her sister to defend themselves even more fiercely.

"No offending customers, little Lex."

If he imagined employing the childhood nick-name softened his admonitions, it didn't. Not a jot.

Allie had to speak. He might be the family swashbuckler, but she'd been running—or help-ing to run—the shop while he and Eve were off on digs or traveling on antiquity hunts.

"I am not a child, Dom. And if you worry about how I run Princes, perhaps you should stay and do it yourself. I've managed things on my own for years, and no catastrophe has befallen Princes."

"No one denies that you keep things afloat for all of us." Eve chose that moment to step in. "Do they, Dominic?"

As the middle child, Eve had honed her role as mediator over many years. And Allie was grateful that at least one of her siblings would defend her. But it was time that Dominic began trusting her judgement too.

She might never accomplish anything astonish-ing, but she knew how to manage Princes, even if she longed for something more.

"You do a fine job running the shop." He flicked his steel-blue gaze toward Eve and then focused on Allie again. "But the incident with Lord Corning—"

"I only wished to be helpful."

Eve moved to stand in front of Dom, facing him. "We should get to the station, don't you think? Don't want to miss our train."

Dom sidestepped Eve. Color had risen into his cheeks. "You confronted the man in Parliament."

"His lordship tried to sell us a forgery and admitted that he'd already sold some onto his friends. I did him a kindness by letting him know, and I went to his private office," Allie pointed out. "You make it sound as if I stormed the House of Lords."

"I wouldn't put it past you."

"I'd offer more than a few coins to see that," Eve said, and then burst into a low, mischievous chuckle.

Allie found herself smiling despite her irritation.

Dom rolled his eyes and marched forward to pull Allie into a brief hug.

"Just keep out of trouble while we're gone. For my sake. Will you?"

"Of course," she told him once he'd released her. Though a man of her brother's reputation urging anyone to be cautious felt slightly absurd.

"And you too." She glanced at her sister. "Both of you. Be safe."

"I think we can handle the wilds of Norfolk," Eve said with her usual confidence.

Like their mother, Eve was gentle natured and even-tempered. Allie often wished she could be more coolheaded herself.

Impulsive. That was the condemnation thrown at her by Dom more often than any other.

She did believe in rushing in if the situation called for it. Wouldn't anyone?

They were off on an expedition to find an Anglo-Saxon hoard. A few documents they'd acquired from a deceased duke's estate indicated there might be one present in a coastal section of Norfolk. Eve had been doing her own research for years on a potential hoard in Yorkshire, though Dom doubted they'd find much there.

Their parents had thrived on travel and the allure of digs too. Allie was far more interested in historical documents than jewels or coins. Still, she could understand the appeal of taking a brush and trowel, digging into the soil, and coming up with something of historic merit. Every single piece that came through their shop held value because it told a story of the past. That was an aspect of running the shop that she did love. Passion for history was her birthright every bit as much as Princes of London.

Eve stepped close and bent to whisper to Allie. "Your time will come. I promise."

It was a painfully familiar sentiment. *One day*, she had been told, she'd be able to accompany Papa too. She never had, but she'd collected a lifetime of memories like this one—saying goodbye and being left behind.

Eve wrapped her in a long, warm hug and pressed a kiss to her cheek. "We shouldn't be away any longer than a fortnight."

The hired coach to carry them to St. Pancras already waited outside, and it took them only minutes to secure their traveling cases and start on their way.

Allie stood on the pavement, waving until they were out of sight. She swallowed against a lump in her throat. She'd done this so many times, and yet watching them depart without her always carried a sting.

Perhaps she could propose her own expedition, not to seek treasure, but to further her research on lady pirates. She stood pondering that possibility until the autumn breeze kicked a few leaves her way, then she went inside.

Back in the shop, she finished off the usual tasks to be accomplished before opening. The shop cat, Grendel, watched her with unusual interest.

"Nothing to worry about, Gren." It was as if the feline could sense her disappointment. "I know I'll have my turn one day. *My time to shine*, as Papa used to say."

She placed the final pieces in the main glass case, a parure of large, glittering diamonds and emeralds nestled on a platform of black velvet— the most expensive gems in the shop—with care. Allie could admire the beauty of such pieces, but they never struck her imagination the way the eighteenth-century flintlock pistol in a nearby case did. Lady pirates Anne Bonny and Mary Read might have used such a pistol themselves.

A door opened in the back room, and Allie smiled.

Mr. Gibson was their resident jeweler and repairman—his passion was horology and clock repair, but the man could fix almost anything presented to him, and he cut and set jewels to perfection. He was also an antiquarian with a breadth of knowledge of history and antiques that rivaled their father's. The two had been friends, and Alister Gibson had insisted on staying on after their father's death, despite Dom's urging that the man should take a well-deserved retirement.

"All on your own, are you, Miss Prince?"

"Now that you're here, I'm not." Allie greeted the older man with a smile.

He normally remained in his workshop, restoring recent acquisitions or setting gems, but his presence still made Allie feel less alone while her siblings were off on expeditions.

"I think coffee and scones are in order. What do you say?"

Under his silver mustache, his mouth twitched as if he might grin. "Cannot ever turn down a cup of that brew from next door, can I?"

None of them could. Princes had been blessed with the serendipity of having a coffeehouse snugged up next door. The scents that wafted over drove them all to pleasant distraction most days, and Hawlston's coffee and baked goods were every bit as delicious as they smelled.

"Back in a jiffy," Allie called while bundling into her coat.

She glanced up at the wall of clocks in the shop. Just enough time to collect coffee and treats before her friend Jo arrived for their usual Wednesday morning chat. They'd taken to meeting an hour before the shop opened to discuss books and catch up beyond the watchful gaze of Lady Wellingdon, Jo's mother.

The coffeehouse was buzzing, but Mrs. Cline, who ran the front of the cafe, smiled when she spotted Allie crossing the threshold.

Allie raised three fingers and mouthed, "Lavender scones."

The dark-haired lady manager nodded and tipped her chin toward the seating nook where Allie was allowed to wait for her order. It was just inside the kitchen, a little carved-out space big enough for a single chair. Customers weren't generally allowed in the kitchen, but since the Princes were neighbors and patronized the shop daily, Mrs. Cline made the exception.

With such a crush of customers, Allie knew she'd have a while to wait, so she pulled out the notebook she carried with her everywhere. She immediately began jotting down ideas for research expeditions she might propose to Dom when he returned.

She was done waiting for her time to shine.

CHAPTER TWO

Scotland Yard

DRAKE STRODE down the hall toward his superior's office with confidence in the work he'd done and certainty that he would finally be rewarded.

He had sacrificed sleep and meals and any semblance of a life to focus entirely on the blackmail scheme and the tangled, messy business of a prince's peccadillos. If the payoff came today, it would all have been worth it.

He'd entered the force with nothing more than empty pockets and a hunger to lift himself and his sister out of the nightmare fate had dealt them, but he was never content as a foot patrolman. Rising through the ranks had always been his goal.

Hell, he might aim higher than chief inspector one day. But for now, it was the title and role he'd sought for years, and he'd savor it. The youngest man to ever rise to such a rank, just as he'd been one of the youngest to rise to detective inspector.

He considered what he'd say when Haverstock offered him the promotion. Among colleagues, Drake tried to show only stoicism and self-control. Displays of emotion were nothing but a distraction in police work, and in the special cases that Haverstock handpicked him for, he couldn't afford distractions of any kind.

But the chief constable would expect gratitude. *Thank you, sir* seemed too little. *It's damned well time* was far too honest. *I will not disappoint you, sir* was, he knew, what Haverstock truly wished to hear. The older man had taken Drake under his wing, mentoring but also leveraging him. He used him for the cases requiring the most discretion. Cases that might require him to maneuver carefully along the bounds of the law, and even step over them if needs must.

Haverstock understood how far a man would go for ambition, and he'd been waving this promotion under Drake's nose for years.

But this case had gone beyond what had ever been asked of him. Hellish weeks without proper sleep. False leads. Last night and into the small hours of the morning, after working on Howe for a week, the thief had led him to a boarding-house. A violent confrontation with another of M's minions ended with the discovery under the floorboards of letters purportedly written by the prince and one photograph that was undoubtedly of the queen's heir in a state the Crown would never wish the public to see.

It seemed the blackmail itself had been thwarted, but M had not been identified or apprehended. And that rankled so much that Drake had taken to grinding his teeth until his jaw ached.

Like any detective, he loathed loose threads.

At the door of Haverstock's office in the deepest recesses of the New Scotland Yard building, Drake took a moment to right himself. He'd had only a moment to tidy after the night's events, but it would have to be enough.

Haverstock had demanded to be updated immediately. So Drake strode into his superior's office and handed the white-haired man a report he'd just typed himself, pecking away at the too-tiny keys through bleary eyes, and the documents found in the rooming house.

He stood, as he always did, with his shoulders as square as the window frame. He ignored his aching muscles and bruised knuckles and clasped his hands behind his back. He was well practiced at this ritual of standing tall and silent, waiting for the older man to cast judgement on the work he'd done.

His superiors might quibble with his methods, but he always did his damnedest to get results. For Drake, no other option was worth considering. He'd failed monumentally in his past, so he couldn't stomach anything but success now.

And Haverstock knew it. Drake was tagged for delicate cases because he'd proven his loyalty and discretion. Only the blackmail case had caused him to doubt the older man's decisions.

Which was why the elusive M and the drive to catch the man would keep him awake at night. He'd find him, and he'd use whatever means were required. That's what separated Drake from those he competed with for promotion and favor.

The chief constable had been seconded to Special Branch and relished the work of protecting the realm and the family that sat at the top of it. Drake preferred his work with Scotland Yard, solving crimes against everyday citizens of London, but the damnable, half-resolved blackmail matter was the case that would bring him the promotion he craved.

"Come in, Drake." The snow-haired man took the report and began to peruse it immediately.

"Hmmm," Haverstock murmured, one wrinkled finger tracing the typed lines.

Years ago, such a sound might have shaken Drake's certainty, causing his gut to twist. Today, he was exhausted and ready for the formalities of this briefing to be finished so that he could begin planning how to take on his new role.

"You continue to impress me, Drake," the old man finally said and looked up at him.

"Pleased to hear that, sir." He didn't smile. Didn't preen. Didn't allow the flare of pride he felt to soften his stance or allow himself to rest for a single moment on the commendation.

"I shall inform the relevant parties that the threat has been eliminated." He tapped the pages in front of him. "And we're certain that *all* the blackmailer's *proof* has been found and destroyed? That there are no copies extant?"

"As certain as we can be, sir. Using my informant's details, I found the photo and the two letters, which is all the blackmail letters ever referred to. My further questioning of Howe was vigorous enough that I believe he's told us all."

"Very good." He spared the photograph and letters little more than a disgusted glance before swiveling in his chair and tossing the lot onto the fire blazing in the grate. "Thank God, that distasteful matter is at an end without tarnishing the Crown and the royal family."

"Not at an end, sir. There's still the matter of M. I will find him." He felt the truth of it, even if he didn't yet know where to look for the man next. Still, he'd solved every one of his cases in a decade-long career. He'd solve this one too. "You know I won't stop until the last thread is tied up."

"I suspect the man lost his nerve and will shrink back into obscurity after his failure to cause real harm to the prince. You've done well." Haverstock allowed a rare smile. "You never fail me, do you, son?"

"Never." At the word *son*, a stab of old fury skewered into his gut. He fisted the hands he still held behind his back. Memories tried to push their way into his mind.

Breathe. Just breathe. He fought back the panic that reared up when he allowed his mind to wander those old paths. The past was cold and done. There was no life in it. Only his future mattered. Only the accomplishments he meant to stack up, only the power he hoped to wield by rising as high as Haverstock's title one day. Hell, maybe higher.

And Haverstock meant well.

God knew he wasn't *that* man who used to call Drake *son* when he'd done no more for the privilege than bed his mother and eat their food and take up space in their too-small lodging room. *Fool, vermin, a waste of space*—the vile man's favored condemnations were always followed by a strike or a kick for emphasis.

Until the day Drake had grown taller and stronger than his mother's paramour. Until the day he'd taken his siblings away from that dingy room and never returned.

His true father was a phantom. A thing of myth and wild stories his mother had conjured to give his child's mind something to latch onto. She'd claimed he was a nobleman—a duke—though Drake had never believed it. Yet sometimes he'd used it, a kind of currency to garner respect, though just as often it had backfired into ridicule.

As a green recruit on the force, he'd told a mate the story and had been nicknamed Duke ever since. At first as a form of ribbing, but now, after his peers had seen what he could do and how relentless he was about doing it, the moniker was only ever used familiarly. Respectfully.

Not by Haverstock, of course. The man relished rank above all else. The implication that Drake held a duke's blood in his veins would make it harder to treat him paternally, to feel the full weight of his power and superiority.

So Drake allowed the occasional *son* in their conversations, and endured the man's delusion that he would court his daughter one day. He'd do a

great deal to climb the ranks to sit where Haverstock did, but using a young lady as a pawn held
no appeal.

"I know what you're aiming for, Drake. But I
can't offer it to you." Haverstock seemed to note
the muscle that tightened Drake's jaw and lifted a
finger in the air. "Yet."

"When?"

"Soon, Drake. Soon. Your day will come. Stanhope will move up by year's end. That will leave
one slot for a chief inspector."

Haverstock danced enticingly over the words
while his gaze remained glued on Drake.

The man saw him as a tool. Tempered with praise
and honed by ambition. He knew the older man
understood he played a balancing act between
giving him a bit of power and always holding
something back. He wanted to keep him hungry
so that he'd work harder to prove himself, and yet
the game couldn't drag out too long.

A starving hound eventually bit back.

"I'm counting on soon, sir," Drake told him, then
shifted his stance, assuming he'd be dismissed so he
could get a bloody hour of sleep, if he was lucky, in
his office chair before the others arrived for work.

"Join us for dinner on Saturday evening, Drake.
We'll be attending a party hosted by Lord Wellingdon. He's long been a proponent of child labor
laws and is now pressing that working-class housing law I know you're keen on. Mrs. Haverstock
and Lavinia would be pleased to see you."

Drake had heard of Wellingdon. Like his sister,

he kept an eye on any laws and policies meant to help those who struggled, as they had in their youth, to keep a roof over their heads and their bellies full. He and Helen and their younger brother, George, had worked long hours when they should have been enjoying childhood.

"I would like to meet Lord Wellingdon. Thank you for the invitation. What time shall I arrive?"

Haverstock waved his hand in the air, almost dismissively. "Whenever your day here is done and you've tidied yourself. If you arrive at our home early, more time for you and Lavinia to speak awhile before we depart."

"Very good." Drake nodded and lifted a brow. "Anything else, sir?"

Haverstock reached out and laid a hand over a document on his desk. "There is one last thing. I thought you'd wish to know." He flipped what Drake recognized as a handwritten police report. "Howe was found a few hours ago."

"That's not possible." His mind ran through the memory of his last encounter with the man. "He was going to leave London."

Drake had given his reluctant informant the funds for a train ticket himself, though he thought it best not to tell Haverstock that part. The chief would see it as weakness.

"Well, he didn't do so soon enough, it seems."

Drake snatched up the paper, scanning quickly over the neatly printed words. A cold chill froze his blood, and then a boiling fury rushed in to replace it.

Howe had been found in the East End. At one of the brothels he favored. And he'd had his throat cut, just as he'd warned Drake would happen if he revealed M's identity. But he hadn't. Howe had provided clues that allowed Drake to find the blackmail materials, and yet the thief had steadfastly refused to give away the mastermind behind it all.

And he'd been terrified once Drake released him.

"I realize the man was a useful informant, but I didn't know you'd be so affected." Haverstock watched him with an assessing frown.

"I saw the man alive hours ago. Bit of a shock, sir. Nothing more."

Haverstock seemed satisfied with that reply and settled back into his chair.

Drake lifted the report regarding Howe. "I'll take this and add it to the case file."

Haverstock waved as if glad to be rid of it.

"That will be all, Drake. Won't be long before Ransome and the others get in."

Drake strode back to his desk, intending to use the few moments before the office filled to close his eyes. His chair groaned as he dropped into it, and he let out a sigh as he lifted his boot heels onto the edge of his desk. Leaning back, he let the worn leather catch his head and closed his eyes. But he couldn't find true rest.

He regretted Howe's death. The man would steal your wallet as soon as look at you, but he'd never killed anyone, as far as Drake knew.

He'd given him funds to leave London because

he'd believed Howe's claim that M would come after him as soon as the plan was thwarted. Why the hell had he bothered with a brothel rather than getting himself on a train as he'd vowed to do?

The conversation in Haverstock's office played in his mind too, and he gritted his teeth.

Soon. The word had sounded more like a taunt than a promise. He loathed being a puppet pulled along by Haverstock's strings. If he could maneuver past the man, he would, though he suspected the chief constable could thwart any such attempt.

The chief had him exactly where he wanted him, but the bit was starting to rankle.

One thing was certain. He wasn't going to court the man's daughter.

Indeed, he had no time for romancing anyone. He had a criminal mastermind to find, and he sure as hell didn't need any distractions in his life.

CHAPTER THREE

ALLIE CLOSED her notebook, satisfied with the list she'd made, though not feeling particularly passionate about any of items on it. Indeed, the idea of reorganizing the back room and the upstairs storage space at Princes intrigued her more.

If she was going to be left to run the shop, then she might as well do it her way.

She glanced up at the counter, wondering if Mrs. Cline had forgotten her. Though, in fairness, the shop was still buzzing with customers and the din of conversation had only grown since her arrival.

Then one man's voice cut across the cacophony, sounding desperate, raspy, and deep as a foghorn.

"Quiet, man! Talk like that and you'll see us all hang."

"Hangin'? Lose our bloody heads, we will," a higher-pitched masculine voice offered in a panicked whisper.

Allie stilled but the men's voices got lost in the hum of conversation. They were close, and she dared a peek around the corner of the nook she sat in. Most customers in the coffeehouse were gentlemen hunched in conversation. She wondered if the trio at the table nearest the nook were the ones she'd heard. All wore dark clothes and two sat elbow to elbow with their backs to her, blocking her view of a third man in a black derby hat.

"Most pathetic thieves I've ever known." This voice came more clearly in a clipped, elegant style. Not the London accents of the two other men.

"Guv, nobody gets the Crown's jewels," the deep-voiced man muttered in a near whisper.

"We could." The man with the upper-crust accent tsked disgustedly. "Such a lack of boldness." The words were hissed and then someone slammed a cup on the table with a thunderous thunk. A moment later, chair legs screeched on the tile floor.

Allie dared another glance out of her corner nook.

The derby-hatted man swung about, his black great coat flapping out like raven wings, and headed for a door that customers rarely used. Allie knew it led to the back alley. She'd suspected Mrs. Cline kept it locked during business hours as there was another door through the kitchen for staff to receive supplies.

But the tall man in the black coat slipped through the door as if he did so every day. His compatriots scrambled up from their table, one hesitating and loudly slurping down the last of his brew before shoving a crumpet in his pocket and then following Mr. Derby Hat out the back door.

Allie stood up so fast, her journal slid off her

lap. She bent to snatch it up and nearly collided with a kitchen staff member carrying fresh-baked goods to replenish the case at the counter.

"Watch yourself, miss."

"Yes, of course. My apologies." Allie arched back, allowing the man to pass, then pushed past the customers queuing to place an order and made her way out the back door.

The trio were clustered together not ten feet away, and the tallest lifted his head when the door hinges squeaked. He wore dark glasses that obscured his eyes, and a beard and mustache concealed the rest of his face.

After seeming to hold her gaze for a moment, he turned and strode quickly down to the far end of the alley. The two other men followed, struggling to match his long-legged gait.

Allie stood thunderstruck. Though she hadn't seen his eyes, having the tall man's attention on her for a moment made her skin crawl.

Were the trio truly planning an attempt on the Crown Jewels?

As mad as the prospect was, something told her that the man in the dark glasses could pull it off. Everything about him felt sinister, and he moved with a confidence neither of his companions seemed to share.

In a sort of muddled daze, Allie found herself at the front door of Princes and only then realized she hadn't acquired the coffee or treats she'd promised to bring for Jo and Mr. Gibson.

"There you are!" Jo stepped out of Princes and

ushered Allie inside. "What were you doing waiting at the door?"

She wrapped an arm around Allie and chafed her opposite sleeve, trying to generate some heat. Then her friend pulled back, her blue eyes widening.

"Heavens, how long were you out there? You're pale as chalk and look as if you've seen a specter."

"I overheard something disturbing, Jo."

Was she mad to give it any credence? A trio of suspicious men who didn't look equipped to pull off the robbery of the century didn't equate to a real threat. Probably just idle talk.

Except for the thread of fear in the one man's voice, and the unrelenting ominousness of the other's presence.

Jo perched a hand on one hip. "Are you going to tell me or must I guess?"

"Three men were sitting at a table and . . ."

"And?" Jo prompted impatiently, already intrigued.

"They spoke about stealing the Crown Jewels." Allie whispered the words hesitantly as if someone might overhear, though she hadn't even put the OPEN sign out yet on the shop door.

"Steal them?" Jo said, her forehead puckering under a fringe of dark hair. "The Crown Jewels? In the Tower of London? Guarded by a dozen tower warders?"

A rumbling chortle drew both of their gazes toward the entry to Princes' back room. Mr. Gibson stood in the doorway, giving in to a rare moment of mirth.

Allie had seen him smile plenty, but breaking into unbridled laughter? Almost never.

"A wild delusion even for the wiliest thief."

Jo chuckled too. "It would be impossible, and you certainly wouldn't sit about plotting at a public coffeehouse."

"Oh, they weren't plotting. In fact, two of them were quite set against it. Or even discussing it. But the other was—" A shiver stopped Allie midthought. If she described the man, she'd sound fanciful and silly.

"Only one man has tried and failed," Mr. Gibson intoned thoughtfully. "Not much to inspire future thieves."

"Was he beheaded?" Jo asked with the same bloodthirsty eagerness she always showed for one of the colorful stories from history that Allie tended to regale her with.

Gibson let out a bark of laughter. "Not at all, Lady Josephine. Indeed, Thomas Blood was pardoned by the king."

"Really? Then it's a wonder no one tried after him," Jo opined.

"A fair point." Gibson laid a rag he'd been wiping his hands with aside and strode toward the front door of the shop. "Shall I collect our coffee?"

"Yes, thank you, Mr. Gibson," Allie told him. "I wandered out in a bit of a daze."

Once he'd gone, Jo drew Allie over to the upholstered mahogany Chippendale chairs they usually sat in for their chats. "You're shockingly quiet, Allie. What's upset you so?"

"I know it's madness, but I feel as though they were serious."

Jo looked dubious, but she had her thinking face on—pursed lips, one finger tapping the edge of her chin.

"*If* one could successfully steal the jewels, and that seems an extraordinary *if*, what could a thief do with such recognizable pieces? As soon as they sold them, they'd be immediately apprehended."

"They'd break them apart," Allie told her. "You remove the individual gems, perhaps have them cut. The sapphire in the queen's coronation crown is over a hundred carats alone. Then you'd melt down the metals. Nothing would be sold as is, unless perhaps to a foreign head of state who would consider it a coup. Or to recoup the treasures taken from them, like the Koh-i-Noor, which I believe was added to the Tower display several years ago." Allie realized she was rambling and looked up to find Jo watching her intently.

"Heavens, you sound as if *you're* planning the heist."

Allie smiled and a bit of the tension in her chest loosened. "My father dealt in gems and Mr. Gibson is an expert goldsmith. We learned about the royal jewels as children, of course."

Rising from the armchair, Allie found she couldn't sit still. The pressure in her chest built again, an urging, a sense that she must do something.

"I feel as if I must tell someone what I heard."

"Can you identify any of the men?"

"I'm not certain, except perhaps by height and build. And their voices, which were quite distinct." Though she'd seen little of the tall man's features, Allie felt she'd know him upon seeing him again.

"If it would ease your conscience, perhaps you should."

"Dom told me to keep out of trouble, but I seem to stumble into it by merely going for coffee."

Jo chuckled. "You're not embroiled yet. Tell someone and be done with it." She frowned in contemplation. "Actually, I may know just the person you can speak to. My father's friend, Sir Felix Haverstock, is quite high up at Scotland Yard." She drew a pretty engraved case from the pocket of her skirt and slipped one of her calling cards free. "Tell him Lord Wellingdon's daughter sent you."

"And if he laughs me out of his office?"

"Then I'll tell my father his friend treated mine poorly, and you know Papa adores you. Oh, that reminds me. Dinner on Saturday. Will you join us? Come to think of it, Haverstock will likely be there."

"Should I wait until then?"

Jo shook her head firmly. "No, I know you, dear Alexandra. You'll fret about this until you've taken action. So go and tell the man everything you can remember while it's still fresh."

"DUKE?"

The voice of his colleague seemed to come only a moment after Drake slid his eyes closed. He willed it away. A few more minutes of sleep and his brain might feel less sluggish.

"Duke?" DS Ransome said more loudly, and a thread of impatience came with it.

"I'm awake, man. What is it?" Drake cracked one eye open and then the other. "Something urgent?"

It had to be. Ransome wouldn't be rattling his door otherwise.

"A lady here to see you, guv."

Drake frowned and stared at the sergeant as if the man had lost his mind. Their offices did not generally take walk-in visitors.

Then worry twisted his gut and he was up and out of his chair, despite his body protesting with pops and cracks.

"Is it Helen?" The clinic where his sister worked was in a dangerous part of the city, and despite her insistence that she could care for herself, he worried.

"No, never seen the young lady. Says she was sent to speak to Haverstock, but Boss isn't in. Says she must speak to someone and wouldn't tell me more."

Drake let out a sigh and pinched the bridge of his nose. He wanted to tell Sergeant Ransome to send her away. He wanted to find any flat surface and sleep for even ten more minutes. But the damnable part of being a detective was a relentless curiosity.

Despite himself, he needed to solve the mystery.

"Send her in."

Ransome gave him a once-over, flicking his gaze across Drake's rumpled clothes and no doubt wildly mussed hair, then ducked back out the door.

Drake yawned and scratched a hand across his jaw. The lady, whoever she was, would have to take him as she found him.

At the sound of footsteps marching toward his office, he straightened his suit coat, took a deep breath, and—

A whirlwind burst through his office door. A petite, flower-scented whirlwind.

He registered the purple of her dress, the glossy chestnut shade of her hair, and the scent of sweet flowers and fresh rain-clean air, and then she was talking so fast and animatedly that his exhausted brain couldn't assemble the words into any sort of sense. Something about a theft and jewels and a suspicious gang of men.

"Slow down, miss, and take a seat."

"I don't think I can sit still." But she did fall silent and planted her hands on her hips, dipping her head and breathing deeply as if she needed a moment. When she lifted her gaze to his again, she seemed less agitated. "Forgive me, Inspector. Traffic was a tangle, and this matter felt more urgent the longer it took. I suppose it is urgent if the men I heard were in earnest."

He'd honed the skill of memorizing faces, cataloging details that distinguished one from another. The lady had a birthmark near her left temple that drew one's attention there, and her eyes flared at the edges with a little upward tilt. An inch-long faded scar marked the skin above her mouth, but it only served to emphasize the curved peaks of her upper lip.

Indeed, her lips were so enticing, he found himself staring. Then he inwardly chastised himself. Fatigue was addling his brain, chipping at his self-control.

The lady possessed a face of interesting and memorable details, but simply describing them wouldn't capture what intrigued him most. She vibrated with energy.

"Let's start again. Tell me your name."

"My name?" She looked at him as if he'd confounded her. "Did you hear what I just said?"

"Frankly, not a great deal of it." He pointed to the chair in front of his desk. "Sit. And let's start from the beginning, Miss . . . ?" He prompted for her name again.

"Alexandra Prince." She took a step closer, and the gaslight on the wall behind him revealed the unique color of her eyes.

They were a cool, muted blue, almost lavender, and shadowed by thick lashes. She ran her gaze down him in one scraping assessment, and his unshaven, unpressed state didn't seem to stand him well in her estimation. Her forehead scrunched in a frown.

"You have blood on your cuff, sir, and bruises on your hand."

Drake glanced down, surprised at the spots of

blood. He'd changed at his flat before meeting Haverstock.

"It was a long night," he admitted.

Such proofs of violence must have shocked her. As they should.

Miss Prince was well-dressed, her voice cultured, her gleaming hair tucked neatly into pins. She seemed a lady of quality, and her assessing gaze unsettled him. Being studied by her felt like sitting for an exam he wished he'd been better prepared for.

"Shall I start at the beginning again?" she asked, perching on the chair in front of his desk. She sat reluctantly, shifting the moment she did. Indeed, her whole body hummed. Her eyes held a spark of it, a kind of determination that he recognized in himself. It called to the part of him that needed to solve every mystery. Fix every problem.

"Tell me what brought you here this morning."

"I overheard something suspicious not an hour ago," she started as she settled into her chair. "There were three men in a coffeehouse next to my family's shop. I was waiting for coffee and scones, you see. Hidden in a nook where most of the shop's patrons couldn't see me. Certainly not this trio. They were intent on their conversation."

"Where's the shop?"

Her brows, a darker shade than her hair, knitted in confusion. "Yes, of course. They might return. Is that what you're thinking? It's in Moulton Street. Hawlston's Coffeehouse. But the most important part is what I heard the men say." She tapped one neatly tapered finger on his desktop to emphasize her point, somehow unerringly finding the single spot that was clear of files and papers.

"And what did they say, Miss Prince?"

She flicked her gaze to where he'd crossed his hands and settled them on his desktop.

"Don't you wish to take notes or make a report?"

"I'd like to hear the story first."

She shot him a dubious look but continued.

"The men were speaking heatedly, though it was clear they were trying to keep their voices down. I only heard them because I was sitting so near, you see? Though they couldn't see me. I was in the—"

"The nook, yes. Go on."

That earned him the merest jump of one brow. He suspected he'd won a sliver of trust from her by proving he was listening. But he'd still heard nothing that would merit completing a report or taking any action.

"One man, the only one I truly saw, told the others that they were pathetic because they weren't keen on what he'd proposed."

Now it was Drake's turn to lift a brow.

She leaned forward, locked her blue eyes on him, and whispered, "They plan to steal the Crown Jewels."

His lungs deflated and all the tiredness he'd barely kept at bay swept over him. Something else rushed in too. The frustration he usually felt when dealing with a member of the public who believed their neighbor was plotting treason, or the local butcher was secretly a murderer, or that a dream they'd had portended danger for the queen.

Over the years, there had been more than a few hysterical citizens bringing him fanciful stories. Though none, he had to admit, as pretty as this one.

He leaned forward to match her, close enough to notice the sprinkle of freckles across her nose and cheeks, to notice that her lips were flushed, and that the sparks in her eyes were like threads of silver hidden in pale violet.

She held herself tensely, almost defiantly, as if she expected his reaction.

Even as tired as he was, he could appreciate her loveliness, her vividness. She made the gas sconces in the room blaze brighter.

He almost regretted how thoroughly he intended to disappoint her.

"Miss Prince . . ." he started slowly. Delicacy and taking care not to offend weren't his strong suit. "If there were truly a group of thieves planning to steal the Crown Jewels—"

"Please—" She interrupted him, as if to stave off what he intended to say next. And that one word, the desperation with which she said it, made him hold his tongue for a moment.

But only for a moment.

"Allow me to finish?" he asked when he rarely asked anyone for permission for anything.

She seamed her lips together.

"The possibility that thieves would seriously

discuss such a plan openly in a crowded coffee-house where others could hear seems very unlikely. I'm certain that many dream of such a feat, or even boast of it. But it's never been successfully accomplished, nor truly attempted except—"

"Yes, Thomas Blood in 1670. I know the story. Perhaps they do too. Look." She shocked him by rising from her chair and picking up his inkwell.

"Do you mind?" He didn't like it when people touched his things or mussed up his desk. Some might see the piles as chaos but they made perfect sense to him.

"I'm just borrowing it," she declared as she moved it to the edge of the desk, then she had the audacity to pluck up a bottle of glue. When she reached for the polished river stone paper-weight his sister had once given to him as a gift, he lifted his hand to stop her. But her fingers were already curving around the edges of the rock, and he found his own fingers clashing with hers.

Something jolted in his chest at the contact. Her skin was warm and deliciously soft and he quite liked the feel of her fingers next to his.

When she sucked in a shocked breath, his wits returned to him and he pulled his hand away, relinquishing the stone to her.

He knew he should apologize. Fully intended to, in fact. But when he looked up into her wide eyes, the silver threads among the violet seemed to shimmer. He searched her face for offense, shock. The lady simply looked as befuddled as he suddenly felt.

But she gathered herself and shot her gaze down to the rock, then positioned it catty-corner to the inkwell.

"You see? I was sitting here." She pointed to the inkwell, her voice a bit breathier than before. "This is a wall that separates the kitchen from where the customers sit." With her index finger, she tapped the flat river stone. "And this is where the trio were hunched." She indicated the glue bottle. "They didn't know they were sitting close enough for someone to hear."

"What was the plan they unfolded?" Even attempting such a brazen theft would take months of planning, and more importantly, gaining the trust of at least one confederate on the inside. Probably more. *That* seemed impossible since the Tower Yeomen were a notoriously staunch and loyal bunch.

She wilted a bit, her shoulders dropping an inch. "There were no details about the plan." With one swift pivot away from his desk, she began pacing again. "But one gentleman was angry. Another was worried, I'd say. It must have been something they'd seriously discussed."

"You said you got a look at one of them."

"Yes, the angry one."

Drake pulled a slip of paper toward him and reached for his pencil. "Describe him if you would."

She approached again and lifted a hand to tap a finger against her lips. "Tall. Dark coat. And a black derby hat. He had a dark beard and mustache, and he wore glasses with smoky lenses."

Drake stilled his pencil and arched a brow. "So you didn't truly see him at all. It sounds as if most of his face was obscured. This description is vague enough to fit half of the men on any London street."

"The glasses were unusual," she said defensively. "An odd square shape."

"And they served to further hide his features." Drake set the piece of paper aside.

She'd come because she thought she'd heard men conspiring to commit a crime, and for that he admired her. Londoners had plenty of cause for apathy and many would hear such an exchange and think nothing more of it.

But if she couldn't identify any of the men, Drake had virtually nothing to proceed with unless he wished to haunt Hawlston's Coffeehouse, hoping the trio might reconvene and repeat themselves. He'd alert those at the Tower and inquire about whether there'd been any word of a plot afoot, but there wasn't much more he could do.

"Unfortunately, even if I showed you photographs of known London thieves, he's not a man you could identify."

Miss Prince let out a sigh so full of frustration that he had the urge to comfort her, but she recovered almost instantly, crossing her arms and tapping one foot against the floor.

"Are you saying I'm a fool to have come?"

He didn't think that. She was obviously a spirited young woman. One who acted independently, which was intriguing considering her age and the lack of a wedding band on her finger. Impetuous, perhaps, but intelligent and with every good intention.

Drake frowned. He usually didn't assume the best of anyone. His mistakes and his work had made him jaded. But apparently, this vibrant beauty had unearthed a shred of optimism he still possessed.

That fascinated and unsettled him in equal measure.

CHAPTER FOUR

THE DETECTIVE inspector was gruff and hard-edged, as if all the features of his handsome face had been sculpted by a sharp chisel. He had a maddening stillness about him, and she suspected it would take a great deal to ruffle the man. As troubled as she'd been by what she heard, his reaction had been . . . lacking.

It certainly hadn't generated enough concern to read it in his expression, though she'd searched for some sign of disquiet.

And then she'd got lost in studying him—the long angle of his jaw, the contrast of such full lips, and the cleft in his square chin—which troubled her even more. He was distractingly appealing and didn't even seem to know it.

He stood from behind his desk, and Allie braced herself for the same sort of admonitions she'd heard from her brother. Warnings about acting on impulse. Or worse, Inspector Drake might be the kind of gentleman who assumed ladies were given to hysteria and overreaction by their very nature.

She was struck again by his height and the

breadth of him. Wide shoulders stretched the fabric of his suit coat, and whatever muscles hid under his shirtfront, they were substantial enough to cause the fabric around his buttons to pull taut whenever he shifted.

Every time they did, her gaze riveted on the spot, wondering if one might give way. And then what? She had a scandalous curiosity about what might lie beneath the starched fabric. But every time the thought struck, she'd gather her wits and look up to find him watching her with a hard stare.

Inspector Drake could intimidate by brawniness alone, and she wondered at the fresh abrasions on his knuckles and the drops of blood on his shirt. She wouldn't favor any criminal's odds when faced with this man's wrath.

He was precisely the opposite of what she'd expected. If Haverstock was Lord Wellingdon's friend, she'd expected a man of a similar age. Wizened and yet dignified. Somehow, she couldn't imagine Inspector Drake answering to such a man. To anyone. There was a sort of controlled power about him. He struck her as a man who followed society's rules but didn't much like to.

"Miss Prince . . ."

Allie clenched her jaw and steeled herself.

"I haven't known you an hour and yet I cannot imagine you as anyone's fool."

"Oh."

He paused as if he wished to let his assessment sink in.

"I have no doubt you heard the conversation exactly as you described, and I can understand the impulse . . ."

"It wasn't simply impulse—"

"Allow me to finish." He held up a hand. "I think," he continued, "that you truly wished to do the right thing. And you couldn't ignore that impulse."

For a moment, Allie stood speechless. Stunned. He stated so simply what she struggled to make her siblings understand. Nothing about the inspector led her to believe he might understand her in the slightest. Indeed, he possessed a coldness she'd expect of a man with blood on his hands. And his jaw was rigid whenever she spoke, as if he was biting his tongue to repress the urge to toss her from his office.

"I appreciate that you don't think me foolish," she finally managed when her shock began to wane. "But is there anything that can be done?"

He'd just pointed out that she wasn't a fool, and she quite agreed, so she already knew the answer to her question. She'd given him very little to go on and could not identify any of the men. Inspector Drake seemed to imply that the tallest man may have been purposely obscuring his appearance.

"Never mind," she put in before he could answer. "I've given you no thread to chase, have I?"

"I can't imagine the men you overheard will make a habit of discussing such a plot in the same coffeehouse."

"No. In fact, two of the men didn't want to discuss the matter at all."

Drake nodded slowly, as if pondering that fact. "Then perhaps what you witnessed was a proposed plot falling apart. Such a venture would be the greatest of risks and only the most committed of confederates could carry it off."

"Yes, that makes sense." Allie felt a bit of relief and an odd flare of luck that she'd been directed to Inspector Drake rather than Sir Felix.

"I'm glad you think me sensible," he said with utter seriousness.

"Detectives must be, mustn't they?"

"Ideally, yes." His square jaw shifted and for a moment Allie thought he might smile.

She was breathless for it to happen. What might this imposing force of a man look like with a smile softening his features?

But the moment dissipated like smoke from a doused candle flame, and he tightened all his hard edges, squaring his jaw, rising impossibly taller, and hardening those eyes that were so dark in the low light that she couldn't discern their shade.

"I have a good deal to be getting on with, Miss Prince."

Allie couldn't resist a glance at his injured hand and her imagination conjured wild possibilities of what Inspector Drake's workday might entail.

"I won't take up any more of your time." Allie offered the man a nod. "Good day, Inspector. I hope those cuts don't sting too much."

He shot a look down at his hand, almost as if

he'd forgotten the appendage was attached to his brawny arm.

She turned on her heel, headed to the door, and felt an odd sense of disappointment. Just as Dom claimed she had a terrible propensity to do, she'd rushed in. Logically speaking, she had no real cause to involve the police when the trio might have merely been chattering with no real intent beyond their bluster.

And yet something in her gut told her otherwise. She sensed that somewhere in London, a plot was unfolding. If not involving all three men, then at least the tall one. The menace she'd felt when he'd stared at her in the alleyway made her shiver even now.

"Miss Prince." Drake had followed her out into the hallway.

"Yes?" When Allie turned, he loomed just beyond the frame of his office door, and a sconce lit all the features of his face. She swallowed hard because she could tell now. His eyes. They were moss green but laced with streaks of amber.

"I must warn you—"

"Green amber," she heard herself say.

Out loud.

Good heavens, she'd blurted the words, and of course he hadn't a clue what she meant. Actually, it was probably less mortifying if he *didn't* know that his eye color had inspired her outburst.

He glowered and tilted his head a fraction in confusion. "I beg your pardon."

"It's very rare," was all she could manage before her cheeks lit on fire and she spun and rushed away from him as fast as her legs could carry her.

She exited the building and kept walking, rushing so quickly she inspired a few shocked looks from passersby.

Across the street and around a corner, she finally stopped to catch her breath. To lean against the chilled stone of the building at her back and will her cheeks to cool.

She closed her eyes and wished for the thousandth time that her tongue didn't occasionally mumble whatever popped into her head.

Green amber.

Allie let out a huff of exasperation. The man had been kind enough to tell her she wasn't a fool. She was absolutely certain her little outburst had changed that assessment.

Of course, what she'd said was true. Green amber *was* rare. They'd taken in a vase made of it once, a thousand-year-old beauty crafted in South America, and she'd been heartbroken when her father sold it soon after to a collector.

None of that explained why she'd been possessed with an urge to destroy whatever meager goodwill the detective had for her.

Luckily, they'd never cross paths again, and she was done with blurting and rushing in and making mountains out of molehills.

She set off toward Princes, thankful for the mile-and-a-half walk to put distance between herself and the gruff police detective with injured hands and lovely eyes.

When she reached Trafalgar Square, she got distracted by a cart selling roasted chestnuts and the minute she slowed her pace, a thought popped into her head.

Inspector Drake had tried to warn her about something, and she'd cut him off.

Warn her about what?

"You LOOK A GREAT deal worse for wear, Benedict."

Drake looked up to find his sister standing over the wingback he'd dropped into as soon as he got home. He hadn't even heard her come into the townhouse they shared.

"I must have dozed off." Hours ago, he'd stoked the fire in the grate and slumped into his favorite chair and hadn't moved since. The dog he'd rescued from M's townhouse hadn't moved from where he'd settled near Drake's chair either.

He reached down to scratch the dog between the ears. Helen suggested they call him Cerberus after the guardian dog of Greek myth. Drake had taken to calling him Bedford after the square where he'd found him.

"I suppose I should be glad you got some rest. I've hardly seen you the last few evenings." Helen worked long hours too, yet she always managed to look entirely put together and ready to take on the next task. Even now, she examined him with a bright, assessing gaze, the way she might a prospective patient at the clinic she practically ran.

"Is that your blood on your clothes or someone else's?" She bent for a closer look. "Someone clipped the edge of your jaw, didn't they? There's the merest hint of a bruise. Those abrasions on your knuckles need to be cleaned properly."

"Anything else, Doctor Drake?"

"Don't tease me on that score today." Sniffing in irritation, she strode to a side table where their chessboard sat. Alma, an elderly cat Helen had rescued months ago, sat in a perfect rounded loaf beside it.

He and Helen played each other at a leisurely pace, but it had been days since either had made a move. Helen selected a pawn as if to move it, but seemed to think better of it and set it down again. Instead, she stroked Alma's orange-striped fur.

"Dr. Porter reminded me today that I am not a doctor and have no say when it comes to treatment for our patients."

"Bloody pompous fool. You could be an asset to him if he'd allow it." Drake sat forward in his chair. "We've saved enough between us, Helen. You should apply to medical school—"

"Oh, I fully intend to." She gestured across the hall to the small room she'd claimed as a study. "I've begun working on my application materials, but there will always be those like Porter who believe men should retain the highest rungs of power, whether in medicine or politics or industry."

He had never met a more capable woman than his sister, but he knew she was right. He also knew society was changing as the new century approached, and he welcomed that change, especially if it meant increased opportunities for many rather than privilege for a very few.

"If we're lucky, progress will steamroll right over such men."

She scooped up another of her rescue cats, a kitten she called Milly, and shot him a dubious look as she settled into the chair next to his and gestured toward him. "Are there more injuries I can't see?"

"Nothing to fuss about."

His sister made a little grumbling noise as she always did when he deflected one of her questions. "I know you won't divulge details of your cases, but can you at least tell me if the one that caused you so many sleepless nights the past weeks is at an end?"

"It is." *For the most part.* He couldn't tell her, or anyone, about M, but the conundrum of how to catch the man was ever on his mind.

"Thank goodness for that."

The relieved sigh his sister let out echoed in Drake's chest too. He wanted done with any matter involving royals and the sins of the heir to the throne. It cleared the way for other cases.

"And what does Haverstock say about advancement?"

Drake worked his jaw and fought the biting response uppermost in his mind. "He said not yet but 'soon.'"

Helen frowned. "Well, that's utter bollocks."

He chuckled. "My sentiments exactly."

"I'm sorry, Ben. But what you do still matters a great deal. Many of your cases have stopped men from doing further harm and achieved a measure of peace for their victims."

"Yes, but forever answering to Haverstock or another superior isn't my goal. I can do more from the top than from the middle."

"You'll get there." She inhaled and smiled. "I smell stew. Did Mrs. Pratt get any of it down you yet?"

They could only afford a staff of two and were blessed with a housekeeper who was also a fine cook.

"Not yet. I suspect she left me to sleep until you came home."

"Indeed, I did, Mr. Drake." The tall, steel-haired woman who managed their household with the same efficiency with which Helen ran her clinic appeared in the drawing room doorway as if she'd been waiting for mention of her name. "Everything's been laid out in the dining room. Unless you'd prefer trays in here."

Taking supper together in front of the fire was a habit built in childhood when meals were irregular and they didn't know when their next might come. Now they both put in long hours, and meals were catch-as-catch-can. It was rare for them to gather to eat together in front of a fire as they had so many years ago before they'd fled their mother's lodgings.

"Dining in here sounds nice," Helen told Mrs.

Pratt, who returned soon after with two prepared trays.

"Were there many cases waiting for you when this one was done?" Helen asked after her first bite of stew.

Ben shot her a look and she returned a soft smile.

"I suppose the better question is how many are you juggling at once?"

"Plenty. As are you." Ben swallowed a swig of tea and shifted to study his sister. "You look a bit put out yourself. Is it Mrs. Dowd?"

Among her many patients, one had found a special place in his sister's heart.

"Actually, she's been sent home." Helen's voice cracked and she sipped tea to cover it.

"Is she well enough to be on her own?"

"Of course not, but I'm not the consulting doctor and the argument was made that we need the space for other patients."

"You know as much as that bloody doctor, if not more, particularly about Mrs. Dowd."

"Mmm." She stared into the fire as if giving the whole matter thought, though he knew she wouldn't push as he would. She wouldn't demand that Dr. Porter give her the respect she deserved. It wasn't his sister's way.

They were different. Helen preferred to work quietly, her head down, helping as many as she could and did not worry overly about being recognized for any of it. She knew her worth.

Her conscience wasn't burdened like his was.

"We could take turns visiting Mrs. Dowd," he offered quietly.

His sister turned a surprised look his way. "You really wish to add something more to your load?"

"You do charity work, your nursing duties, your studies, and yet I'm sure you've already made plans to visit her. I can stop by and visit from time to time too."

She pressed her lips together—usually a sign that she wished to decline but struggled with a polite way to do so. "I'm not sure that's a good idea, Ben."

"Why not?" In this respect, he found his sister maddening. Not asking for help and not accepting it when it was offered were quite different, and she was stubbornly independent to the extreme.

"She's a fragile older woman and, frankly, has a nervous constitution. You can be rather . . . gruff. And a strange man at her door might frighten her."

"A strange, gruff man," he grumbled teasingly.

Helen waved at hand at him. "Stop being difficult. You know what I mean." Then she seemed to soften. "I know you are capable of great kindness, enormous care." She glanced down at Bedford as if seeking proof. "And I know most of all that you always try to do the right thing. Believe me, I know that."

Ben swallowed hard. "Let's not talk about the past tonight."

By mentioning *the right thing* he knew that his sister couldn't fail to recall the time he did precisely the wrong thing with regard to their younger brother, George. He'd been too high-handed, and yet also oblivious to how lost their brother had become. As the eldest, he should have protected him, guided him, better. He'd failed George, and the consequences haunted him still.

"I didn't intend to bring any of that up." More quietly, Helen added, "But I forgive you, and one day you must forgive yourself."

Ben took a long draw of tea, not meeting her gaze. "Let us solve it this way. You ask Mrs. Dowd if I may visit, and I'll go if I'm wanted."

She winced. "I shall try, but the poor dear may not recall our conversation by the time you arrive." She shook her head and tears welled in her eyes. "I feel for her so. Loss of memory must be terrifying, especially when you're alone."

"Yes." Though there were memories Ben would far rather forget, the sharpness of his mind was his main tool. One he planned to use to find M and, one day, reach Haverstock's position. And higher.

"Well, I'll await word from you, but I will visit if it would help."

"Thank you. It's good of you to offer." Helen pushed her stew bowl away and clasped her hands around her teacup. As soon as she settled back in her chair, Milly resumed his napping spot on Helen's lap. His sister studied him until the back of his neck began to itch from the intense assessment.

"What?" he finally asked.

"I don't know. You seem . . . different."

Ben swallowed down a bite of stew. "Perhaps it's the case. It took a bit out of me."

"No, no, I didn't mean it in a bad way. You asking to visit Mrs. Dowd." She shrugged. "You're usually so focused on your work that you'd never consider giving time to anything else."

Ben tensed, fearing where this conversation may lead.

"You don't even take time for friends or other engagements." She shot him a speaking look. "Perhaps you should. There is more to life than work."

He laughed at that, the sound bursting out of him. "Have you met yourself, Miss Drake?"

Her brows dipped and her mouth set in the stubborn way he'd known since childhood. "I do have friends, brother. I have friends I see when I do charity work, when I attend my ladies' clubs."

There was no denying that she had one of the busiest calendars of anyone he'd ever known. No one could do as much with a twenty-four-hour day.

Contemplating him a moment longer, she finally approached the point she often did. "One day, you'll want more than work."

Ben let out a groan. "Please, Helen, not tonight. No mention of wedlock."

She crossed her arms. A sure sign that she'd not yet finished haranguing him. "Very well. I won't say the word, especially as I appreciate you not mentioning it to me. Many older brothers would to their spinster sisters."

"Thank you." He eased back in his chair. Bedford settled down too, stretching out in front of the hearth and emitting a contented sigh. They all seemed to relish the fire's warmth.

But Helen was musing. He could all but hear her mind whirring. "What about Lavinia Haverstock? Is she what's caused the change I see in you tonight?"

He pinched the bridge of his nose and wished he'd never mentioned Haverstock's preoccupation with pairing Ben with his daughter.

"It is *not* Miss Haverstock, I assure you."

Helen busied herself selecting a biscuit from the plate of treats Mrs. Pratt had provided for dessert. "Is it another lady, then?"

Ben glanced at her and then forced his gaze back to the dregs of his tea.

In that single look, she'd seen something, because her face lit with a mischievous smile. "It is," she said in whispered wonder. "I knew something had gotten under your skin."

"There is nothing under my skin, thank you very much. And it's not a lady in the way you think."

"Then how is it?"

"A young woman came to my office today." Mentioning her allowed him to fully recall the details of the encounter, thoughts of which he'd been pushing away all day. "She was surprising. Memorable."

"Pretty?" Helen asked, still smiling.

"Very pretty," he told her honestly. "She had a spark about her."

"Good heavens, now *you're* smiling."

"I'm not." Ben tried to wipe away all emotion as he did at work.

"So why did this lady call on you? Do members of the public often come up to those offices?"

"They don't. The whole encounter was out of the ordinary."

"And memorable." She lifted the teapot and poured him more when he nodded, then filled her own cup.

"She had something to report that she thought the police should know."

Helen scrutinized him, waiting for more. "If you won't tell me what she said, tell me why she made such an impression? Other than being very pretty, of course."

"Something she blurted as she left." He looked at his sister, feeling as befuddled as he had in that moment. "Green amber. Have you ever heard of such a thing?"

Helen pondered and then shook her head. "I can't say I have. I've always thought amber was gold or umber in color."

"She mentioned that too." He leaned forward in his chair. "She said it's rare."

"As she must be to have so preoccupied your prodigious mind," Helen said thoughtfully with not a little glee in her tone.

Ben ignored the provocation, but Miss Prince was there, vivid and full of life in his mind. He'd rarely met someone who exuded such vibrancy. And he liked that there was no pretense about her, no fussiness about etiquette and propriety. He recalled how

she'd initially refused to sit and told him plainly
that she was too agitated to remain still.

Some feared him upon sight. He was aware that
his size and dislike for pleasantries could be off-
putting. Gruff, as Helen pointed out. But Miss
Prince showed no fear.

If only things hadn't ended so awkwardly, he
might have—

"So, when will you see this rare spark of a
young woman again?" Helen asked quietly.

"I doubt I will." Saying as much aloud irked
him, though he knew it was logical and for the
best.

To his surprise, Helen chuckled a moment later.

"What?"

"Benedict Drake, you're one of the most trustworthy men I know, and yet I doubt the veracity
of that pronouncement." She sipped her tea while
watching him over the rim, trying to read his reaction. "And I think you do too."

CHAPTER FIVE

Princes of London sparkled on the tidy London street where it sat. Not only were its windows clean enough to gleam in the glow of autumn sunlight, but the bits and bobs on the other side shone in gold and silver and the rainbow glint of faceted gems. The shop had a charm about it. Its two front windows bowed out slightly, beckoning passersby to stop and stare at the treasures within, and in the few minutes Drake had been standing across the street, hidden under the awning of a bookshop a few doors down, several had paused to behold the gewgaws beyond the glass.

He didn't give a damn about antiquities, but he could appreciate the shop's appeal. And he told himself it had nothing to do with the lovely young woman he'd likely find inside if he ventured in.

But, of course, he wouldn't enter the shop or seek out Miss Prince. That's not why he'd come. Her visit to headquarters *had* prompted this one, but he didn't need to see her again. In fact, he knew he should avoid her. He'd replayed her visit to the office and that moment when he'd touched her often enough to recognize that the lady was a distraction he needed to get out of his head. Even if curiosity made him wish to solve the mystery of whatever the hell *green amber* meant.

His goal was to get a look at Hawlston's Coffeehouse, though he knew the odds of encountering the same men she had with a single visit was unlikely. Which was precisely why he'd decided to employ another set of eyes and ears to spend a few days in the place.

Though, currently, his hired eyes and ears was running late.

Ben stepped through the alleyway between the buildings opposite of Princes and slid his watch out to check the time. As he returned it to his waistcoat pocket, a familiar figure ambled toward him, hat brim pulled low and collar stood up against the biting breeze.

"Your punctuality has suffered since leaving the force, Fitz."

"Couldn't be helped, Duke. A messy case delayed me. I'm sure you can sympathize." His grin was wide and more confident than Ben remembered. "Haverstock have you under a pile of them as usual?"

Arthur Fitzroy had only been a constable for three years before deciding to leave the Metropolitan Police and apprentice himself to a private agent of inquiry. Two years later, he'd split from that gentleman and started his own business as an inquiry agent.

His ambition was as keen as Ben's own and every bit as impatient.

"The old dragon keeps me busy."

"Aye, I'll bet. Knows what he's found in you, he does." Fitz leaned in. "Though I tell you, Duke, there is coin to be made working for oneself. And no fire-breathing Haverstock to wield power over you."

Ben allowed himself a half smile, though he didn't meet Fitzroy's gaze. It wasn't that he hadn't considered breaking off on his own. He had, especially as he bristled under Haverstock's hold. But more than a path to quick income, he longed for power and position. Respect and achievement. To his thinking, that could only be found within the police force.

"I'll stay where I am for now."

"And take Haverstock's throne one day, you will." Fitz assessed the shops along Moulton Street, his nose twitching and eyes narrowing as he chafed his hands together. "What is it you have for me?"

"How do you feel about becoming a regular at that coffeehouse across the street for a week or two?"

Fitz quirked his brow and moved to the mouth of the alley, squinting at the cafe as if expecting to detect something nefarious from its reddish-brown brick facade and chalkboards listing the day's offerings.

"I can do that, but what for?"

"Observation and the reporting of anything suspicious. This is to be quietly done. Not a word to anyone."

"I do understand discretion, Duke," Fitz drawled, clearly offended by the reminder.

"Good." Ben strode through the gap between buildings again to get a better look at Hawlston's.

"We've had a tip that a group of men were heard discussing a plan to steal—" Ben's brain stalled when he caught sight of her. Chestnut hair, flushed cheeks, hands moving as she talked.

Miss Alexandra Prince stood inside her family's shop and leaned into the front display, moving items aside to place an elaborately decorated vase in a prime spot nearest the window. Whether she was singing to herself or speaking to someone, he couldn't be certain. But in between dusting, she talked and gestured with her hands.

"Steal?" Fitz prompted from behind him.

"Something the Crown would not like to be parted from." Ben thought it best to keep the details to himself.

Fitz whistled. "Stealing from the Crown would require some sizable bollocks."

"Or a taste for risk and an oversized ego." Ben glanced back at his former colleague. "We've both known thieves who overestimated their skill."

"Mmm," Fitz murmured in agreement. "And gadded about as if they had a cat's nine lives."

"We'd like to cut this one off at the planning stages, *if* there is a plan. You'd simply be testing the validity of the tip."

"And you don't care to handle this officially?"

"The moment I know the tip is sound, I will."

"Got it." Fitzroy clasped his hands and stretched his fingers, as if he was about to begin an activity that required dexterity. "Who should I be on the watch for?"

Ben winced. "I have nothing terribly concrete to offer on that score, I'm afraid. Three men in dark clothing. One is tall, dark bearded, and wears darkened lenses."

Fitz jerked back and frowned. "Not a great deal to latch onto there."

"Agreed, but you'll be listening for any talk of theft or jewels." Ben glanced at him. "While blending in seamlessly."

"Jewels?" Fitz's eyes widened. "Stealing jewels from the royals would be wildly audacious. I'm assuming you've taken a look at known jewel thieves."

Ben had reviewed the files of a few and asked Ransome to find others. None that had ever been taken into custody were notably tall.

Fitz stepped forward and darted his gaze around at the various shops lining the street. "I can say I'm a new employee at one of these shops, eager to warm my cold hands around a cuppa."

When Fitz started across the street, Ben tapped his arm to hold him back.

"Let me have a look first." As he spoke the words, he kept his gaze locked on Miss Prince, who still arranged items and then reached out to dust a few. The lady remained in near constant motion, just as she had the morning before. He'd expected she'd soon step back farther into the shop's interior and there'd be less chance of her spotting him.

"What are you waiting for, Duke?"

"The right moment." Ben wasn't certain why tension tightened his gut at the thought of catching Miss Prince's notice. Perhaps because the woman lingered too stubbornly in his thoughts already, and she was the sort of distraction he couldn't afford.

He felt Fitz's gaze on him and sensed the man's impatience, and Miss Prince had finally retreated so far into the shop that he couldn't see her through the glass.

This delaying to avoid her was ridiculous.

"Wait here until I return," he told Fitz and then strode toward Hawlston's, keeping his focus on the coffeehouse's front door.

Inside, dense, warm coffee-scented air enveloped him and he took in the groupings of men gathered around tables. A few seemed like they might be tall in stature, though it was hard to tell when a man was hunched over a cup. None wore the dark glasses Miss Prince had mentioned. Aside from lining up the lot of them along the wall, he couldn't get a good look at most of the men's faces.

Ben entered the queue waiting to order items from the bakery case, and he watched as the proprietress's expression changed when she recognized a customer and when she did not.

"Good afternoon, sir." The lady was sharp-eyed, and he received the same inspection she'd subjected a few other customers to.

"May I speak to you a moment, madam? In private."

There were others queueing behind him, and Ben didn't wish to betray his position to anyone who might overhear the questions he intended to ask.

The woman's brows arched high, and he could see her debating, but after a moment she nodded and called to another young woman to take her place at the counter.

"This way, sir." The lady led him to a nook just inside the door of the coffeehouse's kitchen. Ben suspected it was *the* nook that Miss Prince had described and then illustrated in diorama form on his desk.

"This can't take long. I've customers to see to. I'm Mrs. Cline and I manage Hawlston's. Is there a problem, sir?"

"I have no complaints about the shop, Mrs. Cline. My name is Drake," he told her, omitting his official position. He'd handled none of this as an official inquiry thus far and didn't intend to until he knew a real threat existed. "I'm looking for a man who may frequent this coffeehouse."

The proprietress reached up and fussed with the collar of her high-necked gown. "I can't recall everyone who walks through the front door. We're right busy most days."

"Understood. But this man is distinctive. Quite tall and he wears dark glasses."

She frowned and shook her head slowly. "I can't say I know anyone with dark glasses, though we have tall patrons on occasion. Yourself included, Mr. Drake."

"May I leave my card?" He pulled one of his personal calling cards from his pocket that listed his home address. "If you see such a man, could you send word to me?"

With a tentative expression, she reached for the card he'd extended. She examined the rectangle of paper he'd given her, and she flicked her gaze up to him with one brow raised.

She pitched her voice low. "Has this gentleman done something dreadful?"

"Not that I'm aware of," Drake assured her, "but I'd like to speak to him if he happens to show up again."

"Very well."

"Thank you."

He followed her back out into the main seating area of the coffeehouse, casting his gaze around to ensure the man hadn't entered while they talked. But the collection of patrons looked much the same as when he'd walked in.

"Would you care for a coffee or anything from the case while you're here, Mr. Drake?"

He was a tea man through and through and had never yearned for a cup of coffee in his life. But he'd asked the woman for a favor a moment after entering her shop. The least he could do was purchase a cup of her brew.

Fitz still lingered near the shop across the street,

darting curious glances at the coffeehouse. He'd make this quick, but it was worth taking the time to build a bit of rapport with Mrs. Cline.

"Coffee sounds just the thing."

ALLIE HAD RESISTED HER usual morning trip to Hawlston's. The scents wafting from the shop were just as enticing, but the whole matter of the men and the plot and her encounter with one tall, green-eyed detective had unsettled her completely.

She compulsively retraced the men's conversation in her mind, trying to mine for details. Though there was precious little to unearth. Her two glances at the trio inside the coffeehouse hadn't provided her with a clear view of any of them. The brief encounter in the alley seemed haziest of all. Her gaze had locked on the gentleman's dark spectacles and every other detail of his face blurred in her memory.

Such ruminations had kept her up much of the night, and even now, as she unboxed a set of heavy seventeenth-century Florentine candlesticks, all she could think about was whether those three men were next door, hunched over the same table again.

Perhaps they'd enlisted more confederates and composed an entire gang now.

Stop. She was letting her imagination run riot, and doing so rarely got her anywhere. And the truth was that she did not relish the prospect of seeing the ominous tall man again, despite how much she yearned for proof of what she'd heard.

But one tantalizing thought whispered in her mind. What if she could find a real thread to follow?

She could take those details to Inspector Drake, and *that* prospect made her face heat and her heartbeat jump. Goodness, she'd been so taken with the unique shade of the detective's eyes that she'd babbled like a fool, but if she could gather real evidence that there was a plot to steal the Crown Jewels, she'd overcome any personal mortification to help prevent it.

Even playing a small role in thwarting such a plot would earn her a bit of the esteem that seemed to come so naturally to other Princes. And Dom and Eve couldn't argue with her *rushing in* on this occasion. Not when their own father was best known for retrieving a royal gem.

Perhaps a quick trip over to Hawlston's was in order.

She glanced at the covered coffee mug Mrs. Cline allowed her to take away and return with to refill with their smokiest coffee. From the rear of the shop, Mr. Gibson whistled contentedly while he worked.

Before heading back to ask him if he wanted anything, the bell above the shop's door rang and Jo strode in, bringing the scent of crushed autumn leaves and a gust of cool air with her.

Allie smiled when she noticed the book clutched in her friend's hand.

"Ah, you've come to make up for yesterday's missed book club meeting?"

The shop had been quiet all morning, and she'd happily take her lunch while talking about novels with Jo.

"That's what I told Mama, of course," Jo said as she drew close, keeping her voice low. "But the truth is I must know what happened yesterday with Sir Felix. What did he say?"

Allie came out from behind the counter and led her friend to the two chairs in the corner where they usually convened.

"I didn't see Sir Felix," she admitted. "He wasn't there, or so I was told, but I was directed to a Detective Inspector Benedict Drake."

Even saying the man's name put an odd hitch in her voice. Everything about him was sharp in her mind—his cheekbones, the depth of his voice, the width of his shoulders, and those rare green amber eyes.

Jo's blue eyes widened. "I've heard of him."

"Have you?"

"I'm certain that Lavinia Haverstock has mentioned that name. He's a protégé of her father's. She says Sir Felix is attempting to engineer a match between them, but I can't tell if she favors it." Jo frowned. "The girl is as inscrutable as her father."

A protégé? Inspector Drake didn't seem like a protégé. He exuded confidence and control. She imagined he could run all of Scotland Yard one day if his ambition took him that far.

"So did this Inspector Drake take a report about what you overheard?"

"He did listen and asked questions." Allie shrugged. "But what could he do? As you pointed out, I can't identify any of the men."

Jo stared at the far wall of Princes as if she could see through to the coffeehouse on the other side.

"I was thinking of making a trip over." Allie arched a brow at her friend. "Would you like to join me?"

Jo tapped her gloved fingers against the book in her lap. "If I do, you mustn't tell Mama. She'd never allow me to go into such a place unchaperoned."

Allie chuckled. "Your mother and I are hardly confidantes." She stood and offered her hand to Jo. "Besides, I can serve as your chaperone."

Jo laughed too. "Oh, if only Mama would allow you to take Mrs. Benning's place. Every social event I attended would be much more enjoyable."

Allie pressed her lips together. This was not the time to point out that the countess did not care for her. Lady Wellingdon thought her too untamed. Too independent. And Allie thought Jo's mother kept her daughter too tightly reined.

"Very well. I shall join you." Jo stood too.

"Let me just tell Mr. Gibson." Allie headed to the back room and rapped on the door frame of his workshop.

"So you're finally going over." He glanced at the clock on the wall. "You resisted a good long while."

"I did. I considered the matter before deciding, just as Dominic would have wanted."

He turned and winked at her in reply.

"May I bring you anything?"

"I'm content with my tea, but do have a care, Miss Prince." He tipped his chin and looked at her over his magnifying pince-nez. "Yesterday's encounter seems to have unsettled you."

"Which is precisely why I must go back and break its spell. Nothing can be allowed to separate me from Hawlston's coffee." She offered him a smile, hoping it would suffice to reassure him. "I promise to take care and return as quickly as I can."

"Take your time. I heard Lady Josephine's voice. Sit and enjoy yourselves."

"Thank you." Allie patted Grendel, who was curled up on a chair in the back room, and slipped her scarf off its hook on the wall before heading out to meet Jo.

"Ready?"

Jo's only response was a fretful look.

"What if that fearful man you saw is there?" She laid a hand on Allie's arm as if to keep her from rushing out the front door. "Surely, he'd recognize you."

"We don't even know if he is there. I have a strong feeling he won't be."

The more she considered the man, the more Allie suspected he did not frequent Hawlston's. He wasn't typical of its customers. He was better dressed than most gentlemen who frequented the coffeehouse, the majority of whom were employed in shops and offices nearby.

"Besides, he doesn't know I overheard him," she pointed out. "Only that I stepped into the alley."

"That is a good point," Jo acknowledged, though she still made no move toward the front door.

"Don't fret, Jo. I could go on my own." Allie gestured toward their favorite stuffed chairs. "Sit and read, and I'll make it a quick trip over and back."

"No." Jo shook her head firmly and the feathers on her pretty violet hat emphasized the movement. "What sort of friend would I be if I let you go alone?"

Allie laughed. "I go alone to Hawlston's nearly every day."

"Not since you may have encountered a band of dangerous criminals."

"They mostly sounded like a danger to the royal regalia."

"I suspect men who would undertake such a daring theft *could* be dangerous." Jo reached for Allie's arm and wrapped it around her own. "But no matter. Let us go."

"You're certain?"

"I am."

They walked arm in arm for the short trip along the pavement to Hawlston's. As usual, the cafe was busy, though not as chaotic as it was in the mornings.

When Allie reached for the door, Jo gave her arm a tug.

"What's the plan if by chance we do find them there?"

This had been a consideration much of the morning. "We remain calm, observe them surreptitiously, and get a message to Inspector Drake."

When they stepped through the front door, Allie drew in a long breath. The yeasty smell of fresh-baked bread and the sharp scent of roasted coffee made her smile. Thank goodness she'd overcome her reluctance and returned to a place that usually brought her nothing but deliciousness.

She looked round, scanning for any gathering that resembled the men from the previous day. There wasn't a single table claimed by three men in the entire coffeehouse. Mostly, customers were grouped by two or four, and a few sat alone.

Jo took everything in with her usual voracious curiosity.

One table near the front window sat empty and Allie pointed to it. "Shall we sit there?"

"Yes, but . . ." Jo darted glances around the cafe and then leaned in. "Do you see them?"

Allie gave a slight shake of her head, and Jo let out what sounded like a sigh of relief. That same sense of relief made Allie a bit lighter. Hawlston's felt like the same cozy spot she visited each day.

Until she stepped toward the counter and spotted the man standing beside Mrs. Cline.

Her mouth went dry, and some part of her brain tried to conjure embarrassment for the way they'd parted, but she was too pleased to let it trouble her now.

He was here.

Detective Inspector Drake may not have written up a report about what she'd told him, at least not while she'd been in his office. But he must have believed her, because he was here.

It was so odd to see him in this setting, his tall, broad-shouldered frame tucked behind the blue counter that was Mrs. Cline's domain. Something about him seemed less unyielding in this setting.

Or at least that was Allie's thought until his back straightened as if he sensed her studying him. A moment later, he turned.

When their eyes met, she gulped.

He didn't look at all pleased to see her.

CHAPTER SIX

THE ENTIRE time he'd been on Moulton Street, Drake had been aware of Miss Prince's nearness, that he could stride straight into her family's charming little antique shop if wished. And, very logically, he'd listened to the inner voice that warned him not to risk another encounter with the spark of a woman.

So it was a shock to see her standing in the middle of Hawlston's Coffeehouse. To see her in daylight, with the windows at her back, showing him that her hair, which had seemed chestnut brown yesterday, was in fact auburn. Streaked through with sparks of red, not readily apparent unless the light struck them just right. That suited her entirely. As did the buttery glow of the shop's overhead gas lamps.

It wasn't that the dim light in his office had hidden her appeal, only that this illumination brightened her eyes and highlighted the most shocking bit of all.

Miss Prince wore a decidedly pleased look on her face.

The sort of look one gives someone they haven't

seen in far too long. She was pleased to see *him*. Which caused an odd flicker of awareness in him. He had the urge to reach for her. Which was nonsensical. They were all but strangers.

Yet it was ridiculously appealing—that gentle curve of her lips. So much so that his breath hitched for a moment in his chest, and all the chatter and busyness of the coffeehouse fell away.

Seconds ticked by until his addled brain dredged up a bit of cool logic.

She wasn't pleased to see *him*. His presence proved that he'd listened to her, that he gave her story merit. Enough to venture out and make inquiries. That's what she'd wanted most when she visited his office. He'd sensed her fear that she would not be believed or that he might tell her she was overreacting.

There was still a possibility she'd heard nothing more than idle bluster, some ne'er-do-wells' musings. But if he ignored her story entirely and someone *did* make an attempt on the Crown Jewels? He'd be derelict in his duty, and he could never forgive himself. Not to mention that Haverstock would never give him a bloody promotion.

He glanced at Mrs. Cline to bid her good day, but she was already halfway down the counter speaking to another customer. When he turned back, Miss Prince was striding toward him, and her expression had bloomed into an outright smile.

"You came," she said as she approached.

Drake thought it best they didn't have this or any conversation about the matter in the coffeehouse, so rather than respond to her comment, he strode toward her and then brushed past.

Cinnamon and lavender and the smell of beeswax polish assaulted his senses as he passed her.

"Out front," he told her quietly, hoping she'd take his meaning and follow.

He ignored Fitz, and strode toward her shop, out of view of the coffeehouse windows.

When he stopped and turned back, he found her on his heels and not looking nearly as delighted by his presence.

Good. He didn't need to overthink her smiles. He didn't need the lady stuck in his thoughts at all.

"I take it you haven't seen the men again, Miss Prince."

"I haven't." Her voice dipped and she crimped her brow as if admitting a failing. "But I've only been in the shop for a few minutes." She glanced at the toes of her boots before facing him again. "In truth, I avoided my usual morning visit. I didn't wish to see the three again, but then I realized my foolishness. If I see them again, I could assist you."

"I do not require your assistance." The idea of her involving herself in this kindled every protective impulse he possessed. "Trust that I have the matter in hand."

In his periphery, Ben saw Fitz staring at them from across Moulton Street without any subtlety or attempt to conceal his gaping.

"I was the one who heard them, Inspector, and they might return to Hawlston's."

"They may."

"And you won't visit every day," she pointed out, "but I will."

"As will a man who will be reporting to me if he sees or hears anything of interest." He glanced in Fitz's direction.

She did too. "Oh, I see." One brow peaked, and she seemed to reassess him on the spot. "Good. That's more than I expected, if I'm honest."

Ben imagined Miss Prince had a difficult time being anything but honest. And he felt an unwelcome flare of pleasure at the fact that he'd managed to exceed her expectations.

"Now, I hope you can put this business out of your mind." He couldn't order the lady about, but he damned well hoped she'd refrain from meddling. Though, only having met her once, he would most definitely place her in the category of ladies most likely to meddle.

He waited for some reply. Prayed for the merest acknowledgment that she would content herself with running her shop and whatever else usually occupied her.

"I will do my best, Inspector Drake."

"Excellent. Then I bid you good day."

"Good day to you." She made no move to return to the coffeehouse or to enter her shop, just stood and watched him as he waited for a carriage to pass and then made his way toward Fitz.

The urge to turn back nearly overwhelmed him, but he'd trained himself to avoid temptation.

"I'm confused, Duke. Did you come to inspect the coffeehouse or court that pretty redhead?"

"She's none of your concern." Ben frowned. Hadn't he just said as much to himself?

Fitz chuckled at that. "But she's yours, it's clear to see."

The glower Ben gave the man seemed to quell his merriment.

"Can I finally have a cuppa?"

"As many as you like. Use your discretion to decide how long to stay but do visit daily. Track your time and provide me with a report." Ben withdrew a pouch he'd filled generously. "A deposit for the fortnight."

Fitz bounced the coin-filled bag in his palm. "Generous as always. I'll start straightaway."

Ben waited until Fitz had entered Hawlston's and then allowed himself one final glance at Princes of London.

She was back in the coffeehouse. Seated but moving, of course. She chatted with a young dark-haired lady at one of the tables near the window. He noted how she had a tendency to reach up and push stray strands of hair behind her ear, and it made his fingers itch.

How would those glossy auburn strands feel against his skin? Would she blush if he reached up to tuck her hair behind her ear?

No. Those were things he could not have. He needed to put Miss Prince out of his mind.

Yesterday, she'd made an impression. Today,

he'd been transfixed by watching her. If he kept encountering the woman, she'd only consume more of his thoughts.

FOR THE REST OF the afternoon, Allie busied herself with tidying. The back room now smelled of polish, and the inventory room was better organized than it had been in months. She'd even found a few pieces that Dominic had received but never listed in their inventory ledger. The great cost of being as single-minded as her brother was that he couldn't be bothered with details. The mundane bored him to tears. But in running a shop, doing the mundane tasks well meant a great deal.

One of the items she unearthed was a Japanese vase she knew one of their regular customers would adore, so she finally allowed herself a moment off her feet and sat down to pen a letter to the dowager countess who Allie suspected would snap the vase up.

From her spot at her work desk in the back room, she could see Mr. Gibson at the front counter. He'd taken a tray full of watch parts out with him, though the steady stream of customers had kept him busy. As the winter holidays approached, they always got busier.

Allie finished her letter and had begun writing out the countess's address when the bell rang above the shop door.

She looked up to catch sight of a gentleman dressed for the evening in white tie and a dark ebony coat. He looked as if he was ready for the opera or dinner at an expensive restaurant rather than a browse at an antique shop. Mr. Gibson greeted him with the same measured tone he offered each new customer.

Allie began her search for a stamp among the piles of notes and papers on the desk they all used. She found one, apparently their last, and scribbled out a reminder in her notebook to buy more.

Then the customer's voice filtered in from the front of the shop and she froze.

It was a voice she recognized.

Her pen skidded across the page, streaking ink, and she held her breath, straining to hear.

"I do not believe in simplicity, and I demand perfection."

Allie laid her pen aside and concentrated on listening. Yes, there was no denying it. He sounded very much like the ominous tall man at Hawlston's.

Moving as quietly as she could, she tiptoed over and positioned herself near the threshold. Then she peeked through the half-open door.

The customer was indeed tall, but he looked nothing like the man in the alley. She could only see him in profile, but he was clean-shaven with light brown hair. And he seemed wider, less lean, though his layers of clothing could account for the change.

"If I provide you with a gem," the customer said to Mr. Gibson, "can you cut it to my specifications?"

"Of course, sir."

"Show me some of your work, if you would."

The man flicked a gloved hand out and Mr. Gibson reached for the calling card he offered.

Allie noted the jump of Mr. Gibson's brows after he glanced down at the details on the card. "I will be pleased to, my lord," he said. Then he led the man to the jewelry counter.

Pressing her back against the wall, Allie willed her breathing to steady, willed her mind to stop leaping to conclusions.

The man's accent was clipped and precise, and that made sense if he was a nobleman. But why would a nobleman involve himself in a scheme to steal jewels from the monarchy that gave his very title legitimacy? But, of course, that might be the heart of the matter. Perhaps the man was not loyal to the Crown. His sympathies might lie with the Irish cause for home rule or with one of the workers' unions.

Allie glanced at the man again as he followed Mr. Gibson to the locked case where they displayed their finest objects and jewels.

The similarities were undeniable. He carried himself with the same confidence as the man she'd seen—albeit briefly—outside Hawlston's.

"Do you have a loupe?"

"Indeed, my lord." Mr. Gibson handed the man the magnifying monocle he carried with him everywhere.

Allie watched as the man lifted the loupe to his face, and her belly dropped into her boots. It was him. She had no doubt. Something about the curve of his cheek as it met the lens. He *was* the man she'd seen at Hawlston's.

The nobleman lifted his head and snapped his gaze toward the back-room doorway as if he sensed her perusal. Allie sprang back, flattening herself against the wallpaper and holding her breath. She prayed he hadn't seen her.

Several minutes ticked by, and every moment she feared the man would burst into the back room and . . . She wasn't certain what he'd do, but surely he would not wish for someone who could identify him if he was going to engage in such a brazen attempt at thievery.

Her breath rushed out and her heart felt as if it was trying to leap from her chest, but all she heard from the front of the shop was Mr. Gibson's voice as he described two of the rings he'd cut and a matching sapphire necklace. The other man murmured quietly in response. Then the men's voices faded, as if they'd both stepped toward the front of the shop.

She dared not peek out again, for fear the nobleman would spot her.

A moment later, the bell chimed, and she could only guess that the man had departed.

Still, she waited, straining to hear. Finally, she could make out Mr. Gibson's footsteps cutting a path toward her. His eyes widened when he stepped into the back room.

"Are you all right, Miss Prince?" He examined her with genuine concern. "I heard scraping around back here and thought you might have encountered a mouse."

"No, not a mouse. Grendel would have heard the creature before either of us." Allie blew out a few long, relieved breaths and pressed a hand to her chest, willing her heart rate to settle. "Do you have the card he gave you?"

"The customer?"

"Yes, I need it."

"It's up front."

Allie rushed past him and spotted the gilded rectangle on the counter and snatched it up. It was printed on scarlet paper, thick and expensive, with elaborate gold details.

It read *Lord Thomas Holcroft, Belgrave Square, London,* and Allie's hand shook as she examined it.

Finally, she had something. Some tangible proof that the man existed, and she needed to get it to Inspector Drake immediately.

"Is something amiss?" Mr. Gibson had followed her to the counter.

"What did he say?"

"That he wishes to bring me a gem, a diamond, to cut to his specifications."

"Did he say when?"

Mr. Gibson nodded. "He said he would deliver it to me tomorrow afternoon."

"Personally? He himself will return?"

"That seemed to be his implication, yes."

"Tomorrow afternoon," Allie repeated breathlessly. "There's not much time. I must go."

"Miss Prince, will you please tell me what's upset you so?" He gestured toward his own face. "You've gone as red as a ruby, and you're breathing as if you've just won a foot race."

"I believe that man may be up to something nefarious." She didn't want to tell him more. No need to cause him to worry when Inspector Drake would no doubt wish to keep the matter quiet.

Mr. Gibson frowned. "Do you know the man? What gives you reason to suspect him?"

"I'm afraid I can't say more. Not yet." Allie drew closer. "I may be wrong, but it's worth getting this information to someone who can sort the matter out."

"Shall I decline Lord Holcroft's custom if he returns tomorrow?"

"No, not at all. We need him to return, and we need to be ready." Allie reached for her coat and scarf and donned both while Mr. Gibson regarded her with a mixture of concern and doubt.

"I know I'm not making a great deal of sense, but I must go. Would you mind closing up on your own?"

"Not at all, but I am concerned about you, Miss Prince." A sigh escaped him, and it seemed weighted with sadness. "I'm afraid this is just the sort of thing your brother feared before he departed."

Allie's shoulders tightened and she clenched her jaw at the reminder. "I know it may seem that I'm acting impulsively, but I'm not."

At his dubious expression, she gave a tiny smile. "All right, perhaps I am, but I must. This matter is urgent, and if it turns out well, I vow that Dominic will be proud of me."

He nodded but offered her a warning look very much like her brother—or her father—would have.

Allie slid the nobleman's card into her coat pocket and made her way out to the street to hail a hansom. This afternoon, she'd told herself she'd likely never see Detective Inspector Benedict Drake again, but it seemed she would. She had exactly what he needed—a clear lead that would allow him to properly investigate the matter.

This time, at least, he would be pleased to see her.

CHAPTER SEVEN

*B*Y SIX in the evening, Drake had completed much of the paperwork he'd ignored during the blackmail case and set two detectives to make further inquiries regarding M—a challenge when he could tell the men virtually nothing about the high-discretion blackmail case. There were few clues to follow, but the empty townhouse in Bedford Square was a start. He'd begun working on two new cases in earnest too, questioning suspects and visiting the site of a young man's murder.

But even with a day of busyness, the demands of his job did not wholly occupy his mind.

His thoughts strayed again and again to one petite, talkative antique shop owner. He retraced the memory of her smile, the way pleasure had brightened her eyes and echoed in his own chest when he'd seen her at Hawlston's. Flashes hit him at the oddest moments. The way she'd commandeered the objects on his desk. The way her hands danced through the air while she talked. The temptation of her lips curved in a smile.

Yet each time he got lost in such musings,

he forced his mind back to the more pressing matter—his advancement.

Normally, he took Haverstock's word on any matter without challenge. But he'd checked on Stanhope, who Haverstock claimed would be "moving up" soon.

Turned out the man had already moved up, and not just up but out. He'd left his role at Scotland Yard and was now at the Home Office.

It appeared that Haverstock was obfuscating to hold him back, and Drake refused to be hobbled professionally by anyone. Even by a man who'd mentored and championed him as Haverstock had for the past few years.

In truth, he did not want to work for Special Branch. It had seemed an intriguing opportunity and Haverstock had encouraged him, but after the business with the blackmail scheme and the death of Howe, he'd found much more satisfaction in dealing with the cases he'd set aside the last few weeks. Those cases dealt mostly with working-class Londoners.

He identified with their struggles, and he was looking forward to discussing the working-class housing bill with Lord Wellingdon at the dinner he'd been invited to.

For the first time in a long while, he was finishing work at a reasonable hour. But as he donned his overcoat, raised voices in the hallway outside his office drew his notice.

The moment he reached for the handle of his office door, he recognized one of the voices.

A distinctly feminine sound.

Miss Prince was back.

Unbidden, a grin stretched the muscles of his face, and he could not will it away.

He was beginning to think he'd never pass a future day without encountering her, and he was terrified at how much the thought delighted him.

Someone twisted the latch on his door. He pulled the door open and she came with it, stumbling against his chest.

He wrapped his arms around her, and her hands went to his shirtfront, as if to brace her fall. But he wouldn't let her fall. He held her steady, and she hesitated as if stunned, her warm breath gusting against his neck.

The sort of adrenaline that rushed his veins when he was on a case heightened his senses now.

Long lashes. Pink lips. Those tip-tilted eyes. Curves that snugged against him as if the two of them had been made to fit together. He dipped a hand lower, pulling her just an inch closer. So close he could count her freckles. So close he could feel the fierce thud of her heartbeat. So close he could kiss her if he dipped his head but a few inches.

Stop, some distant warning voice told him. *She's not yours.*

"I wished to see you," she whispered.

It was at that moment that he noticed Ransome in the hall behind her, hands on his hips and a glower on his face.

"I tried to stop 'er, Duke."

"No need," Drake told him, then tried to ignore the way the sergeant gaped at him in slack-jawed shock.

"Are you all right?" he asked her quietly.

She nodded and then pushed away from him, past him, and strode into his office.

He followed her and glanced down at his chest—he felt the imprint of her soft curves there still—and everything in him wanted her close again. He licked his lips and shoved a hand through his hair. Her nearness shook him more than he could fathom.

"I must speak to you, and you'll want to hear this, Inspector."

Her eyes were wide and blood had rushed into her cheeks. She looked very much as she had yesterday morning. As if whatever she wished to say was all but ready to burst out of her.

"Go on."

"He came to Princes," she said with quiet intensity. "The tall man from Hawlston's walked right into my shop."

Drake worked to give nothing away. He'd honed the ability to withhold reactions, especially any emotion. It wasn't out of a desire to be cold, merely a necessity of the job. Emotion clouded judgement.

But she'd already broken through, aroused him, confounded him, and the fight for cool dispassion was harder now.

Fear, which he'd learned to beat back years ago, made his pulse tick in his neck. All the heat of their momentary collision turned to a trickle of ice down his spine.

Nothing about the man visiting her shop made sense except in the worst of scenarios. If this was the man she'd overheard, and he'd had the audacity to go to Princes, Drake suspected there *was* a plot afoot. Perhaps the thief wanted no witnesses who could connect him to the mischief he was about to get up to.

"Did you speak to him?" As forthright as she was, he imagined she might confront him on the spot.

"No. In fact, I stayed in the back room and did my best to remain hidden." She swallowed hard as if recalling the moment. "Mr. Gibson dealt with him. He's our resident goldsmith and gem expert, though he knows antiquities too."

"Did he buy anything?"

"No. He inquired about having a gem cut."

Drake arched a brow and his mind spun with possibilities. The one difficulty of stealing famous jewels was disposing of them to buyers who would not recognize them as filched gems. That required a jeweler and gem cutter of skill and discretion.

"Is your Mr. Gibson a trustworthy man?"

"Of course he is." She crossed her arms and glowered at him. "He ran the shop with my father for years and is all but a part of our family."

"Very well." He raised a hand and softened his tone. "I meant no offense. So you saw this customer from a distance? Could it have been another man with a dark beard and dark glasses?"

That was the most sensible conclusion. The description was vague enough to fit a hundred men.

She drew her lower lip between her teeth rather than answer, and he felt a bit of the dread in his gut ebb away. Perhaps it wasn't the same man after all.

"You're not certain?" he guessed.

"I am." She curled her hands into fists. "But he did not . . . look exactly the same," she finally confessed.

"Ah."

"But it *was* the same man. You yourself implied that he might have been concealing his appearance the first time I saw him."

"He may have been, which makes this identification all the more dubious." In most cases, he'd dismiss the matter now, and he wasn't sure why he found himself willing to entertain her story.

"I know his voice. I've replayed the whole thing in my mind over and over, hoping to remember something new or find some additional detail."

Good grief, the lady sounded like him when a twisted case gnawed at his mind.

She held his gaze and said nothing. In those blue eyes of hers, he saw certainty and could not detect a single flicker of doubt.

"I know it was him. Do you ever get a sense here?" she asked him, pressing a hand against her chest. "Or here?" She moved her hand lower, splaying her fingers over her middle.

He was transfixed. His imagination spun too-vivid thoughts—his own hand spread across her body, encircling the gentle curve of her waist, gripping the curve of her hip, pulling her against him. He still felt the heat of her, of that brief moment of holding her in his arms.

Then he cursed his wayward thoughts and racked his brain to remember what she'd asked him.

"The sharpness of my memory tells me it was the same man, the same voice, but my intuition knows too," she said.

"I do know that feeling." The insistent tug of intuition, the hunch that led him to hidden facts.

"Then please believe me, Inspector." She took a step closer, then another. Soon she was near enough to touch again.

Madly, he considered reaching for her. Though he had no right at all.

"I have more for you." A mischievous grin curved her lips. "I have a lead."

For a detective, there were no more enticing words in the English language.

She drew a card from her pocket and offered it to him. When he grasped the edge, his fingers brushed hers and a shock of pleasure shot through him.

She was so damnably soft, so enticingly warm.

So he focused on the card in his hand, the thick, fine paper in a deep crimson shade, gilded so excessively as to be gaudy. And a name: Lord Thomas Holcroft of Belgrave Square. The lack of a house number was odd. It reeked of arrogance, implying that anyone living in Belgravia would know Lord Holcroft by reputation alone.

Miss Prince watched him expectantly. "It does

seem strange that a nobleman would set out to steal from the Crown, doesn't it?"

"He wouldn't be the first aristocrat to cross his monarch, though it rarely ends well for them." He recalled a few lords and ladies known to support the Fenian cause, but the name Holcroft did not strike him as familiar.

"Will you question him?" She made the query sound very much like a suggestion.

"Not yet. First, I'd like to see what I can uncover about the man."

A nobleman would be easier to find than most suspects, even without a house number listed. Though it made little sense to question or confront the man. A simple denial would surely follow. The wisest course was to have Holcroft watched and discover whether his activities or associates could be linked to any sort of plan.

She frowned, clearly not satisfied with his strategy.

"Thank you for the lead, Miss Prince," he told her. "May I keep this?"

"Yes, of course." She made no move to depart and the expectant look remained.

He sensed she wished him to begin the hunt for Holcroft now and that if he'd asked her to join him, she would have eagerly agreed.

But as grateful as he was for a potential lead that might allow him to settle the matter, she had involved herself too much already. Especially if the man had gone from whispers in a coffeehouse to visiting her shop.

"I was just on my way out for the evening—"

"Please don't tell me that you don't need my assistance, Inspector, and that I should go on my way and forget the entire matter."

He'd considered saying exactly that. "You brought me a lead, Miss Prince. You've done a great deal."

"I could do more." Her eyes sparked and her mouth curved in a cat-in-the-cream smile. "You may not wish to question him, but would you like to get a look at him? He's coming back to Princes tomorrow afternoon."

SHE'D DONE THIS TO herself, all but insisting that Inspector Drake come to Princes and wait for Lord Holcroft's return in order to get a good look at the man.

And now that the Scotland Yard man was here, just where she'd wanted him, she'd never been more distracted in her life.

He'd strode through the front door at half three while she was helping a customer. The wealthy industrialist, Mr. Snodgrass, was seeking a gift for his wife.

Allie usually took care with Snodgrass. He'd come to Princes many times for gifts or unique items for his home. But the minute Inspector Drake walked in, her attention was entirely his.

Not that he sought it. Like any polite customer, he noted that she was with another patron and busied himself with browsing the shop.

But she was too curious not to watch him. Too

pleased to see his handsome face again not to follow him with her gaze. She had a knack for knowing what sort of object might intrigue a customer, but with the inspector she was at a loss. He didn't linger over the furnishings, vases, coins, books, or gems. Just took everything in. Assessing.

"I say again, Miss Prince, could you put it in special wrap? Perhaps add a ribbon?"

"Forgive me, Mr. Snodgrass." The poor man had been speaking and she'd heard it only distantly. "Yes, of course. I will package it with care."

"Very good. Send it to my office as you have the others, and it must arrive by Tuesday."

"I promise that it will." Allie flicked her gaze toward Inspector Drake. She'd momentarily lost sight of him. "Good day to you, Mr. Snodgrass."

"And to you, Miss Prince. Excellent choice, as always." His mustache wiggled as he offered her a smile, then departed.

"What did you choose for him?" Inspector Drake emerged from one of the back aisles and sauntered toward the counter where she stood.

"An opal-and-amethyst ring for his wife's birthday."

"He must trust your judgement a great deal."

"I'm good at choosing what a customer might like."

He shot her a look. "So you're good at assessing people." Drake inspected the Roman coins arranged beneath glass in another display, then lifted his green gaze to hers. "What would you choose for me?"

Allie's mouth went dry, and her heartbeat galloped in her chest. Something in his eyes, the low intensity of the question, felt like more than a challenge. It felt a bit like an invitation to solve a particularly interesting puzzle.

The distinct note of challenge in his tone thrilled her.

"Hmm." She tipped her head as if she was the detective and he was her case to solve.

He held still for her perusal, watching her with an intensity that made her skin prickle, and when she took her time and didn't immediately offer up a suggestion, a hint of a smile lifted the edges of his mouth.

Oh, he was enjoying this. But so was she.

This close to him, she noted aspects she'd missed in their earlier encounters. The glint of bronze in his hair where the waning sunlight bounced off a mirror and caught the color. A scar at the edge of his mouth and another on his chin. And two grooves between his brows as if he pondered very hard and very often.

"Am I so very baffling, Miss Prince?" He pitched his voice low and teasing.

As soon as the sound rumbled over her, she knew.

"Not at all. I'd never concede so easily." She crooked a finger at him. "This way, Inspector."

She led him to a shelf where several unique objects were arranged. They weren't the items that generally caught customers' notice, but Allie thought them some of the most interesting pieces they carried at Princes.

"This, I think." With both hands, she lifted a polished wooden box off the shelf and held it out for his inspection.

"It is a pretty thing."

The box was covered with elaborate carvings and accented with inlaid abalone shell.

"It's more than pretty," Allie told him. "It's a puzzle box imported from China. In order to open the box, you must solve the mysteries of the box's design."

A smile flashed across his face, and Allie felt as if she'd seen a burst of sunlight on a cloudy day. She felt a bit of pride for inspiring that stoic face of his to ease into joy. If even for a moment.

But soon the pensive frown came again. "It does seem a very obvious choice, Miss Prince. Detective. Mystery box."

Allie laughed. "You impugn my skills." She pointed at the box. "But you are intrigued, aren't you?"

His hands were large enough to all but enclose the box completely and yet he handled it gently, turning it this way and that. Allie found herself mesmerized by his deftness, and she noted that the abrasions on his knuckles had already begun to heal.

"I am absolutely intrigued." The look he shot her from under his brows made her doubt he was talking about the box and hope he was talking about her. A syrupy warmth spread through her body.

She tried to say something in reply, but for once in my life, she struggled to form words.

When she heard movement in the back room, it was as if she'd been tugged out of a trance.

"Mr. Gibson." Panic welled up and she reached for Inspector Drake instinctively. "I haven't explained your presence to him. Give me a moment?"

Drake had locked his gaze on her hand where she held him. When he looked at her again, his eyes seemed brighter. "Of course."

"I don't want to alarm him, but I think he needs to know the truth."

Drake's brows knitted. "The difficulty is that we don't yet know the truth. This Holcroft may or may not be the man you saw previously."

Allie gritted her teeth. He still doubted her.

Then he shocked her by laying his hand over hers. "But even if he is, what he said at Hawlston's does not constitute a genuine plot."

Drake stepped back and fixed his gaze over her shoulder. She turned to see Mr. Gibson emerge from the back room.

"I've returned from lunch, Miss Prince. Just letting you know." Mr. Gibson offered Inspector Drake a brief glance. "Pardon me for interrupting."

Before he could return to his workshop, Allie called to him. "Mr. Gibson, this is Detective Inspector Drake of Scotland Yard."

"I see." The goldsmith observed Drake with new interest and what seemed a degree of respect.

"He's come to . . . observe Lord Holcroft. We'll remain in the back room during his visit." Allie suspected Drake might decide to follow the man after his departure too.

"Do you plan to apprehend the man inside Princes?" Mr. Gibson's jaw tightened, and Allie imagined that he feared for the shop's reputation. She did too, of course.

"Not at all." Drake glanced at each of them. "I merely wish to get a look at the nobleman for now."

"Very well. Shall I take over up here, then? And I am still to accept the man's gem and cut it to his specifications?"

"Yes, we should treat him as we would any customer. At least for now." Allie counted herself lucky that Mr. Gibson was willing to aid them without delving much deeper into the details.

Twenty minutes later, he'd settled into his spot behind the counter, and Allie found herself sequestered with Inspector Drake in the back room. The area was spacious, but the detective's size made the room seem shockingly diminutive.

Allie watched as he subjected each item in it to the same intense perusal he'd given the antiquities on display in the front of the shop. He even stopped to read the clippings, mostly about Dominic's finds and Eveline's talks, that she'd pinned to the wall above her desk.

"I take it this is your work area."

"Seems an obvious deduction, Inspector. Shopkeeper. Desk in the shop's back room," she said pertly, daring to tease him as he'd teased her.

"A shopkeeper who likes flowers, is running out of ink, and enjoys reading." He side-eyed her and then bent his head to read the spines of several books she kept at the edge of her blotter. She waited for his reaction. The pile mostly contained pirate histories.

"Your taste in books runs to the criminal, Miss Prince. Should I be concerned?" When he looked up again, his mouth was curved in a mischievous grin that revealed dimples. Allie had the mad impulse to trace them with her fingertips.

"I've been researching lady pirates," she told him, then bit her lip when his dark brows shot up with interest. She licked her lips and blurted the rest. "Perhaps one day I'll write a book about them."

His grin softened to an expression that was less mischievous and full of sincerity. "I'd like to read your book."

The comment felt like a warm breeze rippling across her skin, and then all that warmth rushed into her cheeks. It shocked Allie how much his comment pleased her. It shocked her how much the detective's nearness made her body hum with awareness.

"Then your taste in books runs to the criminal too, Inspector?"

That flash of a smile again. So quick she might have missed it if she'd blinked.

"Even before I joined the force, I tended to favor stories of adventure or detective tales."

"Are they what inspired you to join the Metropolitan Police?"

"No." He said the word so sharply, she snapped her gaze to his eyes. They had darkened to a stormy green. "I wanted to stop feeling powerless. Thought perhaps I should devote my energy to seeing justice done."

Allie took a step closer. "I admire that impulse," she told him earnestly, "and I understand it. The desire to do what's right."

He matched her approach by taking a single stride himself.

"Is that what you wish, Miss Prince? To do what's right?"

At the moment, all she truly wished was for him to grin at her again, to see those dimples carved above his sharp jaw. This close, she could smell his cologne, feel the heat of his body just a few inches away.

No man had ever overwhelmed her senses the way he did.

When she didn't answer his question, he stepped closer. The toe of his boot brushed the edge of her skirt.

"Miss Prince?" His gaze traced her features, then settled on her lips.

Her breathing quickened and she searched her addled brain, trying to focus on the question he'd asked rather than the effect of his nearness.

At the distant chime of the bell, they both stilled. Allie strode toward the half-open door, expecting to see Lord Holcroft. Instead, she recognized the postman who delivered their afternoon mail each day.

"Not him," she told Drake. He'd positioned himself behind her, a spice-scented wall of masculine heat at her back. She held still a moment, savoring the warmth of him, then tipped her head back. "Not long now."

They both glanced at the clock on the wall. It would be four in less than a quarter of an hour.

"Will you follow him?" Allie asked, finally turning to face him.

He stepped back, giving her space that was entirely appropriate.

"That is my intention," he told her. "Though it may take others to maintain watch and days to determine anything of use."

"I suppose there's nothing to confront him with at this point."

"No, and if I did, he'd simply issue a denial."

"Yes, he would. This gem he's bringing Mr. Gibson to cut. What if it's stolen? If they were plotting to steal the Crown Jewels, perhaps jewel theft is their stock-in-trade."

"Once I've seen the gem and know the details, I'll make inquiries to see if it matches any reports of stolen gems."

Allie began pacing. It was her usual method for working off agitation when she had nothing else to do.

In contrast, Drake settled into a straight-backed chair. "Is that an antique or used for play?"

He'd chosen a chair in front of the chess set that their mother had used to teach Allie and her siblings how to play. It had been Allie's idea to put it in the back room, where she could play Mr. Gibson on the long days they spent in the shop.

"It's both. My mother used it to teach me and my siblings. Do you play?"

"Occasionally, though my sister is a fierce competitor and has an unchallenged string of victories against me."

Allie laughed. She found herself intrigued by his chess master sister. "Perhaps you need a few pointers."

"Teach me how to beat her, and I'll be forever in your debt."

Allie gulped down the lump that had suddenly formed in her throat at the thought of having Detective Inspector Benedict Drake indebted to her, and she pushed away the notions that came to mind of how he could repay her because they involved intimacies she had no right to.

In repayment, may I trace your dimples with the tip of my finger?

Good grief, less than an hour alone with the man and she was becoming a wanton.

The multiple clocks on the shop's shelves as well as the pendulum wall clock in the back room all dinged in near synchrony, indicating the four o'clock hour.

Allie peeked through the door, which stood ajar by a few inches.

Mr. Gibson shrugged and glanced at his watch. "Perhaps he's running late."

"Perhaps he is."

Allie turned back to find Drake had picked up the white queen and was examining the intricate details of the marble piece.

"I suppose I have time to teach you a few tricks." Allie settled into the chair across from him and reset the board. Though she usually took white, Drake sat on that side today, and she quite liked the notion that he'd move her usual pieces around the board.

"Show me one of your opening moves, Inspector."

He slid a pawn forward as did she. Then, after a few moments' consideration, he advanced another pawn. A sacrifice.

Each time he slid a piece from one square to another, he hesitated, tapping his index finger atop the marble figure. Allie found even that small tell fascinating. He surveyed the board, even in these early moves. Detective Inspector Drake was not impulsive. He took his time, then slid his piece toward her with utter confidence.

When he put his knight in play next, he shot her a questioning look.

"A potentially disastrous gambit." Allie beamed. "It's one of my favorites."

"I'm playing as Helen does."

"Your sister is quite clever."

"Tell me why it works."

For the next while, Allie showed him why the gambit *could* work to white's advantage. She felt as if she was giving away arcane secrets by showing him how black could thwart the aggressive maneuvers.

They practiced a few variations, not truly playing a match. Drake asked excellent questions and seemed to genuinely appreciate her knowledge of the game.

"Still no sign of him," Mr. Gibson informed them, peeking his head into the back room. "But there is something odd."

"What's that?" Drake asked, curiosity deepening the two grooves between his brows.

"Another man has been watching the shop from across the street for the last forty minutes."

CHAPTER EIGHT

At GIBSON'S words, Drake felt the tug of intuition that Miss Prince had spoken about. A twisting in his gut that demanded a response.

He moved past the older man and strode into the shop, taking care to remain behind a high row of shelves lining the main counter. A scan of the shops across from Princes revealed working-class Londoners moving past and one couple who lingered in heated conversation outside the stationer's located one shop down.

No sign of anyone watching Princes.

But then a cloud of smoke came into view, and the answer to that tug in his middle emerged from the haze.

A figure stood receded in the mouth of the alley where he'd met with Fitz. The short, barrel-chested man took another draw on his pipe as Drake observed him. Recognized him. A moment later, another gray cloud wafted up, and when it had cleared, he had no doubts.

The well-known thief's presence here, watching Princes when Holcroft should have appeared, did not bode well.

"Do you see him?" Miss Prince had emerged from the back room and came to stand behind him.

"I do, and I know who he is."

"You do?" She gripped his arm in her eagerness and then began to push forward as if she yearned for a look herself. He reached out to keep her back.

She made a huffing sound of protest but remained concealed.

He turned, took her hand, and led her to a corner of the shop completely out of sight of the front windows.

When they'd stopped, she made no move to withdraw her hand. He found himself enjoying that simple point of contact too much and released her.

"He's a known thief called Jack Demming. Usually to be found around the docks or across the river in Southwark, so it's odd that he'd be here."

Her eyes widened and excitement all but rose off her like the smoke from Demming's pipe. "Maybe it's one of the other men I saw. I need to get a look."

She moved quickly, and he reached out to stop her, but she'd already crept up toward the window. Cleverly, she kept to the side wall and then finally approached a large tapestry that mostly hid her from view. Peeking around, she let out a thoughtful *hmm*.

"He could be one of them. The right stature and size."

"Come away from the window, Miss Prince."

The frown she shot back at him was full of irritation.

"Why is the man here, Detective Inspector?" Gibson had resumed his spot behind the main counter and stared at Ben expectantly.

"That's a very good question. And believe me, I intend to ask him." Ben offered Gibson a nod and then turned to Miss Prince. "If you'll excuse me."

He meant it as a sufficient leave-taking and immediately made his way to the Princes' back room, heading for a door that he assumed led into the alley behind the shop.

Behind him, he heard the firm, rapid footsteps of the lady he suspected wouldn't let him depart without further explanation. Unfortunately, he didn't have the time to provide one.

"Inspector, the thief is out front. Why are you back here?"

Shooting a glance over his shoulder, he told her bluntly, "If I approach the man, he'll bolt."

"Oh yes. He'd recognize you, wouldn't he? You must sneak up on him. I quite like that plan."

He chuckled despite his sense of urgency. "Finally, you appreciate my methods, Miss Prince."

He'd pitched his voice low without meaning to, and her cheeks flushed the loveliest shade of pink. He liked sparking that reaction in her, liked the way her eyes locked on his, then flicked down to his lips.

Twisting the doorknob, he turned and allowed himself one last look at her. "Stay here, Miss

Prince. Let me handle this. Demming isn't a man to be trifled with. I need to determine why he's here and your lordling isn't."

"Of course." The innocent look she returned didn't truly reassure him, because her eyes glinted with far too much curiosity for him to believe she'd contentedly remain in the shop.

"I insist you remain here."

"Do you indeed?" Her arched auburn brow was an enticing challenge. She was a quite untamable lady.

He worried about his ability to keep her safe. But the way she had taken up root in his thoughts and the way his body responded every time she looked his way meant he was the one in grave danger where she was concerned.

"Wait for my return." The door spilled out into a narrow alley, but there was no obliging passage between buildings. Ben had to go a ways to find a passage out onto Moulton Street. Which was probably a good thing. He was far enough down that Demming didn't see him as he sprinted across the street and then continued even farther to find a way around the row of buildings so that he could come up behind the thief.

There were no other passages that broke through the line of buildings, so he sprinted toward the cross street and then cut into the mouth of the alley.

Carts, boxes, and other detritus blocked his way in spots, and a recent rain had filled every depression in the muddy throughway with a pond of muck. He was forced to proceed slowly and feared Demming might abscond before he could question the man.

ALLIE NIBBLED AT THE edge of her nail as she stood in the shadows along Princes' far wall and watched the man who watched her shop.

"If he sees you observing him," Mr. Gibson said in a quiet, steady tone, "the man might hie off before the inspector gets to him, Miss Prince."

"I don't think he can see me." As soon as the words were out, several of their clocks on display chimed once to mark the half hour. "Holcroft is either late or he's not coming at all."

"The whole matter of Holcroft and this watcher is odd." Admitting as much seemed to cost Mr. Gibson a bit of his usual equanimity. "Do these men intend to steal from the shop, do you think?"

"I don't know, but I don't think they do." The very idea of anyone invading Princes for nefarious purposes made her feel as determined as she had ever been in her life.

Princes wasn't just a shop. The rooms upstairs had once been her home. Her grandfather had built the shop's shelves with his own hands. Her mother had chosen the wallpaper and curtains and every modern fixture.

Stealing the Crown Jewels might offend her sensibilities as an Englishwoman and antiquarian who appreciated the regalia's history, but the notion that these men might bring harm to her family's shop filled her with a fierce need to thwart them. However she could.

"I think there's a great deal more going on," she whispered as much to herself as to Mr. Gibson.

The nobleman's visit was sharp in her mind. The pomposity in his voice. His very unique calling card.

Inspector Drake still hadn't appeared, and the thief in the alleyway had begun looking bored, gazing around the street, his notice drawn by a shapely lady walking a regal-looking hound.

An idea struck and she made her way to the back room, searching the shelf that contained dozens of shop ledgers and several reference books for their thick-spined copy of *Debrett's*. She flipped the pages quickly, searching for Lord Holcroft's entry.

She found a viscount by the name of George Holcroft, but among the brothers, uncles, and sons, she couldn't find a single Thomas listed. If the black beard and dark glasses had been a disguise, perhaps the presentation as a haughty aristocrat had been too.

She rushed back into the shop to tell Mr. Gibson and immediately noticed that their watcher was gone.

"Where is he?"

Mr. Gibson scanned the opposite street and pointed. "He seems to be departing."

Without hesitation, as if some inner force propelled her, Allie strode out onto the street. Mr. Demming hadn't gotten far and twisted his head when the bell above their door sounded.

Spotting her, his eyes bulged under the low brim of his hat. He stopped and looked increasingly confused as Allie strode toward him.

"I wish to speak to you, sir," she said as she pushed past other pedestrians on the busy London street.

As quick as a flash, Demming turned his back on her, tucked his head, and rushed away at a pavement-eating stride.

Allie picked up her pace and wished she wasn't hampered by the length of her skirt and the weight of her petticoats.

At the corner, the thief cut right and disappeared from view.

An omnibus had just dislodged passengers, and a sea of people started down the pavement toward Allie, stalling her progress.

"To hell and rot." Her brother's favorite curse came out unbidden and an elderly lady nearby gasped.

Allie ignored the woman's outrage because she'd spotted an opening. Like Demming had done, she tucked her arms in and pushed past the gaggle of new pedestrians. A moment later, she rounded the corner and found the cross street even busier, clogged with carriages and those making their way to and from shops along the busy thoroughfare.

Demming had disappeared into the crowd, and she couldn't distinguish one burly dark-coated man from another.

Except for the one man who she couldn't fail to notice.

Drake emerged at the end of the alley, and she felt a rush of relief to see him. His long cloak arced out behind him as he ate up the distance between them in his approach. His color was high, his dark hair wild. He looked breathless and frustrated, and when he spotted her, his expression transformed to ire.

"You vowed to wait for me, Miss Prince."

"I didn't vow anything. You insisted and I . . . changed my mind."

"Of course you did."

"You hadn't appeared, and then Mr. Demming departed, so I pursued him."

He scanned the street one way and then the other.

"Unsuccessfully," Allie added, as if the fact wasn't obvious. "I'm sorry."

Drake closed his eyes, ran a hand through his hair, mussing it further and in a way that set a few curls free.

Allie felt a wildly inappropriate urge to stroke her fingers through them. Why could she think of nothing but touching the man?

"I lost him too. You've nothing to apologize for." His voice had gone deeper, warm, almost reassuring. Then he shocked her by releasing a half smile. "Except, perhaps, for doing precisely the opposite of what I asked you to."

"I was trying to be helpful."

"I know. That's why I cannot fault you."

"And I did discover something."

"What's that?"

"I checked *Debrett's*. Lord Thomas Holcroft isn't listed. The copy is only three years old. I suspect he may not be a true nobleman."

He began nodding before she'd finished speaking. "I suspected as much when he didn't turn up."

"Why do you think he came to the shop posing as a customer?"

Drake worked his jaw, his gaze locked on hers, holding back whatever suspicions were percolating in his mind.

"Please tell me what you're thinking." He had no reason to divulge all the workings of his detecting mind to her, but this was about her shop now, and she needed to know as much as he'd reveal.

"I have a few hypotheses but not enough information for any conclusions." He glanced around them again, still scanning for Demming.

"What shall we do next?"

"I'll escort you back to Princes and urge you, once again, to—"

"Let me handle this," she said in an overly gruff imitation of his voice.

What sounded very much like laughter rumbled in his chest as if trying to burst free. Then he cleared his throat and gave her a rueful glance. "You find me repetitive, do you?"

"A bit. I know you think I do not listen, but I do. It's just that—"

"Please, Alexandra." He reached for her, just a hand against her upper arm, but the weight and warmth of it slid through the sleeve of her dress and spread all the way to her toes. Though his voice had dipped low, pleading, there was nothing soft in his gaze. His green eyes had gone hard, his jaw set.

If he'd wished to shock her into silence, he'd succeeded. The use of her name had set her pulse racing, and whatever she'd meant to say drifted off in the cool autumn breeze.

"Forgive me for the liberty, but I am asking you to step away from this for your own safety. I want to keep you out of danger. And in this case, I know the man and his methods well."

She understood that it was his job, his duty even, to protect her as he would any citizen of London, but he spoke with such warm sincerity in his voice. Such yearning in his gaze. He wanted to protect *her*. Given her family's tendencies, that should have rankled. But somehow it didn't feel at all like her family's usual brand of overprotectiveness.

Drake had never once made her feel foolish or even chastised her for the impulse to help.

"I will find Demming before the night is out. I promise you that. I know the man's haunts. Give him a few hours, and he'll be tucked up at his favorite pub near the Southwark bridge. And I'll be waiting."

Allie believed him, trusting that he had methods for persuading the man to talk. She could even concede, if she allowed logic to have the last word, that her presence would add nothing to the evening's pursuit.

"Very well," she finally said. "You'll send word if you learn anything from him?"

"Of course." He raised his head and glanced back in the direction of Princes. "And I'll put a man on Princes. A constable who can see you home at the end of the night."

"I don't think that's necessary." But as soon as he heard her tone of protest, one sharp inhale told her that she wouldn't win this one either.

"Demming was watching your shop for a reason. I intend to find out why." His tone had turned ominous, and she couldn't help wondering if he'd add new abrasions to those knuckles of his tonight.

She almost felt sorry for Mr. Demming. Almost.

"I need to return to the Yard, so let's get you back. Gibson will be off his head with worry." He slid the hand at her arm around to the small of her back as Allie turned to make the trip back to Princes.

Once they'd set off, he stopped touching her, and she decided instantly that she far preferred it when he did.

As NIGHT FELL AND they began preparations to close Princes for the evening, Allie noted a new wariness in Mr. Gibson. After decades of association with her family, he'd seen her father and siblings go off on voyages and expeditions that many might consider dangerous, and had barely blinked an eye.

But after the visit of the man calling himself Lord Holcroft and the ominous observer, Mr. Demming, he perceived a threat to the shop itself.

And she knew that he cared for it as if it was his own.

She'd decided she had to take him into her confidence.

He'd taken her explanation about what she'd overheard at Hawlston's in his usual stoic stride. Much like Inspector Drake, he seemed dubious that an actual plot to steal the Crown's regalia was afoot. But a threat to Princes? That seemed to gnaw at him as the day wore on.

"Shall we see about a man to serve as night watch until all this business is done, Miss Prince?"

"We could." Though Drake had sent for a constable as promised, the young man had grown bored after an hour and dozed off in one of their chairs near the front window not half an hour ago.

His presence hadn't made her feel any safer, only that his time standing guard in their less than busy shop had bored him to tears.

"I'll look into it if you approve."

"I do." If it put Mr. Gibson's mind at ease, it would be worth the expense.

She suspected Drake would uncover and thwart this plot in short order, judging by how bumbling the main participants seemed to be.

"Very good." Mr. Gibson breathed a little easier.

"Constable Walker is to see me home, so I'll leave now if you don't mind. I can put him out of his misery and let the poor man go on his way." She smiled and Mr. Gibson turned a withering look toward the young constable.

"I shall be seeking a guard who doesn't nod off, I assure you."

"I know you will. Good night."

"And to you, Miss Prince."

"I live close by, Constable, so I usually walk if that suits you."

"Of course, miss." The young uniformed officer scrambled to his feet when she approached.

Once they'd set off, Allie felt the pointlessness of putting the young man to such trouble.

"What did Inspector Drake say to you about why you were sent to my shop?"

"That I should stand watch and see you home."

"But did he tell you why?"

The young man looked at her oddly. "The inspector needn't explain any more than he needs to and rarely does. Tight-lipped is that one." As soon as that judgement was out, he cleared his throat and set his jaw in an attempt to strike the same unaffected mien Drake sometimes wore. Perhaps policemen practiced it.

"Is he good at what he does?" Allie side-eyed the young man as they walked.

He chuckled at her question. "I've never seen anyone better. Some say he's fearless, relentless when he's on a lead. And they say Duke's never failed to solve a case."

"Goodness, that is impressive." She swallowed hard at the thought of Drake's relentlessness. "But why did you call him Duke?"

Constable Walker shrugged. "A nickname. That's all I know." He shot her a sheepish look. "I've only been a constable for half a year, miss. I've a lot to learn."

"Then I'm sure you will."

When they reached her family home in Manchester Square, the constable insisted on waiting until she was safely inside, despite her hope she could part from him near the corner.

Once inside, their housemaid, Lottie, greeted her eagerly, her eyes alight with curiosity. "Good evening, miss."

"Evening, Lottie." Allie allowed the girl to help her with her coat and gloves. "Before you ask, no, I'm not courting a constable. May I count on you not to tell the rest of the household about my escort tonight?"

Their housekeeper, Mrs. Taunton, had seen a great deal over her decades as manager of the Prince household, but they'd rarely had a policeman at their front door. And their elderly butler, Conroy, loathed any kind of disruption to their usual routine.

"Of course, miss, but . . ." She drew closer, Allie's coat still clutched in her arms. "You're not in any sort of trouble, are you, Miss Prince?"

Allie had come to adore Lottie, but the girl loved nothing as much as gossip.

"Not a single bit of trouble. I promise." In her head, she debated whether preoccupation with an imposing, relentless detective counted, but of course, he was determined to keep her *out* of trouble. "I do think I'll take supper in my room. Could you send up a tray?"

Once Lottie had gone, Allie headed up to her room and paced the floor in front of the unlit fireplace. Normally, she'd be eager to remove her day dress and slip into something cozy, but she didn't tonight. She felt unsettled, full of a strange compelling energy. As if there was something she needed to do, though none of her usual evening activities held any appeal.

Tonight, all her thoughts were on Southwark—on Benedict Drake—and she had the wild impulse to go there herself.

She imagined his reaction to her doing so and shuddered.

Still, she couldn't shake the oddest sensation. A ridiculous notion, really.

That, somehow, Benedict Drake needed her, and if she went to Southwark, she could help him.

CHAPTER NINE

THESE RIVERSIDE haunts were familiar to Drake.

Too familiar.

Though it had been years, the memories were still as sharp as the wind that whipped the sails of ships being loaded and unloaded in the London docks.

He'd worked in a factory in Southwark at thirteen. At fifteen, he'd looked for work at the docks not a stone's throw away on the other side of the river. It had been brutal labor—with employment secured for only a day's duration. Each morning, one had to compete to be chosen, but the odds were often in his favor. Even at fifteen, he'd been tall and muscular and strong, and he'd been selected for work frequently enough to feed and lodge all of them—himself, Helen, and George.

And then, after the heated argument he would always regret, his younger brother had come to the docks too. But George had never spoken to the foreman Drake had directed him to. George wasn't interested in seeking honest work. The Thames-side gang that his brother found his way into was a dangerous, desperate lot—picking the pockets of drunk sailors or filching goods from warehouses and ships along the river.

When George had been fool enough to steal from the gang, it had been the last mistake his brother ever made.

Drake couldn't untangle his own folly from his brother's dreadful choices. Anger, guilt, and grief were tied up in a knot, and coming back to this place did nothing but twist the pain.

But he needed to speak to Demming. He needed to know why he had parked himself outside of Princes of London, and what connection, if any, the thief had to the man who'd come into Alexandra's shop. He knew exactly where he'd find Demming.

Dusk had only begun to settle over the city, but The Anchor Pub was already bustling. It was a beacon in the fog and had been for centuries. The odds were good that Demming was nestled up inside. The man was even known to take up residence in the pub's upper rooms at times.

The greatest danger for Drake was that he'd be recognized. He hadn't worked this area as a constable or foot patrolman, but there had been cases during his early days as a detective that brought him into contact with those who considered Southwark their territory.

One couldn't do this sort of work without making enemies. He and Demming had met over the years when the thief was brought into the station where he worked, but as far as Drake knew, Demming had no reason to loathe him, no special grudge to bear against him. And Demming certainly had no reason to know Ben had been in the back room of the Princes' antique shop all afternoon.

Once he stepped inside The Anchor public house, he was grateful for the busyness of the place. One could hide among the crowd, but a man of Demming's size and boisterous nature couldn't hide for long.

Not ten minutes after finding a table in the corner to tuck himself into, Drake recognized one of Demming's known associates. Ichabod Kean matched Demming for size and ruthlessness, and not long after Drake noticed him, the man slammed his glass on the table and made his way out of the pub.

Drake debated whether to follow. Kean might lead him to Demming, or Drake could wait instead to see if the two returned together. But he wasn't in a waiting mood. Before giving the barmaid time to come over and ask what he wanted to drink, he stood and made his way out of the pub again. Somehow, though he'd been inside for only a quarter of an hour, the skies had grown impossibly darker, and a thick fog clung to the ground.

Luckily, Kean was a friendly sort and had run into some associates the minute he exited the pub. He stood with the men in jovial conversation, hunching together against the wind off the river, and breaking out into laughter now and then. Drake made his way around the opposite side of the building. The technique hadn't worked earlier with Demming, but he hoped he could come up behind Kean, wait, and watch for where he went next.

After a few more shared laughs, the men headed off together, just as Drake hoped. He suspected they'd make their way to one of the gaming hells or perhaps one of the dens where they could bare-knuckle box, and those were just the sort of places a man like Demming could be found.

He followed the trio as closely as he dared. All of them seemed in high spirits and were perhaps full of spirits. Kean and another man stumbled a bit as they walked, weaving as if whatever they had consumed at The Anchor was already taking effect.

To Drake's surprise, they cut through the main road and ducked into an abandoned building. He stood debating whether to follow the men inside or wait until they emerged. The absence of Demming unsettled him. He couldn't help wondering if he was in the wrong place. Demming might be standing outside of Miss Prince's home, continuing his watchfulness there.

He waited a good twenty minutes, chafing his hands against the evening's chill, watching for movement inside and around the building. A dim light had been lit in the building's upper story, and something told him Demming was inside. The decision to enter might be foolhardy, since the men inside outnumbered him. But he had to find Demming. If he wasn't with them, they could direct him to the man.

His revolver sat heavy in his pocket, and he hoped he would not have to use it or even threaten to.

This was Demming's territory. Surely, a man seeking him here wouldn't be entirely out of the ordinary.

On the ground floor, he found the building all but pitch-black inside. He used his hands to guide himself along the wall until his eyes adjusted. That's when he noticed a single window high on the opposite wall that allowed a bit of moonlight to leak in.

The building had once been a factory of some sort, though all the machinery now sat derelict.

Footsteps crunched on gravel to his left, and Ben spun toward the sound, body tensed.

Light burst out of the darkness, blinding him, and he lifted an arm against the glare.

"Expected a bit more of you than this, Drake." The low, gruff voice was exactly as he remembered Demming's.

"Just wanted a word with you, Jack." Ben blinked as his eyes adjusted and he could make out the shape of the man behind the bullseye lantern. He sensed the nearness of other bodies in the darkness too. He guessed it was the three men he'd followed who stood in the shadows.

"A word, is it? Just the one?" At his taunt, one of the other men laughed, allowing Ben to gauge that he was but a few feet away.

"More than one, I'm afraid," Ben told him. "I need to speak to you about your presence on Moulton Street today."

"Not in the mood for being questioned." Demming grunted and signaled at one of the men. "Take him."

An arm thick as a tree trunk wrapped itself around Drake's neck. He thrust an elbow back into the man's belly.

"Get 'is hands," the man behind him shouted.

Ben shoved up to break the man's hold on his neck, but his release was only momentary. Before he could fully break free, the arm lashed around him again and the thug only squeezed tighter. So tight he couldn't catch his breath.

Another man emerged from the darkness, jerking one of Drake's hands into a loop of rope.

Ben swung wildly to catch the man with a blow, but he ducked agilely and caught his other hand, wrapping it with the rough binding. The knot he tied was as tight as the hold on his neck.

Once the man in front of him nodded, the one behind him loosened his hold a fraction.

Ben gulped in air.

They'd tied his hands in front, and he calculated how he might reach for his revolver.

As if reading his mind, Demming stepped closer and reached into Ben's empty pocket and then the other, pulling the revolver out by its barrel.

"Seems you 'ad more than talk in mind, detective." Demming stared at Ben with a menace that felt deep, personal. "Tie the bastard to the gears."

Ben had more than a couple inches of height on Demming's men, but they outweighed him in combined brawn, and the one behind him dragged him as if he weighed nothing at all.

Together, the two men slid a chain around his

middle. Ben fought to keep his arms free, but they forced them down and under the chain. The hard, unforgiving wedge of metal at his back felt as if it would leave a permanent dent.

"Consider carefully whether you want to do this, Demming. Assaulting a Met detective isn't something you want added to your record, is it?"

"Oh, I've thought of this moment awhile, I 'ave. Bleedin' dreamed of it."

"Why?"

"Forgot 'im already, 'ave you?"

The beast at his back alternately tightened and loosened his hold on Drake's neck, as if it was some sick game.

"Who?" he managed, though his voice had gone hoarse.

Demming drew close, a fearsome glare on his bearded face. "Amos Howe."

Drake's mind had gone fuzzy, his thoughts scattered pieces he fought to assemble. Howe in that empty townhouse in Bedford Square. The unanswered questions about M. Haverstock handing him a report detailing Howe's death. All of it swirled in his brain.

"You knew Howe?" Drake willed the scraps of information to assemble into solid facts.

"'E was my brother, and you got 'is throat slit."

"I'm sorry." Drake meant it with utter sincerity. Howe wasn't a great man or perhaps even a good one, but he'd done the right thing in the end.

He thought he'd learned a great deal about Howe

during the investigation, but he'd never known he was related to Jack Demming.

Demming spat. "To 'ell with your sympathy. Can't bring me brother back."

Demming drew back and punched Ben in the stomach.

He hadn't braced for the blow, and it reverberated to his spine. His body attempted to curl in on itself, but the behemoth at his back held tight to his neck and shoulders.

"Tell me why you were on Moulton Street," Ben rasped.

They might beat him, torture him, toss him in the Thames, but he at least needed to know the answer to that single question. He needed to know how to keep Alexandra safe.

"I 'ad my reasons. Maybe I was waitin' on you." Demming scoffed. "Then that crazy little bitch came at me like a terrier. Nipping at me 'eels."

Ben closed his eyes, thankful Demming had been there for him. Even if he found Alexandra's audacious determination to confront the thief maddening, he admired her bravery. She was extraordinary.

"Do you know Holcroft?" Ben had no intention of volunteering details about the attempted robbery, but any connections he could gather would help.

"Never 'eard of 'im. Enough talk." Demming stepped back toward the shadows, then bent to strike a match and light his pipe. He sucked on the thing, generating a cloud of pungent smoke.

He finally looked up at Ben. Then he shifted his gaze past Ben to the men surrounding him.

"Do your worst, boys."

SOUTHWARK AT NIGHT, DRENCHED in fog, was a kind of dark Allie had never experienced.

Little tremors raced across her skin when the hansom driver departed and she stood alone, listening to the lapping sound of the Thames, trying to distinguish the nature of the stew of smells that emanated from the water and ships' cargo.

She'd told the driver to drop her near the bridge. A pub near the bridge—that's what Drake had called Demming's favorite haunt.

And, sure enough, she noted one corner of a building glowed with light and life. A few men stood outside arguing even as two more passed them to enter its doors. The Anchor. She could read the sign painted in deep red letters even through the night's haze of soot and smoke.

She'd never been to Southwark before. Dominic had, and Eve too. They'd set out on journeys from here or met shipments containing antiquities they'd acquired for the shop. In the past, their father had even rented a warehouse nearby to store the relics he'd acquired on his expeditions, some of which would be shipped ahead before he made his trip home.

Allie never had a reason to come, though she'd begged to visit once. Her parents were setting off on a trip to the East, and she'd wanted to join her siblings to see them off. But she'd only just recovered from one of the colds that plagued her as a child and was considered too fragile to make the journey to the docks.

Fragile little Allie. Always left behind.

That thought made her glad she'd come tonight, no matter how angry the inspector would be with her. That same nagging insistence in her middle still told her that she needed to find him, help him if she could.

She headed toward the pub. In the fog, all the sounds were muffled. Bits of conversation. Men's voices carried to her on the breeze. Underneath it all, the sound of the water lapping against the docks and boat hulls was strangely lulling, making the night seem less ominous. The men milling about mostly paid her no notice as they went about their business. She was shocked to see so many working even at this hour.

Lanterns hung on posts, and there were barrels with fires lit that a few workers gathered around to warm themselves, but the gaslights were few and far between. Though where the lantern light ended, The Anchor's glow led the way.

She'd worn a black dress left over from the year of mourning her father, thinking it might make her less noticeable. But the moment she stepped into The Anchor, she noted that the only other women in the pub were garbed in vivid-colored gowns. She stood out like a crow would if it landed on a branch of canaries.

Most of the pub's patrons, however, were men, and she felt their perusal as she made her way toward the bar.

"Hello, sir."

"What can I do for you, miss?" The publican wore the same assessing look as every other man in the pub, though his expression soon softened as if she'd passed muster somehow.

"Would it be terribly strange to ask you for tea?"

The older man laughed, his eyes creasing in genuine amusement. "Would be strange but not unheard of. The missus is in the kitchen this evening and makes an excellent brew, so you're in for a treat."

"Sounds perfect."

"Food?"

"No, I don't think so." Allie had scanned the room when she walked in but took a moment to do so again. She knew detectives sometimes disguised themselves, but she'd never yet been in the same room with Inspector Drake and not felt his presence keenly.

He wasn't here. But had he been?

"I'm looking for someone."

"Oh, aye? And who might that be, miss?"

She felt the urge to overexplain and stifled it. "Drake." She said the single word more quietly than any she'd spoken to the man so far.

He immediately shot a look toward a corner table and then the other end of the bar, where a barmaid was loading her tray.

"If you're asking after the man I know, he was

here not an hour past." As he wiped the counter, he stepped closer. "Came and went quickly."

"Went where?"

"'Fraid I can't help you there, miss. Never spoke a word to him as he never stopped to take any refreshment at all."

If Drake came and went quickly, perhaps he'd seen Demming and pursued him. Or somehow realized he'd find the man elsewhere.

"Do you know a man named Demming?"

"Aye, I surely do, but he's not a man you want to know."

Allie believed him, but she had to ask. "Where can I find him?"

The barman drew in a long breath and sighed. "A tenacious lady, I see."

"I'm afraid so."

"Demming won't have gone far. Holes up in a warehouse nearby or visits a gambling den a few lanes south."

"Thank you." Allie dug a coin from her pocket and placed it on the bar, even though she'd have to forgo the cup of tea.

"Here's advice you've not asked for," the barman called as she started toward the door.

Allie turned back.

The man's expression had gone grim. "Don't go looking for trouble, miss."

If only he knew that she was seeking the one man who'd no doubt repeat a similar sentiment the moment she found him.

She gave The Anchor's publican a nod, then stepped out into the night.

Clouds had gathered, dimming the moonlight to a mere glimmer that outlined the shapes of buildings and people.

The sensible part of her yearned to find a cab, head back across the river, and get warm in front of the fire Lottie had no doubt laid in her bedroom. But a far different feeling was louder—the need to find Inspector Drake.

So she walked south, deeper into this part of London she'd never visited before. To say she was lost was an understatement. Beyond Bankside, the streets were often nothing more than alleyways between warehouses.

When she passed through a covered alleyway, the darkness all but consumed her. She reached one hand out to use the wall as a steadying guide and waved the other in front of her, lest she crash into someone coming the opposite way.

After a few shuffling steps, her foot struck something firm, and she pitched forward just as the object shifted.

"Damnation," a man's voice grumbled, followed by a groan of pain.

Then hands were on her, one grasping her arm, the other her hip as the man rose before her. Stumbling, he caught himself on the wall and then released her.

"Drake." Allie knew. Even in the darkness, she knew she'd found him. She recognized the timbre of his voice, the starch and spice scent of him. The enormous, broad-shouldered shape of him.

She lifted a hand, placed it on his chest, and was relieved to feel the steady beat of his heart beneath her palm. She slid her hand higher, found the hard line of his jaw, and skimmed her fingers along the stubbled edge.

"I found you," she said on a warm rush of satisfaction. She'd found him, and that seemed the most important thing she'd done in a long while.

His fingers slid along the line of her throat. "Is it really you?"

Before she could answer, he leaned in and nuzzled her cheek, grazing his lips all the way to her jaw. "Flowers," he mumbled. "You always smell of flowers." Then he jerked back, though he kept one large, warm hand braced on her shoulder.

"Damned stubborn woman. You shouldn't be here," he hissed. "I asked a constable to see you home."

"He did, and then I thought I should come find you."

"I do not . . ." He hissed as he attempted to straighten, and she noticed that he kept one arm wrapped around his middle. "Require your help, Miss Prince." His voice was deeper, raspier than usual.

"I've heard that before," she told him as she reached for him gently, certain he was injured, judging by the labored gusts of his breath. "Let me help you," she said softly, urging him to relent. "Please."

"You're incorrigible." But he let her get an arm around him and position herself beside him. "My God, woman. Do you ever do what you're told?"

"It may surprise you to know that, yes, I usually do. All my life, actually."

He grunted at that. "I'm dubious as to the veracity of that statement."

"Well, I'm horrendous at lying, so you should believe me."

"So, it's only since you met me that you've decided to become intractable?"

Allie smiled in the darkness, but she doubted he could see her. "I suppose you bring it out in me."

"Wonderful." He let out a grunt of pain as he straightened and drew her toward the mouth of the alley where she'd entered. She felt the unsteadiness of his gait. He was limping, and his breath wheezed in his chest.

Once they were out of the cloister of the covered space, she caught a glimpse of him in the moonlight and gasped.

"What happened to you?"

"Retribution."

"Wait here." She led him to a low retaining wall, and he seemed shockingly content to slump against it. "I'll find us a cab."

The moment she made to step away, he reached for her, gripping her upper arm. "You're not going anywhere in these streets without me."

Allie came back to stand before him, resisting the urge to point out that she'd come here without him, and he was in no state to take on any additional riverside criminals even if one did approach. He held tight to her arm and kept his head bowed.

"We need to get out of here." Under a fall of

dark hair he lifted his gaze to look at her. "To-gether."

In the dim light, she spotted the dark stain of blood near his lip and a thicker trickle close to his eye.

"Mercy, how many were there?"

He emitted a sound that sounded suspiciously like a raspy chuckle.

"Four but only three delivered the beating."

She moved to stand beside him again, then took his hand and hooked his arm around her neck.

He didn't resist and let her nestle close. The heat of his body warmed her instantly, and when she slid an arm underneath his coat and tucked it around his waist, he groaned as if something hurt him there too.

Together, they made their way toward the bridge and soon secured a hansom. When it came time to climb in, Drake disentangled himself and insisted on offering her a hand.

"What's your address?"

For a moment, Allie panicked. "I'm not leaving you here. You said we were leaving together."

"I can catch another."

"No." She'd come this far, and she wasn't leaving him wounded and alone in this place. "Please come with me."

He wiped at his lip with the back of his hand and held her gaze. "Stubborn and incorrigible."

"Call me anything you like, Inspector. Just get in."

Finally relenting, he called an address up to the driver and climbed in beside her. She'd traveled in

plenty of hansom cabs with her siblings and with
Jo, and the seat was always cramped, but not like
this.

Their bodies were seamed together, and she
could not shift without pushing closer to him. As
soon as the cab set off, she was glad for the heat
of that closeness. But more than that, she was glad
to have found him.

Her intuition had been right. She turned to
tell him as much, but he'd leaned his head back
against the wood. Since the man needed rest, she
accomplished the great feat of not asking any further questions as they wound their way toward
his home.

CHAPTER TEN

He DIDN'T want to let her go, and yet he knew he should.

She'd insisted on tucking herself against him again and helping him inside. Once they stood in his drawing room, he should have released her, and yet he still held on because she was sweet and soft and maddening.

He should be furious with her. He should have sent her home alone as he'd intended.

Something about this woman made him forgo everything he knew he should do and give in to what he wanted instead. And that was a dangerous path.

"Where do you want to sit?"

Her very practical question finally cleared a bit of the haze of the last hour, and he lifted his arm to allow her to step away. But she didn't.

"I can manage on my own," he told her, and it didn't even sound convincing to his own ears.

Still, he forced himself to disentangle himself from her curves and the sweet-scented warmth of Alexandra Prince. Even her hair smelled of flowers.

"Of course you can, Inspector," she said in the

tone of one in total disagreement but humoring him to move on. He was quite used to that tone from Helen.

"Where's the kitchen?"

"Why?"

"We need water and clean cloth to tidy you up."

"You needn't mind about that. It's late and your family must be worried. Mrs. Pratt can see to a cab to take you home."

"My family is away on an expedition." She tipped her head. "Who is Mrs. Pratt?"

"I'm the housekeeper, miss." As she had an extraordinary habit of doing, Mrs. Pratt appeared just when she was needed. "What can I get for you?"

"A hansom cab to see her home," Ben said as he peeled his overcoat off. Every muscle protested. Demming's men knew where to land punches and kicks for maximum effect.

"A basin with water and some cloth for washing up, please, Mrs. Pratt." Miss Prince's voice was quiet yet determined as she directed his housekeeper and ignored him entirely.

"Of course, miss." Even as she spoke the words, Mrs. Pratt moved past Miss Prince to get a look at him. She gasped when she did. "Oh no, sir."

"All's well. I assure you."

"Should I send for Miss Drake or Dr. Porter? She'll wish she'd been here to help."

"No." Ben lifted a hand. "Don't send for her or that damned doctor. Promise me, Mrs. Pratt. It's a few scratches. Nothing more."

The housekeeper stared at him skeptically, then finally dipped her head.

"I'll return with the items directly," she told Miss Prince on her way out of the room.

"I take it that Miss Drake is your sister. The one who's brilliant at chess."

"Yes, and she's also a nurse at a clinic in Whitechapel. She'd subject me to a medical once-over, and I don't need it. I've had worse beatings, and far worse nights."

Miss Prince approached and bent at the waist to get a good look at his injuries. As soon as he met her gaze, a strange energy buzzed between them. She traced every inch of his face with her eyes, though not with the same cold scrutiny his sister would have.

Miss Prince's gaze was soft, appreciative, as if she quite liked looking at him, even when his face was a garish mess. And he hated how much he relished having her close. She was a delectable distraction he could not afford in his life.

And he needed no clearer evidence than tonight to prove that an association with him was a danger to her. Good grief, what if she'd showed up in Southwark half an hour earlier? What if she'd followed him into that bloody warehouse? After over a decade of police work, there was no doubt a passel of men like Demming who'd line up for a turn at doing him harm. Or doing the same to those he cared for.

He wouldn't expose her to that.

"Whatever happened here came dangerously

close to your eye," she whispered, reaching up to brush her fingers gently along the edge of his face. He felt the stroke down the length of his body and shivered.

"One of them wore a ring." He held her gaze a moment longer. "Miss Prince—"

"I don't think there will be a bruise, though that cut may take a few days to heal."

"You should go."

She straightened and tipped a sad smile down at him. "You're wasting your breath, Inspector. Unless you mean to heave me over your shoulder and toss me out, I intend to stay and clean those cuts."

She thought he did not want her to stay, and perhaps that was for the best. Though the opposite was true. Each time he urged her to go, it was far more effort than it should have been. He did so for her benefit, not for his.

Having her near had ignited something in him from the moment he'd met her, and he could no longer tell himself anything different.

"Here we are." On the tray Mrs. Pratt delivered were clean bandaging, a basin of water, sticking plaster, and a pot of tea.

"This is perfect. Thank you, Mrs. Pratt." Miss Prince beamed at seeing the teapot, immediately poured two cups, and handed him one.

"I'll be near if you require anything else, though you seem to be in fine hands, sir." Mrs. Pratt's mischievous wink was, thankfully, offered while Miss Prince had her back turned.

He couldn't blame his housekeeper. In the seven years they'd employed her, he'd never invited a lady visitor into their home. Indeed, he'd avoided the very idea of involving himself with a lady for the very reasons that he could not let himself get used to Miss Prince's company.

"Let me have a look," she said in a near whisper, and then she was touching him again.

She cupped his chin and nudged his head up, then she drew so close the skirt of her gown brushed his knees. He spread his legs and she moved between them to get closer.

Her movements were efficient, but her touch was light. As if she feared causing him more pain.

He'd never allowed anyone to fuss over the injuries he'd sustained on the job over the years, but her touch lulled him. Soothed him.

"There. The cut near your lip is slight." Her thumb swept along the edge of his mouth. "But I could put sticking plaster on the one near your eye."

"Don't bother."

She moved away from him, and he stood, stifling a groan when his body protested.

"Then I think I've done all I can," she told him as she folded the cloth neatly and stepped away to lay it beside the basin's edge.

Ben couldn't resist taking a step closer to her, touching her. He reached out and she slipped her hand into his. "What possessed you to come tonight?"

She lifted her gaze to his and looked at him

with an earnestness he rarely saw from anyone. "I had to. I can't fully explain it. Something told me I could be of help." She looked away for a moment and smiled ruefully. "And perhaps something in me didn't want to be left behind."

Her honesty, without any pretense or caution, was refreshing.

"You did help, but it was reckless. And now you must—"

"Leave it to you, I know." She slipped her hand from his and crossed her arms. "It involves my shop now, Inspector. Did Mr. Demming say why he was watching Princes?"

"He claimed that he was looking for me." Ben shrugged because the explanation felt as inadequate now as it had when Demming offered it an hour ago.

"You don't believe him?"

She could read him now, and that, if nothing else, told him the dangerous effect she had on him. He prided himself on withholding his emotions, not letting them cloud his reactions or judgement. Somehow, after a few days' acquaintance, that necessary, practiced mask was slipping. At least with her.

"Not entirely, no. But Alexandra . . ." Ben reached for her again. It was ridiculous how natural it felt. "Try not to worry."

She let him take her hand and then drew closer, until their chests were but an inch apart.

"This will become an official investigation

now. Demming will go to ground, but I will find him again. And Lord Holcroft."

"So I must wait to hear from you?" She seemed to hate that notion and didn't try to hide it.

He wondered if it was that she wished to hear from him or merely wanted an end to this matter.

One thing he knew—he needed to devote more resources to resolving it, to finding out if there was a plot and ensuring that none of those involved posed a threat to her and her livelihood.

"I'm not patient either, but I'm asking you to be." He stroked his thumb across the backs of her fingers. "In a few days, I promise you I'll know more."

"Oh, but I am patient." She lifted her hand to trace her fingers across his knuckles, almost absentmindedly. Her touch was delicate and yet tantalizing. When she encountered an abrasion atop one knuckle, her brow puckered. "Well, about certain things. I've been waiting all my life. Usually, it's only my tongue that gets me in trouble."

"Is it?" He locked his gaze on her mouth. How could he not?

Her breath quickened as did his own, and her fingers stilled atop his hand, though she made no move to pull away. When he lifted his gaze to hers, he saw heat there. A spark of the same desire he felt whenever she was near.

"What I mean to say is . . ."

Ben slid his fingers along the curve of her jaw as she'd done to him not ten minutes past.

"What you mean to say is . . . ?" he prompted.

"Sometimes I blurt out whatever is on my mind. People don't like it."

"I rather like it."

She blinked. "You do?"

"Mmm. I don't know what you've done to me." He trailed his fingertips along her bottom lip. Touching her was addicting. The more of her skin he traced, the more he wanted to explore.

When he reached up to cup her nape, she closed her eyes. The sign of trust made him swallow hard.

He did not want to harm her, endanger her. But good God, how he wanted to kiss her.

"Alexandra." The word slid over his tongue like rich whiskey. He loved speaking it aloud, and that she allowed him to.

"Yes." Her thick lashes flicked up, and she looked at him with what seemed like yearning. She drew the edge of her lower lip between her teeth, then reached out to lay her hand against his shirtfront.

"I know I should go," she whispered, "but nothing in me wants to." She studied his shirtfront, teasing her fingertips along the line of buttons. When she looked up at him again, he couldn't stop himself.

He traced the backs of his fingers along her cheek, then bent to kiss the skin he'd touched. Tracing his lips up to the delicate shell of her ear, he told her the rawest truth.

"I don't want you to go."

The words seemed to set something loose in

her. She reached up, threaded her fingers through his hair, and arched against him, letting her body fall into his. She closed her eyes again, and her lush mouth trembled slightly.

He'd never been hungrier for a woman in his life. But if he kissed her, he'd lose the ability to protect her. To protect himself.

But she was far more tempting than he could resist. All reasonable arguments fled, and it was only him and her and this precious closeness. A desire so strong it blotted out everything but the need to taste her lips. He'd never wanted to kiss anyone more. Never seen a woman and known in that same moment that he wanted her—and he could admit to himself now that the attraction had been there from the moment she strode into his office, talking so quickly that his brain couldn't catch up.

He stroked her cheek, and she opened her eyes. He saw everything amid the silvery blue—her curiosity, her boldness, her willfulness, and desire too. For him.

He bent his head, and she responded with a kiss so eager that it stole his breath. With both arms wrapped around her, he pulled her closer. She arched onto her toes, and he all but lifted her off them so that her soft curves melted against his body.

When he teased his tongue along the seam of her lips, she opened to him immediately. And she learned quickly, tracing her own tongue against his lower lip.

Her scent drove him mad, and he wanted to find the spot where she'd dabbed the floral concoction on her neck, between her breasts, behind her ear.

He traced a path down to the base of her throat, just above the collar of her high-necked gown, and yearned to release each bloody button that kept every inch of her from him.

When he reached for the first button, he heard a scratch at the front door and stilled.

Helen was home.

It took all the willpower he possessed to stop touching Alexandra. But he forced himself to, gently setting her back on her feet and then lifting his hands from her body.

Her eyes slid open when he did, and shock was soon chased by disappointment in her eyes.

"What on earth has happened to you?" his sister called from the drawing room threshold, her gaze assessing his wounds, the blood on his shirt.

Helen still wore her overcoat and stared from Alexandra to him with curiosity and concern knitting her brow.

"I'll be right as rain tomorrow," he told his sister.

She lifted one dark brow and then strode forward, offering her hand to Alexandra.

"Hello. I'm Helen Drake, and you are?"

Ben winced at her curt tone. It wasn't unkindness, just his sister's usual efficient manner.

But Alexandra, in her own straightforward way, didn't seem to mind. "I'm Alexandra Prince, and I'm pleased to meet you. Apparently, we're both better than he is at chess."

To his shock, Helen immediately softened, even chuckled. "I'm glad to hear he admits that to someone. He rarely will to me." Still holding Alexandra's hand, his sister added, "Perhaps together we can give him enough pointers to bring him up to snuff."

"That sounds like a worthwhile challenge." Alexandra looked back at him as she released Helen's hand. "It's late, and I should be getting on my way. Good evening to both of you."

She offered him a nod, and then strode from the room.

"I should see that she gets off safely," he told Helen, but Mrs. Pratt appeared in the hallway. She'd collected Alexandra's coat from the hall rack.

"I'll make sure of it, sir," Mrs. Pratt told him.

When the two of them had headed toward the front door, Helen stepped closer, scrutinizing his injuries.

"Apparently, you were wrong, brother dear," she told him archly. "You did indeed see her again. Your lady with a spark."

DRESSING FOR THE WELLINGDONS' dinner party took Allie far longer than she'd intended.

She kept getting lost in thoughts of the previous night. The wild impulse she'd followed to go to Southwark, and the overwhelming relief she'd felt when she found Ben, despite the state Jack Demming's men had left him in.

And then that kiss. The memory was sharp and bright in her mind—she imagined she could still catch the scent of him on her skin, still feel the hardness and heat of his chest against hers.

Had he reached for her first? Or had she pulled him closer? She'd never experienced anything like it in her life—one moment they were two people with an odd magnetic pull between them and then they were kissing. And it changed everything. It no longer mattered if she had been too bold or if he had broken some rule of etiquette by touching her too freely.

The kiss hadn't been awkward or hesitant or anything she'd imagined her first kiss might be. As soon as she was in his arms, she felt that it was right where she was meant to be.

The clock struck eight, and she realized she'd gotten caught up in those moments again.

She forced herself to finish washing and dressing, and then patted the pretty assembly of curls and jeweled pins that Lottie had arranged her hair into at her nape.

Ten minutes later, she alighted from the carriage the Wellingdons had sent to fetch her, wondering if she should keep the details of the previous night from Jo. They told each other almost everything, and Jo could read her as others couldn't. But her friend would be happily distracted this evening.

Jo was always happiest in her element, surrounded by her siblings and her books and all the musical instruments she so excelled at playing. And because Lord Wellingdon was that rare sort of father who was as kind and encouraging to his daughter as to his son, he engaged Jo in the sorts of political conversations that were common at their dinner parties.

The challenge came when Lady Wellingdon was about.

Jo's mother had taken against Allie, or more accurately against the Prince family altogether. The countess thought her father's and brother's exploits were "unseemly," and the lady seemed to fear that Allie would lead Jo into a life of dangerous adventures, stubbornly ignoring the fact that Allie had never had any of her own.

Lady Wellingdon was never cruel. She steered toward the chilly edge of civility and never offered any true warmth. Still, for Allie, spending time with Jo made it all worthwhile.

"Miss Prince, I'm so pleased you could join us this evening." Lady Wellingdon welcomed her as soon as she entered the family's sumptuous drawing room.

"Thank you for the invitation, my lady." Allie smiled and watched as a series of expressions played over the countess's features while she assessed Allie's dress.

"What a vibrant color you've chosen for your gown."

"Thank you, my lady." The raspberry-colored gown was cut well, and Allie loved all its flounces. Since she didn't read ladies' magazines or care particularly about fashion, she wore what pleased her.

"Heavens, you look divine," Jo enthused as she came up behind Allie, wearing a rich blue gown that matched her eyes.

"So do you."

They exchanged a quick hug, and then Jo pointed a look at her mother over Allie's shoulder. "I'm taking her to the library, Mama. I want to show her my newest bookstore acquisitions."

Lady Wellingdon harrumphed lightly. "Don't dally, Josephine. More guests will arrive soon, and you two mustn't cloister yourselves among piles of books forever."

"She has no idea she's just described my idea of heaven," Jo whispered as soon as they were past the drawing room threshold.

Allie tried suppressing a chuckle, but it didn't work.

Once they were inside the Wellingdons' impressive library, Jo slid the door shut and turned eagerly to Allie.

"Has there been any news from Inspector Drake?"

"News?" Allie's stomach flipped, her cheeks flushed, and it took everything in her not to confess all that happened the previous night.

"Was he not looking into what you overheard? If he hasn't, tonight you can take your concerns to the man I sent you to at the start."

"Haverstock?"

"Indeed, Sir Felix and his daughter, Lavinia,

have both been invited. You can tell me if you find her as difficult to converse with as I do." Jo collected a book from a table near the door and came back to show it to Allie.

"Do you think if I proposed this to our bicycle club, we could convert them to a book club for the winter?" Jo handed over *Bicycling for Ladies*, a dark blue clothbound volume with a cheerful lady bicyclist on the gilded cover. "I ordered it from America and can send for more if we choose it."

Allie flipped through distractedly. Bicycling had given her a sense of freedom and independence when she'd sorely needed it after emerging from a childhood feeling as if her body was weak and illness-prone, but tonight she struggled to think of anything but Benedict Drake.

"It looks perfect," she told Jo with as much of a smile as she could muster. "You have my vote, and I'm sure the others will agree."

Jo beamed. "Excellent. I'll put an order in for more straightaway." She set the book aside and gestured to the shelves her father had designated for her collection. "I don't really have any new acquisitions you haven't heard about. I just wanted a moment to chat with you on our own. But if you see anything you'd like to borrow, you know you're always welcome to."

"Do you have anything on travel to Ireland?" The ideas for a trip that she'd scribbled down in her notebook that day in the coffee shop felt distant now, but she still dreamed of a journey to Ireland one day.

"Are you planning a trip?" Jo all but bounced with excitement.

"I thought perhaps a research trip for my book."

"If you need an assistant, I'll beg Papa until he relents."

Allie laughed. "You'd be an excellent research assistant."

"I'm quite serious." Jo laced her arm around Allie's to lead her out of the library. "Mama will be entirely focused on Olivia's coming out next year, so I might be able to escape."

Allie doubted Jo's mother would allow her that much autonomy or that Lady Wellingdon had given up on matchmaking her eldest daughter with an eligible nobleman.

Indeed, as they made their way back to the drawing room, Allie heard distinctly masculine voices.

"Who did she invite this time?" Allie watched her friend's face for a reaction.

"Lord Echolston." Jo swallowed hard after pronouncing his name. Allie sensed that she quite fancied the handsome young viscount but had yet to admit it.

"He seems kind and always wants to talk with you about books," Allie said encouragingly, and Jo returned a mysterious smile.

From the drawing room, the low timbre of one male voice stood out from the rest. Allie jerked to a stop, and an electric ripple of awareness chased across her skin.

Jo clutched her hand. "Oh heavens, I thought

it a possibility, but I swear I didn't know for certain." She cast a fretful glance at the drawing room threshold. "It seems they've brought Inspector Drake."

Jo's eyes widened as Allie picked up her flounced skirt an inch and strode into the drawing room.

He'd been on her mind since she'd parted from him the night before. Since the moment when she'd touched her lips to his and been kissed so extraordinarily for the first time in her life.

He was lifting a glass to his mouth when he saw her.

Allie knew the exact moment because his body jolted the way hers had when she heard his voice. Everything around the edges of her vision blurred, but the sight of him remained clear.

She took two steps forward. He took one. Then he turned a glance toward the young woman and white-haired man beside him.

Miss Haverstock and her father, Allie presumed. In physical appearance, Sir Felix looked exactly as she expected—tall, regal, with snow-white hair and a manicured mustache—but the man's demeanor, even from across the room, telegraphed displeasure. His brow pinched in a frown, and he grumbled something to his daughter, who wore the same serious look as her father.

"Oh, there you are." Lady Wellingdon waved from her spot on the settee. "Lord Echolston has been looking for you, Josephine."

"Go ahead," Allie urged her.

"But I must introduce you to the Haverstocks."

"Your father will, I'm sure." Lord Wellingdon had just entered the drawing room and immediately drew the attention of Inspector Drake and the Haverstocks.

As soon as Allie approached the group, Lord Wellingdon greeted her.

"Ah, Miss Prince. You may find this conversation interesting."

They all watched her as she approached, but Allie's gaze kept returning to Benedict Drake.

He looked extraordinary in an ebony tailcoat and white tie. And if she didn't keenly recall every moment they'd spent together, she might not notice the signs of the beating he'd taken in Southwark. Only a slight mark near his eye remained as evidence. Unless there were bruises underneath his clothes.

Considering him without his clothes made her throat dry, and then he was close enough to touch, and she barely resisted reaching for him.

"So glad you're here, Miss Prince," Lord Wellingdon said, welcoming her warmly. "Have you met Sir Felix, Miss Haverstock, and Mr. Drake?"

She shot a questioning glance at the inspector.

"Miss Prince and I have met," he said immediately, which drew a mildly surprised look from Sir Felix.

"Go on, Haverstock," Lord Wellingdon urged. "Miss Prince will be interested. She's Octavius Prince's daughter, after all."

"Heavens. Is she indeed? A lady with knowledge of history, then." Sir Felix lifted a monocle as if Allie required further inspection. "What do you know of Egyptian history, Miss Prince?"

"Not a great deal, I'm afraid. I've learned a few hieroglyphics and know enough to recommend items in my family's shop." Alexandra replied more thoroughly than the chief deserved, considering his sneer as he inspected her.

When she glanced Drake's way, he offered her a reassuring nod.

"As I was saying." Haverstock directed his words to Lord Wellingdon, all but ignoring Allie's reply. "We've been invited to a soiree where a mummy is to be unwrapped." He side-eyed Allie, as if unwilling to give her his full attention. "I believe your father brought specimens over from Egypt for just that purpose."

"Perhaps we can get you an invitation too," Miss Haverstock put in politely.

A pit of queasiness settled in Allie's middle.

As a child, she'd perceived her father as larger than life and had been awestruck by his achievements. Now she viewed some of his actions more critically.

"He did not bring them for that purpose," she told the group, "but he sold them to collectors, and perhaps that was just as distasteful."

"You speak thus of your own family's livelihood?" The disdain in Haverstock's tone caused everyone to shift uncomfortably. The older man's color was high, his speech slightly slurred, and Allie wondered if the glass of whiskey clutched in his hand had been one of many.

"I speak honestly, Sir Felix. Disinterring human beings for entertainment is disrespectful. Eventually, I believe my father came to regret his involvement in the practice too."

"You disrespect your father by saying so."

Allie pressed her lips together. He was wrong, but she wouldn't convince the man, especially if he was in his cups. Still, she found she couldn't keep silent. "None of us would wish anyone we cared for to be treated in such a manner."

Haverstock scoffed. "You're quite naive, Miss Prince. And you're far too severe in your condemnation for one so young." The white-haired man turned away from her, leaving his daughter looking miserable.

From the corner of her eye, Allie noted Jo's approach. Drake took a step closer before Jo reached her.

"Ladies, would you like to come see the new book Lord Echolston has brought me?" She glanced meaningfully at Allie and then at Drake too. "You too, Inspector."

Lavinia joined Jo immediately, but Allie held back.

"May I escort you over?" Drake asked her quietly.

"Aren't you meant to be escorting Miss Haverstock?"

His eyes widened and he gave one decided shake of his head. "It's not what it seems."

Allie felt awkward and foolish, and she could not bear another moment of Haverstock's sneering looks or Lady Wellingdon's unspoken criticism.

"I'm sorry, Inspector. I need some air." It was all she could manage before she turned away from him and headed for the Wellingdons' back garden.

CHAPTER ELEVEN

Drake didn't bother excusing himself before following Alexandra.

By the time he reached the Wellingdons' broad veranda, the lantern-lit stones were empty. Then he caught sight of the skirt of her raspberry gown as she cut around a row of tall hedges.

He feared she might have rushed off because Haverstock's pomposity had driven her to tears. But when he found her on the other side of the neatly clipped greenery, she was pacing and muttering to herself.

"I know why you've come to find me," she told him when he rounded the hedge. "I'll apologize to Sir Felix when I go back in."

"That's not at all why I've come. And what the hell would you apologize for? Being magnificent?"

She stopped short and stared at him, narrowing her eyes as if she wasn't certain he was in earnest.

"Was I?" She shook her head. "I didn't think through a single word. It just came out. Perhaps I should have been more respectful and tempered my—"

"No, you should not have." He'd admired her

straightforward manner since meeting her, but seeing her with Haverstock, who'd had far too much to drink and was desperate to impress Lord Wellingdon with his boasts, had been spectacular. "You were honest. Perhaps blunt, but you're as entitled to your opinion as the chief is to his."

He stepped closer and longed to reach for her. It seemed he would forever feel the urge to touch her, be connected to her, even if only for a moment.

"Thank you," she said, her voice trembling as if the emotions welling inside her were too much to contain. Then she closed her eyes and drew in a long breath, exhaling slowly. After a while, her expression softened.

He realized she looked at home out here in the garden, her face lit by moonlight, free of all the constraints and expectations even he found confining in aristocratic drawing rooms.

He stroked his fingers along the satiny curve of her cheek, and she opened her eyes, looking much more at ease.

"And it just so happens that I agree with you. Digging up the dead for study is one thing. Doing so for entertainment is something else entirely."

She swallowed and nodded. "Indeed. I attended an unwrapping once. Honestly, I was supposed to remain in a separate room with my siblings, but we snuck a peek over the edge of the stairwell." She grimaced at the memory. "The guests broke off pieces and passed them around. I kept wondering who the Egyptian had been. If they'd had a family who cared for them thousands of years ago, or even descendants now who had no notion that their ancestor had been taken to England."

Though she referred to one who'd lived millennia ago, Drake couldn't help thinking of the ways his own family had failed at caring for one another. That he didn't even know who his own father was.

Alexandra stepped closer. "I'm sorry if I've mucked matters up for you with Sir Felix."

"You needn't worry about that." The man might be standing in a house but a few feet away from him, but he was the very furthest thing from Drake's mind.

"Why wouldn't I worry? He's your superior, is he not?" She moved closer and curled her fingers around the lapel of his tailcoat. "And you're ambitious, are you not?"

In that moment, Drake struggled to find the growling hunger that usually resided in his middle when he thought of his future, his achievements, his yearning for more. All he found was complete and utter focus on Alexandra. She was quite appealing enough to occupy him entirely, and a shocking thought drifted through his mind.

She matters far more than any title.

"Haverstock will get past whatever momentary offense he felt, I'm sure."

"I'm not so certain." She cast a doubtful glance back toward the Wellingdon townhouse. "And since you mentioned that we are acquainted, he may take his anger toward me out on you."

She couldn't know of Haverstock's pettiness or

how he wielded his power, and yet she'd somehow sensed it.

"The man needs me too much to do that."

"And Miss Haverstock would no doubt defend you." Alexandra hitched one brow up in question.

He chuckled, and she frowned fiercely. Adorably.

He slid a hand down to cup her chin.

"Hear me on this point. I did not escort Lavinia Haverstock this evening. I am not courting Lavinia Haverstock, and I promise you that she would never defend me to her father on any score. We're not . . ."

Intimate was the word on the tip of his tongue. And he meant it in contrast to whatever this was. He'd known Alexandra but a few days and yet the connection between them was palpable. Strong. Intimate.

"You're not . . . ?" she prompted.

He slid a hand gently around her nape, savoring the silken feel of her hair, the heat of her skin. He wasn't yet sure he could put into words what he felt, but he could show her.

She tipped her head up, and he took her mouth in a soft kiss. He'd meant it to be no more than that. Convinced himself he could taste her once more and be gentlemanly about it. But there was nothing gentlemanly about his feelings for Alexandra. They were new and raw and undeniable. Powerful enough to chip at the cool stoicism he thought he'd perfected.

And the wonder of it was that she seemed to feel it too. She leaned into him, pulling him closer by his lapels, fitting her lush curves against him. Then her other hand came up as she wrapped her fingers around his neck, stroking his hair and sending a shock of pleasure straight to his groin.

He deepened the kiss, teasing his tongue against the seam of her lips, and she offered him heaven. A deep, drugging taste of her, and he realized his control wasn't just slipping, it had crumbled entirely.

To get her closer, he lifted her off her feet, one hand cupping the sweet swell of her backside.

The kiss flared into more—a wild exploration. Her fingernails traced against his skull and that stroke made him so hard he ached. He pulled her closer, slid a hand down, trying to gather the skirt of her gown. She emitted little moans of pleasure as he stroked his tongue against hers.

"Allie?" Lady Josephine's voice came from far away.

Or perhaps it only seemed that way because he had fallen under some spell. But Alexandra had too. Even after the lady's call, even after he'd set her down gently, they held on to each other, leaning their foreheads together, trying to catch their breath.

"Allie? Is everything all right?" the Wellingdons' eldest called again.

"Quite all right," Alexandra called back, though she made no move to leave his embrace or step out from behind the hedge.

At the sound of footsteps on the veranda paving stones, they finally pulled away from each other, and Alexander swept her hands down her skirt and strode out into view of the house.

"I'm all right, Jo."

"Very well," Lady Josephine said more quietly. "The dinner gong will sound soon, so you'd *both* best return in short order."

"We will." Alexandra nodded and smiled.

Lady Josephine apparently retreated because Alexandra returned to him. And in her usual perceptive way, she could read his expression.

"What is it?"

"Allie," he said, repeating the nickname Lady Josephine had used and that had apparently put an odd look on his face.

"Yes." She dipped her head, momentarily shy. "It's what everyone calls me." Her eyes flashed as a little grin tipped her bee-stung lips. "Except for you."

"Alexandra suits you."

A beatific smile lit her face. "I've always preferred it, but no one else seems to agree. To my family, I'm always Allie. Little Allie. Or little Lex, though only Papa called me that. And now sometimes my brother if he's trying to soften me." She tipped her head. "Why do you prefer Alexandra?"

"It's a beautiful name. Long and luxurious. A bit more complicated than Allie."

"Am I complicated?"

He drew closer, reached up, and tucked a strand of hair behind her ear. "I mean that as a compliment. Complicated in the way that a tangled case can be more interesting than a simple one."

"And what do you prefer to be called?" she asked softly. "Ben? Benedict?"

Drake winced. "Not Benedict. My mother called me that when she was cross. And now Helen does when she's taking me down a peg."

"Ben." She uttered the single syllable with more thoughtfulness than anyone had ever offered his name. "I do like it."

He laughed, full-throated and in a way he hadn't in, well, as long he could recall.

"I'm glad you approve."

Even from the garden, they could hear the sound of the dinner gong.

"We have to go in," she said without an ounce of enthusiasm.

"I suppose we do." Ben felt much the same. He'd forgo the whole dinner and any of the conversation he'd hoped to have with Wellingdon to stay out here with her.

"I'd rather leave now. With you," she told him boldly.

"As would I."

"We'd cause a scandal."

He'd take a scandal if it meant time with her, but he wouldn't subject her to the judgement of the Wellingdons or Haverstock.

He knew they must rejoin the group and held out his arm. She immediately wrapped her hand around it, and he laid his other hand over hers. He already disliked how they'd have to pretend once they were back inside. Pretend they hadn't just shared a kiss that still heated his blood. A kiss that had shaken him. Changed him.

He couldn't walk away from her now. There

was the time before he'd met Alexandra Prince and whatever he was becoming now, and he did not wish to go back.

"I won't provoke him again, I promise."

He was so far gone that it took him a moment to realize who she referred to.

"I wouldn't have you change to suit Sir Felix Haverstock. Or anyone."

Out of the corner of his eye, he caught her grinning.

He vowed to himself then and there that he would make it his mission to evoke such smiles from her again.

And despite all the reasons he knew he shouldn't—despite the feeling that something in him had been torn open and his usual defenses would no longer shield him—he needed to kiss her again too.

DEPENDING ON THE TIME of year, they would close Princes for the day on a Sunday. Shoppers would sometimes come, as the holiday approached, in November and December. But since there would only be two of them in October, Allie had agreed with Mr. Gibson that they'd close on Sundays during the month.

Ordinarily on such days, Allie took care of all the tasks she couldn't get to in the evenings—replying to letters, reading the newspaper, or even sifting through research for her book.

But today wasn't an ordinary day. It was the day after she'd shared the most extraordinary kiss, with a man who'd tempted her from the moment she'd met him.

And now? Her thoughts were consumed with him. And kissing him.

It wasn't supposed to be unforgettable. Indeed, Eve had warned her years ago that a lady's first kisses were often an unpleasant, even disastrous, experience.

But nothing about her encounters with Benedict Drake—Ben—had been unpleasant, not even the remainder of the night at the Wellingdons after their stolen moments in the garden. Oh, Haverstock had snubbed her the rest of the night. And Jo had been miserable because there'd been no time to talk about what had happened in the garden. And Ben had been seated too far away from her too.

Yet she'd been in a kind of warm haze for the rest of the night.

And this morning, she was good for nothing but remembering the heat of his mouth on hers, the way he'd lifted her easily and fitted her against the hard muscles of his body.

She found herself tracing her lips, yearning for more. To be back, hidden in the hedges, with him again.

Could people make love against a hedge?

She was so brazen now that she wanted to find out.

Even as the day's hours stretched on, the hunger to do it all again—to do more—didn't diminish. And she spent hours trying to convince herself that the wild impulse to go and find Ben and kiss him again was entirely reasonable. She'd never been forward, never truly flirted or pursued an interest in any man. Not that she was missish about ladies doing such a thing. Only that no one had inspired her to make the effort.

Until now.

She stood, walked to her wardrobe, and selected her newest walking suit.

Lottie, who'd been chatting in the hallway to Mrs. Taunton, must have heard the squeaking hinges of her wardrobe door.

"Anything I can do to help, miss?" Lottie rapped once and stepped into her room.

Allie stared at the young woman, her mind still spinning with possibilities. She wanted to see him. Indeed, it felt more like a need. Was he at home on Sundays? Or was he working on all the cases that required his attention?

It had been so long since she'd considered any kind of outing beyond charity work and her bicycle club.

"I'm going out, Lottie. No lunch for me today. Though if I'm home by supper, tell Mrs. Taunton a tray in my room will suffice."

"May I help you change?"

Allie was still wearing an old day dress that was soft and comfortable for days at home.

"I can manage the suit, but would you do something with my hair?"

"Of course, miss." Lottie smiled. She relished any kind of work that involved lady's maid duties and had a special talent for arranging hair, choosing just the right earbobs, and picking the best accessories.

Soon she'd transformed Allie's simple chignon into an artistic arrangement of braids and curls.

"Is it the young constable?" Lottie whispered once she'd set the last pin in place and stood back to survey her work.

Allie smiled at her in the mirror. "No, not the constable."

"But you are going off on a little adventure, aren't you, miss?"

"I am." Not quite an adventure by the Prince definition. There was no artifact or buried treasure involved. And yet she was pursuing something of great value single-mindedly with no real certainty of the outcome. *That* was very Prince of her indeed.

"It's about time I did," she told Lottie. Everything in her cheered the sentiment.

The young woman offered her a conspiratorial smile and a wink. "Well, off with you then on your adventure."

BEN TOLD HIMSELF THAT he should regret kissing her.

He was a man with nothing to offer, not even an accurate family history, and she was fond of those.

Toying with Alexandra Prince was unthinkable. He admired her too much to pretend he was the marrying sort. He'd decided long ago that it was something he'd have to forgo until he'd achieved his goals. Maybe someday, but not anytime soon.

And yet he couldn't regret a moment of that kiss. He'd replayed it dozens of times in his mind, allowed himself to imagine freeing her from that red dress, from her corset and petticoats, and laying her out on his bed, taking his time tasting her, savoring every moment—

"Are you finished with the newspaper?" Helen stood in her coat, donning her gloves.

"I . . ." Ben looked down to find the papers he'd collected from the newsstand this morning as crisp and unbent as when he'd purchased them. He'd been daydreaming for bloody hours.

"Never mind."

"No, take them."

"No, no, I have my book to read on the omnibus." She pulled a knit hat on, arranging it at a jaunty tilt, then stared at him for a moment. "Are you all right?"

"Of course I am."

"Very well. I must be off." She started toward the door and then turned back. "Perhaps you'll tell me later what has you so preoccupied."

"Perhaps."

Once she'd gone, he pushed a hand through his hair and forced himself to focus on perusing the newspapers, a task he usually relished on his days away from the job.

He flipped pages, absorbing little, until two words caught his notice. *Crown Jewels*.

The story detailed how the Crown Jewels were

now back at the Tower after cleaning and repair at a local jeweler's, and the new Jewel House where they were encased at the Tower of London was open for visitors.

When he'd contacted the Tower after Alexandra's first visit to his office, there'd been no mention of the removal of the regalia. Then again, as he scanned the news account, he realized it was scant on dates. It could have happened weeks ago and the release of the information had been delayed. The Crown dictated tight control of any information, and sometimes misleading information was released to deter threats against the regent and the other royals.

Perhaps the jewels' movements had been what inspired the men Alexandra overheard. Perhaps they'd planned some move on the jeweler rather than a much more difficult theft from the Tower.

Thankfully, to his knowledge, there'd been no attempt on the regalia at either location.

For the first time in his life, he found himself curious to see the collection. Alexandra could probably recount the history of every gem encrusted in the crown and scepter and orb and whatnot.

A knock sounded at the front door, pulling him out of his ruminations.

As he approached, he could see the shape and colors of his visitor through the patterned glass and his heart began a fierce tattoo.

"Hello," Alexandra said brightly when he opened the door. "You're at home."

"I am," he heard himself say, even as his mind

tripped over how lovely she looked. It was as if he'd summoned her with constant thoughts, and a part of him couldn't quite believe that she was here.

Once she stood in his drawing room, brightening the whole space, she turned to face him and looked suddenly uncertain.

"I thought we might . . ."

His throat went dry, his mind returning to all he'd been imagining for the last twelve hours.

"Go for a walk," she finally said.

"A walk."

"Or take lunch together."

"Lunch." When she began to look around nervously, he took a step closer. She immediately did the same. "Forgive me for sounding like a damned echo."

She laughed, and every single doubt slipped away, every rational argument he might be able to summon if he wasn't entirely pleased to have her in front of him.

"A walk, lunch. Both sound appealing." If she'd asked him to join her to walk a high wire across the English Channel, he would have agreed.

"Of course, I haven't given you the chance to suggest anything either."

He glanced over at the newspaper he'd left open on the top of his desk.

"This may sound mad, but would you care to go visit the Crown Jewels?"

CHAPTER TWELVE

*B*EN FELT as if he was living another version of himself—a lighter, freer version. A man who could enjoy his days away from work, court a lovely young woman, and seek out leisure activities as if he didn't have a care in the world.

Time with Alexandra was everything he had denied himself, but he couldn't shake the sense that some Dickens specter would soon appear to reveal that it was a glimpse of what could be, but only if he chose another path.

But he couldn't. His path was set. His goals could not be forfeited. They'd already cost him too much.

So he told himself these moments were ephemeral. He would savor the day with her, and she'd return to her home and he to his. They'd shared a few kisses, and he'd give in to none of his other desires where she was concerned. Nothing that would lead her to believe he could offer more.

"I suppose it's fitting that we've come to see the Crown Jewels," Alexandra said as they alighted from a cab near the Tower's fortress walls. "In a way, they're how we met."

"They are." He was grateful to the pile of gold and gems for that reason alone.

She smiled up at him, and he saw such openness and warmth in her eyes that his breath hitched in his chest.

He wanted to tuck the feeling away and save it for the days ahead. She'd go back to running her shop and writing her book and eventually going on the sort of Prince-style journeys her siblings did, and he'd go back to his work. But today would give him memories to savor.

"You've never been before?" Ben asked when they joined the waiting queue to enter the Tower grounds.

"My parents never brought us to such places. They always had their hearts set on the next expedition or journey, most of which were outside of England."

He recalled her sadness when she spoke of being left behind while her family traveled.

"Papa's wanderlust was all but insatiable. He grew restless after even a few months back in England." Her hand tightened momentarily where she'd taken his arm as they walked. "Maybe that's why my brother and sister both prefer exploring closer to home."

"I confess that I've never traveled extensively either." He looked at her, weighing his next words, acknowledging that it would reveal him as terribly unworldly. "I've never been much farther than London, in all honesty."

"There's no shame in that. Neither have I. Obviously, there's much to explore, even for those of us who've lived in the city most of our lives."

Inside the walls of the Tower grounds, they discovered that the queue to see the gems was the longest of all. On the carriage ride over, he'd explained about the removal of the jewels and their recent return.

She seemed to think his theory that it may have been the cause of the musings she'd overheard at Hawlston's a reasonable one. Though she'd emphasized that the tall man, the supposed Lord Holcroft, still unnerved her when she gave him more than a moment's consideration.

"Shall we wander a bit or join a tour?" he asked, pointing to a spot where one of the Yeomen Warders was collecting visitors into a group to begin a tour.

"Let's explore," she told him eagerly. Ben purchased a map, and they used it to plot a course to the spot on the Tower Green where two of Henry VIII's wives met their end.

"I can't imagine the horror of putting one's head on a chopping block," she murmured as they stood on the green.

"And the betrayal of one's husband ordering such a thing."

"Thank heavens we've moved past those days."

"Mmm." Ben had a case the previous year wherein a husband had disposed of two wives over the course of five years, the first murder only uncovered because of the second wife's untimely death. There'd been no real rationale for the two women losing their lives.

He didn't tell Alexandra about the case, not wishing to reveal his own cynicism. He wondered if society *had* moved beyond the barbarity of the past. The moment was a stark reminder of how much of his work wasn't fit to share with anyone, certainly not a vibrant young woman who saw the world as a place for hopefulness, improving on its past errors.

It was one of the reasons he'd truly never considered marrying. His work consumed him and showed him a side of humanity few wished to know about.

"I think we can go in there." She pointed to a structure with crenelated towers. "It's where many famous prisoners were held. Supposedly, there are engravings left by them on the walls."

"Are you certain you've never been here before?" he teased.

"I read a great deal as a child," she said defensively and then turned a curious look his way. "You did say you liked to read as a child too."

"Yes, but it was nothing as improving as history books." He found himself yearning to be as open and honest as she was. "We were unable to afford more than a couple of books between us," he admitted. "We relied mostly on penny dreadfuls for reading material."

She leaned in and whispered, "I love penny dreadfuls too." The smile she turned his way was delightfully mischievous and conspiratorial. "So you see, my reading wasn't always of the instructional sort. Actually, I believe I discovered all I know about the Tower from a guidebook my aunt Jocasta left behind after she'd come to visit us in London."

"A truly voracious reader then."

She chuckled. "I was. I wish I still had the time to be."

Once inside the tower, they joined a few other visitors examining the inscriptions of various prisoners, many from the years of the Tudors' reign. Most seemed to have been imprisoned for personal, political, or religious reasons, and he wondered if anyone had ever been imprisoned within its stone walls for actual crimes.

After the tower, they wandered the fortress, and Alexandra pointed out the area where the royal menagerie of animals had once roamed the grounds. She explained that the animals were removed over fifty years ago, some going to the Zoological Gardens at Regent's Park.

He'd never visited that zoo either and allowed himself to imagine inviting her there some other day. Imagining other days with her, other outings, was far too enticing.

Finally, as if they'd saved it for dessert, they made their way to the Jewel House. The queue had shortened, and when they finally stepped into the room that housed the regalia, it did indeed look like a dessert—a pile of gold and gems and utter ostentation surrounded by an ornate iron cage. The regalia was arranged in tiers, the long golden bejeweled scepter lying at the bottom and the largest crown at the top.

Alexandra let out a little gasp when the whole assembly came into view.

"Goodness," she whispered, "now that I see it all laid out, I do begin to understand why there have been so few plots to steal it all."

"They'd have to get through the glass and this iron grate." Ben examined the thing, shaped almost like an enormous birdcage, and looked for weaker spots. He noted its curves and one spot where it hinged.

He couldn't help scanning his gaze over the other onlookers, noting that none of the men were particularly tall. Of course, the coincidence of an attempt on the one day he'd decided to shed his usual work-obsessed nature and have a bit of pleasurable leisure time would be beyond irony.

Stealing the heap of it might be a challenge, but he could see why the sparkling, jewel-laden pieces would appeal to a thief. Hell, popping a single gem out of its setting would satisfy many thieves and certainly every pickpocket he'd known as a child.

"There's simply too much to carry," Alexandra said with utter practicality. "Colonel Blood and his conspirators took the crown, orb, and scepter, but they dropped the scepter."

Ben chuckled deeply, drawing a chastising look from a couple nearby. He bent to whisper in Alexandra's ear.

"If you were to make the attempt and could only manage one item, what would fetch the most?"

She eyed him with a mischievous smile. "Are we plotting now?"

"Just indulging my curiosity."

"The obvious choice would be to take one of the crowns. St. Edward's has the most historic value. Worn at coronations since the thirteenth century. Though it was deemed too heavy for Victoria and thus that crown." She pointed to one encrusted with so many gems that it sparkled from every angle. "The State Crown is likely the most valuable. Look at all the diamonds. Though I bet they're both heavy."

"But you think it the most valuable piece?"

"I'd say so. The most gems, as you see. That sapphire alone must be a hundred carats."

It was an almost mind-boggling display of excess. Ben imagined that if even one item in the collection were translated into pounds, it could house and feed and provide heat for thousands of Londoners. Though through Alexandra's eyes, he understood that each piece possessed a story, a meaning, related to England's history.

"Oh, there it is. I didn't know if it would be on display. Though . . ." She leaned in so far to get a better look at an object set with three clear stones that Ben reached out a hand to steady her. "Mr. Gibson would know for sure, but I think those diamonds may be paste."

"What is it?"

"A diamond armlet. The center one is the Koh-i-Noor from India. I know that one is over a hundred carats. Mr. Gibson is quite fascinated with it and told me of its history."

"It is indeed a replica, madam," a lady who'd approached told them. "The diamond itself was recut and is worn by Her Majesty in a brooch."

"Must be a damned big brooch." The words were out of Ben's mouth before he could stop them.

Both ladies returned a look of surprise, though only Alexandra wore an amused smile.

Once the informative woman had gone, he offered Alexandra his arm.

"Maybe we should depart before I offend anyone else."

"You weren't wrong," she told him as she wrapped her arm around his. "A hundred-carat diamond would be a bit much for everyday wear."

"You wouldn't want a suitor who spoiled you with jewels then?" Another set of words that probably should not have escaped his lips but somehow had.

And he found that he cared too much about her answer.

She took time with it. They'd made their way out of the Tower fortress walls before she turned to him.

"I've never had a suitor." It seemed to cost her something to meet his gaze squarely and offer the confession. He saw her throat working as she swallowed, and her cheeks began to pinken slightly. "So I haven't given much thought to what sort of gifts I'd prefer from one."

Her words shouldn't please him, especially since it was something she found hard to admit. But, more, they didn't make sense. Even as they'd walked through the Tower grounds, she'd drawn the notice of gentlemen.

Perhaps she'd closed herself off from the possibility as he had, but why?

Now was his chance to explain his choice to her. To explain that he'd never truly courted a lady. That he did not have the time or energy to devote to marriage. Not yet. Perhaps not ever.

Haverstock spoke of how his own wife complained of his absences and preoccupation with his work. He wouldn't subject a wife to that. And yet everything in him, everything that caused him to give himself to spending this day with her, wanted to offer more.

Hell, he wanted to offer her everything.

"Alexandra—"

"WAIT," ALLIE STOPPED HIM.

She suspected what he might say and there was something she had to get out too, but they should have the discussion privately. "Can we talk on the return trip?"

"Of course." Within minutes, he'd hailed an enclosed carriage.

Allie reached out and laid a hand on his arm before he could call up directions. "To yours."

"Mine?"

"I'm not quite ready to go home yet."

He hesitated only a moment before nodding,

telling the driver his address, and helping her inside.

"I want to hear whatever it was you were about to say," she told him once they were seated across from each other. She stripped off her gloves because she was suddenly overly warm. "But I have something of a proposal for you too."

"A proposal?" His voice dipped low on those two words.

A little shiver of anticipation rushed across her skin.

All the way to his home this morning, she'd considered why she was seeking him out. What she wanted with him—beyond another kiss, of course.

She'd told him the truth. There'd never been any suitors, and she'd never much minded that fact. Eve often said she didn't wish to marry because she never wanted to give up control of her choices. Allie's work managing Princes, her research and writing goals, her dream of one day doing something spectacular enough to live up to her family name—Eve's philosophy reminded Allie that a husband would have a say in all of it.

Allie had a few hidden romantic yearnings for a marriage of equals, of sharing, and understanding each other as no one else did. She sometimes imagined that's what her parents' marriage had been. But Eve had pointed out that Mama had been a skilled artist and writer, and yet all of that skill had been devoted solely to Papa's endeavors.

But even if Allie could imagine forgoing marriage, she couldn't accept that she'd never experience passion.

She swallowed, steeled her nerves, digging deep for a bit of Prince confidence.

"I'm afraid it's scandalous, what I'm about to propose."

He arched one brow and smiled so quickly that she only caught the flash of it.

"I wish to hear it." Leaning forward, he fixed his gaze on hers and reached for her hand. He wore no gloves and took full advantage of her bare skin, stroking his fingers inside the cup of her palm. "Tell me your scandalous proposal, Alexandra."

"I want . . ."

He waited with admirable patience while she tried to find the words that had seemed so sensible in her mind. For the first time in her life, she wished her tendency to blurt her thoughts would take hold.

But it didn't, and she had to think through each word.

"I don't know when or if I'll marry. I don't even know if I want marriage, but I do want the rest of it." She frowned. Too vague. "With you," she clarified, and her heartbeat sped at the admission that mattered most. "Only with you."

He bowed his head at that and when he looked at her again, his green eyes had darkened. His jaw had gone taut and square.

Oh heavens, had she misjudged what was between them? Or what could be?

"Unless you do not—"

He lifted her hand to his lips, kissed her knuckles, his breath hot against her skin, and then nipped the edge of her thumb.

"You needn't worry on that score." Still *he* looked worried. He'd drawn his brows together as he studied her face. "But your reputation."

"We can be discreet."

He smiled, this time letting it linger. "Nearly everything is revealed at some point, and I would not wish that judgement to fall upon you."

She knew of ladies who did as they pleased— took lovers, published bawdy books, traveled the world. They were the exception and no doubt paid a price for their autonomy, but it *was* possible.

Her own sister aspired to such a life of choices and achievements that were hers alone.

"It's a risk I'm willing to take." All things considered, she'd rather have a reputation as a lady who took a risk than as one who hadn't ever stepped beyond the lines society drew for her. "Are you?"

He kissed her hand again, cupping it with both of his, and she thought she spied the hint of a smile playing at the edges of his mouth.

"A man who takes a lover risks very little. We both know society judges women differently."

"Have you taken many?" It was a question she wanted to know the answer to, even if asking it made her a bit queasy.

"No. And none who I . . ." He seemed to get stuck on his next words. "The answer is no, but the truth is that I have never met anyone like you. Never felt the way I do when I am with you."

Allie let out a breath, leaned forward, and laid her hand against his cheek. "We're the same on that score."

He gripped her hand with his own, turning his face to kiss her palm.

She hadn't doubted her proposal, but now she knew she need not doubt his feelings either.

Just as she was about to reach for him, the carriage slowed. They were already pulling up to his address.

CHAPTER THIRTEEN

A LLIE SQUEEZED Ben's hand when the carriage finally rolled to a stop.

He paid the cabbie and then led her into the house. This time, they didn't stop at the drawing room. He led her straight to his private room.

The spacious chamber encompassed two distinct areas, one he clearly used for work and one that contained a bed.

Ben moved to stand behind her and help her with her coat. He took both hers and his and laid them across a chair nearby.

The fire had gone out in the grate, but her entire body was flushed with warmth. Anticipation. Need. Desire. She'd never felt any of them as fiercely as she did with Ben.

He noticed her glance at the grate and immediately moved to lay a fire, assembling the wood and kindling with care. Clearly, he had a strategy and she waited patiently, watching him.

And watching him kindled a fire inside her too.

The muscles of his chest and shoulders always strained the buttons of his shirtfront, but now she got to focus on the muscles of his thighs. They tensed and shifted as he moved.

He was such a gorgeous man. She'd seen a thousand statues of men in her life—in books, in the British Museum, in her own family's shop—and none of them could compare to Benedict Drake's physique. At least not in her estimation.

As soon as the fire sparked to life, he dusted off his hands. The air immediately grew warmer.

"There. That will cure a bit of the chill."

"Or you could just wrap me in your arms."

He came to her without hesitation and twined his arms around her waist. She lifted her hands to his shoulders.

"You're such a temptress." One of his hands dipped low on her back, almost as far as it had that night in the garden when he'd cupped her backside and lifted her effortlessly against him.

"Are you sure about this, Alexandra?" he asked in a husky whisper.

She didn't answer quickly, wanting him to know that she had given this proper thought. This was a step beyond any choice she'd ever made in her life—something that was wholly her own, against rules others and society had set for her, and carrying consequences she would have to be willing to bear if her siblings or Jo or, heaven forbid, Lady Wellingdon ever found out.

But she was done with doubting herself.

She gazed into Ben's eyes, wondering if a man of such strength and cleverness ever felt as she had for so much of her life.

"Do you ever doubt yourself?" she asked softly as he stroked a thumb across the back of her hand.

"Of course. More than I care to admit." He offered her a soft smile. "Not about you or this moment," he rushed to add. "Not even about my work." He hesitated, swallowing hard, and a pained look came into his eyes that she wished she could soothe away. "My doubts haunt me from the past. Choices I'd change if I could."

The revelation showed that he trusted her, and she understood the preciousness of that. Leaning forward, Allie lifted her hand to his cheek. The green depths of his eyes sparked when he looked at her.

"What would you change?"

He swallowed and ducked away from her a moment before meeting her gaze squarely. "My brother. I . . . failed him. I should have tried harder to save him."

"Save him?"

"From his bad choices."

"I'm certain you tried." Allie couldn't imagine him doing anything but the utmost for those he cared about.

"Not as hard as I could have. I washed my hands of him at one point. Lost faith in him." He'd gone off into memory, staring at the fire once more. "He died many years ago."

"I'm so sorry, Ben." Allie stroked a hand down his arm, feeling the hard swell of his muscles beneath the fabric.

Her touch softened his expression; the haunted look was gone.

"Please don't doubt yourself, Alexandra."

"My siblings doubt me." She wasn't certain why the admission bubbled up, but once it was out, the truth of it made her eyes burn.

"Then they don't see you clearly." He cupped her face, feathering his gaze over each feature as she'd become used to him doing.

"But you do?" she asked on a breathy whisper.

"I do." Leaning forward, he brushed a kiss against her cheek. "I see that you're clever." He slid his hand along her neck, tipping her chin up and then bending to place a hot kiss at the base of her throat. "I see that you're determined." Stroking his fingers across her skin, he reached up to grip her nape. "I see that you're brave."

When he stalled, his breath coming in hot heated gusts against her skin, she barely managed to whisper, "What else?"

A low, delicious chuckle rumbled from his chest, and he lifted his head to look at her again.

"I see that you're beautiful, Miss Alexandra Prince."

"In some ways, it feels as if I've been uncertain my whole life. But in this, I'm not. I want this moment." She curled her fingers along the edge of his collar, stroking one finger up his neck. "I want you."

A tremor rippled through him. She felt it underneath her fingertips.

"And you?" she whispered. "Are you certain?"

"Absolutely." He bent and nuzzled her cheek. "My only struggle is patience."

Allie smiled, tilting toward the feel of his stubbled jaw next to hers. "Are you usually impatient?" He didn't seem to possess her impulsive nature. A detective needed to be methodical, surely.

He lifted his head and stared down at her, his eyes a molten green, the stubble on his jaw highlighting the sharpness of that rigid line.

"Not usually, but I haven't wanted anything this much in a very long time." He lifted his hands to the neck of her gown and slid a button free, then stopped and drew in a sharp breath.

Allie reached for the buttons of his shirt, willing him to continue with hers, but he still hesitated.

"What is it?" she whispered. "Tell me what you want."

"I want to strip off every stitch of your clothing. Pull every pin from your hair. And lay you out on that bed." He flicked his gaze to the spot. "I've imagined you that way."

Allie slid her fingers between two buttons of his shirt to feel the hot, bare skin underneath.

"I want that," she confessed, her breath shaky because her body had begun to hum with a need she'd never felt before. Not like this.

"Nothing happens until you're ready, Alexandra." He rasped her name so deliciously she felt as if he'd stroked her skin. "We'll take it slow."

"But I'm not sure I want to take it slow." Allie reached up to unfasten the buttons at the neck of her gown.

Ben smiled and moved around behind her. "May I help?"

"Oh, most of the hooks are in the front. Just those few at the back."

He placed a hand on her back, one heavy point of tantalizing heat. "Maybe it's best if I don't help. I might be tempted to rip something."

As she continued unfastening her bodice, he moved away from her and over to poke at the fire.

She preferred his attention on her, but his momentary distance allowed her a moment to take in his room more thoroughly. A desk sat near the window, its top covered with intriguing objects. She wandered over as she worked her buttons free.

Much like his desk at work, there was an inkwell and nib pens, a blotter, a jar of glue, even a smooth, flat stone like the one she'd seen at Scotland Yard.

"Your desk at home is just as full of documents as your one at work," she told him with genuine interest. "Do you ever sleep?"

"Not as often as I should."

Even as she pulled the fabric of her bodice free of her skirt, she couldn't resist reaching out with her other hand to run her fingertips along the piles of documents and various objects he used as paperweights.

"You didn't like it when I did this at Scotland Yard," she teased.

"You noticed," he said, his voice deep and husky as he left the fire and came back to her.

"I noticed everything about you." She didn't mind confessing now how much he'd intrigued her. Reaching for his shirtfront, she tugged him closer. "Especially the unique shade of your eyes."

"Is it unique?"

"Green with flecks of gold." Allie lifted onto her toes, letting him take her weight and studied the depths of his eyes. There was a kaleidoscope of colors hidden in the mossy green, but what she liked most was how they blazed with desire now. "Green amber," she said softly. "You may recall that I blurted it like a ninny."

"You were talking about my eyes." He murmured the words as if fascinated by the realization.

"I was struck by them. By you."

"And I by you." He wrapped an arm around her waist, and the heat of him warmed her much more than the fire. "Even when you mussed my desk."

Allie reached up and slid his tie from his neck. Deftly, he helped her slip her unbuttoned bodice from her shoulders.

"So if I made your desk messy again, you wouldn't mind?" she teased.

He answered by wrapping her in his arms and lifting her onto the edge of his desk. "I wouldn't mind at all." With one finger under her chin, he tipped her head up and took her lips.

Allie pressed her hands to his chest, relishing the fierce thrash of his heartbeat. Then her fingers found the buttons of his shirt, and she worked at each one impatiently.

Ben tugged at the fabric of her skirt, gathering it up until he'd raised it and her petticoat up to her thighs.

"How is it possible to be this soft?" he asked,

his fingers sliding along the inner edge of her thigh.

A shiver chased down her spine, but it wasn't cold. Heat spread out from every spot where his skin met hers.

Which made her want his touch everywhere.

"Wait," she whispered, and he instantly stilled.

Allie slid off the desk and onto her feet and turned her back to him. "Will you help with my skirt and petticoat?"

He fumbled with the hook on her skirt, but it might have been because he'd bent to press kisses against her shoulder, her neck, and the wicked spot behind her ear that shot heat straight to her core.

Soon he'd pushed her skirt over her hips, then her petticoat, and she worked the hooks and eyes of her corset at the same time. Soon she stood in only her chemise and stockings and drawers, and he helped her pull the chemise over her head.

She turned toward him, suddenly chilled, and he took her lips. Then he wrapped his arms around her, and she felt safe and warm and knew she was right where she was meant to be.

She reached down for the fastenings of his trousers, yearning to discard another layer of fabric that separated his body from hers.

"Not yet," he told her. "Let me take you to bed."

He bent to scoop her into his arms, but Allie sidestepped toward the desk. "Here," she insisted.

At first, she thought he might disagree. She wasn't certain what had possessed her to demand it. Desire was making her bold.

Ben stunned her by stepping toward the desk, swiping his arm across its surface to topple its contents onto the floor, and lifting her back onto it.

Then he kissed her. A deep, searing kiss. She opened to him, teased her tongue against his, got lost in how a kiss could be wild and tender and dizzying all at once.

Then he nudged her knees apart and moved between her spread legs. He bent his forehead to hers.

"Remind me to go slow if you need me to," he whispered and then he took her mouth again. He gently eased her down until she was clutching at his shoulders, until she lay with her back against the desktop.

He slid the ribbon of her drawers free and tugged the fabric from her hips and down her legs.

She was naked before him, more vulnerable than she'd ever been with anyone. She could feel the heat in her cheeks, but it wasn't from embarrassment or shame. Nor from the fire that filled the room with a flickering warmth. She was flushed with need, her every sense was heightened and every inch of her yearned for his touch.

"You're stunning," he murmured, tracing his fingers down her chest, then dipping to take her nipple between his lips. "And delicious."

She gasped at each stroke of his tongue, then she slid her hands into his thick hair, urging him closer. He was over her, so close and yet still not near enough.

"I want to make this perfect for you," he whispered.

Allie caught the edge of his jaw and tipped his head up until their eyes met. "Not for me. With me. I only want this because it's with you."

Her words stole his breath, made his heart thrash in his chest. And he knew in that moment that he'd never be content with one night of giving her the passion she craved. He wanted her to be his. Wanted this to be the start of something that would not end in a week or a month.

And the trust in her eyes, her eager willingness, undid him. He was hers whether she knew it or not, and now he only wanted to show her.

He unfastened his trousers and slid the rest of his clothing off.

Alexandra fixed her gaze on his body, taking him in boldly, pulling her lower lip between her teeth as she stared at his cock.

"Goodness," she said. Then she flicked her gaze to his. "May I touch you?"

Ben nodded. He wasn't sure he could get words out if he tried. He was already breathless, and when she reached for him, he gasped.

She explored with her fingers, stroking his length, then wrapping her hand around him.

"Tell me what's next," she said on a husky whisper.

Ben chuckled. "Let me show you."

He moved between her legs, slid his hands up her thighs, and then dipped his fingers into her curls. She was wet and hot, and he didn't want to go slow.

Allie bucked against his touch. "Please," she urged as if she didn't wish to go slow either.

He stroked into her heat, slid a finger inside, and she reached up to grip his shoulder.

"Yes," she whispered, "I like that."

"I hope you'll like this too," he told her and as he knelt down before her. "Because I need to taste you."

She made a little sound of protest when he slid his finger from her, but then let out a moan that made his cock ache when he replaced it with his tongue. He got lost in loving her with his mouth, addicted to every gasp and moan and the way she reached down to scrape her fingers across his scalp to indicate her pleasure.

She began to quiver and writhe against his mouth, and when she shuddered against him and called out his name, he felt as if he might spend himself before he was ever inside her.

When the rippling waves subsided, he stood before her again.

Alexandra looked up at him hazy-eyed. "Ben," she rasped, "I want to touch you again."

He rocked against her. He'd never wanted anyone, anything, more than he wanted Alexandra.

She nodded as if she could read his thoughts.

"Only you," he told her as slid into her delicious heat. She couldn't know what his words meant. He was too far gone to think through any of it. This moment was for feeling, and every second of it felt extraordinary. Like a dream of what he wasn't sure he deserved but was somehow lucky enough to find.

He rocked into her slowly, inch by inch, letting her movements and reactions guide him.

"Only with you," she whispered, her blue-violet eyes ablaze.

And the words set him on fire.

He built a rhythm that she responded to in kind, bucking against him, tugging at him with her hand on his shoulder, another gripping his upper arm.

"Ben," she cried out on a gasp, and then crested around him once more.

He was lost then and growled his release. Then he took her to bed, laid her out on it as he'd imagined he would one day. She reached for him, and he lay tangled in her arms, her legs twined with his. Lost in her, in this moment, basking in this wholeness she made him feel.

Chapter Fourteen

"You wished to speak to me, Chief Constable?"

Ben stood stiff and tall, his hands clasped at his back as he always did when summoned to Haverstock's office. Yet he wasn't the same man who'd done so a hundred times before.

The hours with Alexandra—perhaps every minute since he'd met her—had altered him. He felt lighter. As if a weight on his shoulders had eased. It felt odd to sense the drive inside him loosen a bit. And yet he welcomed it because he could not regret a moment they'd spent together.

Haverstock stood with his back to Ben and seemed to be warming himself in front of the fireplace, yet there was nothing like ease in the man's stance. His shoulders were slumped, his hair a bit disheveled, as if he'd forgone his valet's ministrations. Ben wondered if he'd stayed too late at one of the clubs he was rumored to frequent.

Still, the delaying tactic of subjecting others to long silences wasn't unusual for the chief. He used it as a means of displaying his power. When you came to him, you were on his time, and your own ceased to matter.

"I find myself astounded at how quickly all that we've come to expect can change."

"Sir?" Ben eyed the empty cut crystal glass on the chief's desk.

"You were my finest officer, Drake. My sharpest tool." He finally shifted to turn and face Ben.

The man looked dreadful. Not just disheveled but diminished somehow. Less full of life and drained of his usual arrogance.

"How long have you been a detective inspector, Drake?"

Oh damnation, the man was in one of his moods. Asking questions to which the answer was obvious was an indicator of Haverstock's churlishness.

"Three years, sir."

"And you aim much higher, do you not?"

Ben barely resisted the urge to roll his eyes. "You know that I do."

"As high as my office?"

Haverstock eyed him steadily, willing him to buckle.

"Yes, sir, or higher." Ben didn't feel the urgency for it anymore, but he wouldn't back down when challenged.

"I see." The chief constable broke eye contact and perused his desktop as if in deep contemplation. "Then your actions of late confound me, Detective Inspector."

He lifted a document from his desk. "Did you or did you not hear of a plot to steal the Crown Jewels?"

Ben couldn't see every bit of writing on the piece

of paper Haverstock dangled, but he recognized the handwriting as Ransome's. It looked to be a statement of some sort, though not an official police report.

"I had no evidence of a crime. Just a citizen who'd overheard a suspicious conversation."

"And that *citizen* was the woman you chased out into the garden at Lord Wellingdon's? Indeed, based on your behavior that evening, I can only conclude that you're infatuated with *Miss* Prince."

Ben clenched his fists and considered warning Haverstock he'd just stepped onto dangerous ground.

Haverstock tossed the document onto his desk.

"What inquiries have you made?" He gestured to his blotter. "I must ask because there are no reports for me to review."

"There is a report related to Miss Prince's overheard conversation." Ben worked his jaw. "And a report of my altercation with Jack Demming."

Haverstock frowned. "How is Demming caught up in this?"

"He was loitering outside of Princes of London, Miss Prince's shop. But I found him and spoke to him, and I now believe his motives were more personal."

"Personal?"

"He's Amos Howe's brother, apparently."

"Ah . . ." Haverstock's face creased in a deeper grimace. "That matter is resolved."

"It never was. We have still not identified or caught M."

"Put a great deal of time into it recently, have you?" Haverstock held his gaze, unblinking. "Or have you been too distracted with *Miss* Prince."

"Haverstock—"

"You have not followed procedure from the outset, Drake. The chit's report should have been taken immediately. Escalated immediately. But it seems you're more interested in getting under her skirts than solving this case."

Ben bit down hard, struggling to hold back his fury. He eyed the chief constable's door, weighing whether he should walk out before saying something that would end his career with the Met.

"You've nothing to say for yourself, Drake?"

"I have constables attempting to gather information about M while I've attended to the backlog of cases that languished during the blackmail investigation." That damnably tangled case had to be considered a success in one regard, and it was time to play that card. "There have been no further threats to the prince, have there, sir?"

"No." He shot Ben a dire look. "Not to the prince directly. This new threat is to the very monarchy."

"New threat?" No wonder the chief constable looked as if he hadn't slept.

"This matter that will now take precedence over whatever other cases you're working. Delegate all else. Whatever else is causing you *distraction*, set it aside." Haverstock took a seat at his desk and drew a folio toward him, flipping it open, and staring down at the page in front of him with genuine bleakness in his gaze.

"What has happened?"

"It's to be handled with delicacy. Special Branch. The Home Office. All have a concern here." Haverstock lifted a police report from the pile of documents. "An attempt was made on the royal regalia."

Disbelief slackened Ben's jaw. "When?"

"Two days past, the final day before their move from the jeweler's where they were held."

"You said an attempt. Nothing was taken?"

"They overtook two guards and damaged the vault but apparently could not crack it." Haverstock flipped a photograph that showed a damaged metal door. "By some miracle, we've kept it out of the press. Though the jeweler is proud of their vault's resilience, and someone will crow eventually."

"Most likely." Ben didn't see the harm in letting the details out. The thieves had been deterred, and the attempt would put the Tower's Warders on high alert. But it was an act against the Crown, and after the bombings of past decades and the agitation of protests more recently, they'd want no such news in the press.

"Do we have descriptions from the guards?"

Haverstock pushed the entire folio toward the edge of his desk for Ben to collect. "The thieves were disguised, masked, and wearing darkened spectacles. It's all there." He flicked his hand as if wishing to be done with the details himself. "I take it you've discovered no concrete leads from Miss Prince's tale."

"I did not."

Haverstock's face creased in a fierce glower. "If you were focused on your work rather than that girl's charms, you would have questioned her properly."

He was besotted. He could admit that to himself now, but it was far more than mere infatuation. They may have only known each other a few days, but she'd already altered him, made him feel more alive than he had in years. He could not imagine a future without her in it.

"Your work is before you, Drake. I expect your full attention on this matter. Your diligence. Let *nothing* divert you." The man's emphasis was anything but subtle.

"I understand, Chief Constable." Ben offered the man the look of acknowledgment that usually preceded his dismissal from a meeting.

But Haverstock settled back in his chair, hands clasped over his middle, as if he was only just getting started.

"Now to a more personal matter. My daughter, Drake." Haverstock paused as if expecting Ben to finish the sentence.

Unease began to tie itself in a knot in his middle. "Sir?"

"Your behavior at Lord Wellingdon's soiree has caused her a great deal of heartache."

Ben frowned. He had no doubt Haverstock

withheld crucial information when he saw fit, and, more and more, he'd come to recognize that the man worked him like a marionette. But he didn't believe for a single moment that Lavinia was heartbroken. They'd met only a handful of times and had exchanged the most banal of civil chitchat.

"Forgive me, Chief Constable, but I don't understand. Miss Haverstock is a fine young woman—"

"The finest you'll ever have the opportunity to court."

Ben willed himself not to lash out. Haverstock liked getting his own way, and for some reason he was set on this match with his daughter. Which begged the very pertinent bloody question.

"Why do you wish me to court her, Sir Felix? You imply that I barely deserve such an honor. And perhaps you're right. You know the murky nature of my parentage."

Haverstock scoffed. "Ah, Drake. You have moments of brilliance, boy, and then those when you fall far short of your abilities."

Ben rocked on his heels and considered walking out of the man's office. He'd had quite enough of the chief for one morning. The man had never baited him so openly. Never insulted him so plainly.

"Do you think I'd consider you a suitable match for my daughter if I didn't know your history as thoroughly as I know my own?"

"How could you know my history when I don't

know it myself?" Ben's patience with the man and his maneuverings was at an end.

"I know your father, of course."

For a moment, everything in his periphery went black, then blurred. Sounds became muffled. When it all rushed back, he was bent over Haverstock's desk, his fists planted on the man's blotter.

"Explain yourself, Haverstock."

"He will never acknowledge you publicly, but he's a man of noble blood and . . ." Haverstock stroked his beard thoughtfully. "He checks in on you now and then."

"And you never told me." Ben was shocked he'd gotten the words out with his teeth clenched so tight.

Haverstock stood, stretching to his full height, which was still a few inches less than Ben's, and puffed out his chest.

"He asked me not to. He approached me at a gentleman's club, told me he'd been watching your progress."

As a boy, he'd believed having a caring father might have changed all their lives, but now it seemed the man was a coward, one who could beget illegitimate children but did not wish to endure the consequences.

He didn't need some watcher now. He'd needed a father a decade ago.

Ben's breath tangled in his chest. The fear and uncertainty of childhood swept in, but he forced the feelings away and focused on the man he was now. What he'd accomplished. What he'd yet to achieve. Then he thought of Alexandra and wanted nothing as much as to wrap his arms around her.

All that he'd accomplished paled in comparison to how she made him feel.

"I have no interest in courting your daughter, Sir Felix. She is an intelligent young woman and can surely choose her suitors for herself."

"How dare you—"

"And I'd ask you not to share any more details of my *progress* with Lord Whoever, but I doubt you'd heed my wishes."

"You forget yourself, Detective Inspector," Haverstock barked. The man rarely raised his voice and seemed flustered by his own loss of control. "I will allow it because the matter of your parentage is tender. But I mean what I said, man. Leave off trifling with this Prince chit and find these brazen thieves."

Haverstock pointed to the folio Ben had picked up. "You'll see that if you do, you may kill two birds."

Ben frowned. "What do you mean?"

"There was a scrap of paper found. A cutting from a newspaper. A single letter." Haverstock raised both white brows. "Any guess, Drake, what that letter might be?"

Ben flipped through the folio and found a photograph of the piece of evidence. The letter *M* stood in two sharp black peaks, its serifs ornate, as if it had come from the masthead of a newspaper.

ALLIE HADN'T BEEN ABLE to sleep a wink.

After leaving Ben's as the first light of morning dawned, she'd taken a cab home and tried for rest. Not ten minutes later, Lottie had come in to lay a fire, and Allie had given up.

Oddly, she wasn't tired at all. Her mind flowed with energy and ideas, and for the first time they weren't ideas intended to win Dom's approval or impress Eve. They didn't even involve a research expedition or traveling with her siblings on a dig. They were ideas for Princes, to revive interest in the shop, perhaps entice new customers, and the notion that she would go on her trip to Ireland with or without Dom's blessing.

Now she imagined taking that trip with Ben.

It was as if a new clarity had come from those moments with him.

Warmth bloomed in her chest when she thought of the night they'd spent, and she had no regrets. She'd chosen those hours with him, knowing she might face judgement, if only from his sister or the Drake housekeeper, if either of them realized she'd slept over. And, of course, there was the Prince household staff. She suspected at least one of them had noted her absence in her bed last night. But making the choice had freed her somehow, or at least given her a taste of what making a life for herself felt like—a life that had nothing to do with living up to the precedence of her father or siblings.

She and Ben had made no promises to each other, not even plans for when they'd meet again, but she knew they would. She had a brazen kind of confidence now and would go to him this evening if need be.

After washing and dressing, she made her way to the shop. One of her ideas involved reorganizing the shelving. Everything had been the same for so long, and she'd felt a responsibility to maintain it that way, but now she wondered why. The shop was not a mausoleum. It should be a vibrant place, emphasizing color and providing better space for browsing.

Their walk around the Tower fortress reminded her how much visitors brought a place to life. And that each piece should have its place. Princes' shelves should be organized, not cluttered.

By the time Mr. Gibson arrived, she'd made a proper mess, though she felt certain the displays would be more enticing once she'd finished.

"I would offer help, but I have a sense you're possessed with a vision of what you want, and I might simply get in the way," Mr. Gibson offered thoughtfully after removing his coat and opening up his workroom.

"I do have a vision," she told him as she polished a vase that hadn't been dusted in far too long. "And I have a few fresh ideas for the shop too."

"Should they wait until your brother and sister return?"

"No," Allie told him a bit more sharply than she intended. "I'm no longer waiting on Dom and Eve's approval when it comes to matters of the shop."

Though they had an equal share in ownership, they took virtually no interest in its day-to-day operations or its ongoing success. But she did. She always had, and not simply because she'd been left behind while they went off on adventures.

She loved the idea of finding new owners for antiques, especially among those who not only appreciated their history but would also give them a new life or pass them on to the next generation.

Mr. Gibson made a murmuring sound, usually an indication that he was giving a matter deep consideration.

When Allie glanced back at him, he gave her a firm nod.

"You are the heart and soul of this shop, Miss Prince, and I trust that whatever changes you make will be improvements."

"Thank you, Mr. Gibson. Though I think you're a good deal of the heart of this shop too."

He cleared his throat as if the overly complimentary moment had evoked the sort of emotions he was usually keen to hide.

"Well, then. Since you are quite occupied, I shall fetch our morning coffee."

Allie's stomach growled at the very thought of a scone or crumpet or some other baked treat from Hawlston's.

"Thank you, Mr. Gibson. That sounds divine."

"Shall I leave the sign to CLOSED until I return?"

It was more than a quarter hour past their usual opening time, and Allie had been too engrossed to notice.

"No, we should open. I can manage."

Within another twenty minutes, she had the shelving refilled with fewer pieces, but those intended to catch the eye. She'd collected the other items into a crate and lifted it, intending to take it into the back room, when the front doorbell chimed.

She expected Mr. Gibson and set the box down to help him carry whatever treats he'd brought back, but it wasn't Mr. Gibson who watched her from just inside the front door.

"Good morning, miss." The man adjusted his pince-nez with a gloved hand. "You are most definitely not the gentleman I spoke to a couple of days ago."

"That would be Mr. Gibson. I am Miss Prince."

"Are you indeed? Then you must be *the* proprietress based on the name on your lintel."

"I am." A strange feeling worked its way down Allie's back. An inexplicable sense of déjà vu. "And may I know your name, sir?"

"Lord Holcroft. Of the uncut diamond that your man Gibson swore he could fashion to my specifications."

"Lord Holcroft." The air felt tight, as if it was pressing in around her. And Allie realized she was holding her breath. "Yes, of course, Lord Holcroft."

He looked like the man who'd come a few days before, and yet not exactly like that man. His voice sounded similar and yet not as familiar as the day Holcroft had first come to the shop. Not precisely like the man at Hawlston's.

But perhaps her memory had faded over the passing days. Was he as tall as the man in the alley?

And his face—it was obscured by an elaborately fashioned mustache, his jaw blurred by a high fur collar on his coat, and his eyes shadowed by thick ruddy brows and gold-rimmed pince-nez that cut straight across his gaze.

The man chortled. "Late, am I not? You must forgive me for that, Miss Prince. The days get away from me, and I forever overestimate what I can accomplish in a week."

He seemed so . . . amiable. There was a such a bon vivant sense about him. She couldn't tell for sure, what with the fall of his long mustache, but he seemed to be smiling and had been almost since the moment he'd walked through the door.

"Is your man Gibson here?" He bent and held a gloved hand up to his pince-nez as if inspecting the space behind her.

Allie glanced up at their row of antique clocks. It was nearly the top of the hour and Mr. Gibson had been gone far too long for a mere fetching of coffee and crumpets.

"He is not here at the moment but should return soon, my lord." Allie gestured toward the man. "If you have your gem, I can watch over it until he returns."

"Oh, I don't know." The man patted his overcoat pocket. "It's quite a precious little stone to me, and I'd like to make it clear to the man what I have in mind for its transformation."

"I understand." Allie studied the man, who

hadn't taken more than two steps into the shop. "Feel free to browse until his return, or tell me if there's anything you'd like to see. I'm certain he won't be long."

The man cast an assessing gaze around the shop, and Allie tried to study him without being terribly obvious about it.

"He's at Hawlston's," she told him, and scrutinized what she could see of his face for any reaction.

"Is he now?" Lord Holcroft approached the nearest display, all but blocking her view of him.

"Are you familiar with it? It's the coffeehouse just next door."

Holcroft lifted his head and cast a look over the rim of his glasses.

His were the darkest brown. "I'm a tea man through and through, my dear."

Allie swallowed and found herself taking a step back, though the man was nearly the whole length of the shop from her.

He'd picked up the puzzle box she'd just set front and center in the shop this morning.

"Such clever little trinkets, aren't they?" Laughter bubbled up out of him. "I do adore a puzzle."

"That one is a particularly intricate design."

"Indeed. Quite a fetching thing." Holcroft shifted it in his hand, then tossed it in the air, and Allie rushed forward to take it from him. "But," he said, stopping her midstride as he caught it and set it gently back on the shelf, "it's not why I've come."

He took a few steps toward the main counter, pulled a box from his pocket, and laid it atop the glass.

"There we are. The gem is inside, along with detailed instructions for how I'd like it cut. A gold setting, I think, and the chips along the side. It's to be a gift for my daughter, you see."

The more he talked, the less he sounded like the man she'd heard in the coffeehouse. Had she imagined the similarity the first time he'd come in?

He was tall and carried himself with the same air of confidence, though he lacked the menace.

"You'll give it to him, will you not?"

"Of course, Lord Holcroft."

"Very good. Then I should be on my way. So many appointments to attend to." He spun away from her with the adroitness of a younger man, but then stopped, frozen in place, and turned back. "I almost forgot that you may have disposed of my card after my failure to turn up. Here's another."

A crimson gilded calling card appeared between his fingers as if by magic. She hadn't seen him reach into his pocket, and yet the card was there.

He laid it on the counter and then made his way to the door.

"Good day to you, Miss Prince," he all but shouted over his shoulder.

Allie scooped up the box he'd left and slid off the lid. Inside, a rather crude-looking stone sat on a little pillow of black satin. It was larger than she'd expected, and when she took it out, the stone was heavy and cool against her palm.

Lord Holcroft and the whole matter of his uncut stone seemed quite simple now. Quite believable, and she felt like a fool for all the assumptions she'd made about the rather jolly man who simply wished to create a gift for his daughter.

She scooped up his calling card. The same crimson hue with gilded writing, but one significant difference. This one listed an address. Number eight in Grosvenor Square. Perhaps the other had just been a misprint.

Holcroft looked odd, but he was nothing more than a new customer.

Though that left the man at Hawlston's an odd and unsettling mystery.

CHAPTER FIFTEEN

After questioning the night watchman at the jeweler's, Ben felt a bit of sympathy for the man.

Mr. Boscombe readily admitted to drifting off and carried an enormous weight of guilt for the thieves getting as far as they had, even if they'd been unable to crack the safe and abscond with the jewels.

But he'd not seen either of the men's faces and insisted that they hadn't spoken a single word. At least in the few moments of him waking up to the horror of the break-in and being thrashed on the skull until he lost consciousness.

Ben had taken time to examine the area of broken glass and the scratches and dents made on the safe. Though it had, unfortunately, all been tidied, he'd looked for any clue that might have been overlooked—a bit of torn fabric, something one of the thieves unwittingly dropped, or even more of the damned newspaper clippings.

But he'd found nothing.

The only notable aspect of his visit was his examination of the safe. The scratches and dents could all be explained by something as simple as a crowbar, but, oddly, they weren't near the safe's lock mechanism. The thieves had simply gone at the door with brute force, as if they thought they could tear into the metal and didn't bother with the lock itself. *That* made no sense.

He had two detective constables checking in with known thieves who might dare a theft of the Crown Jewels. Though he'd already had a few of his regular informants making such inquiries since Alexandra's first visit to Scotland Yard. Thieves did like to boast, so it stood to reason that word of such an audacious attempt would have already spread.

So far, they'd come up with nothing.

But one man knew something, or at least he'd been close to someone who did, and as much as Ben didn't fancy risking another beating from his brutes, he had to speak to Jack Demming again.

He made his way to Southwark and visited the man's haunts with no success. Then he recalled that Howe's mother lived in Southwark. Ben had memorized everything in the file about the man whose death still weighed on his conscience. And now, from Demming himself, he knew that lady who lived not far from St. George's Cathedral was Demming's mother too.

Ben waited at a park within sight of the woman's address for nearly an hour and was on the verge of simply knocking when he was finally rewarded. Demming strode out the front door, lifted his collar against the nip in the air, and headed north.

He kept expecting the man to hail a cab, but Demming walked like a man possessed by a purpose. Within a quarter of an hour, Ben was warmed from the walk and recognized that Demming was heading toward Waterloo Station.

It was easy to blend in among the crowd filling the busy station, but easier still to lose sight of Demming too. The man didn't go to the main ticket counter, he approached a special station—the Necropolis station.

Ben's gut clenched when he spied the station's familiar sign. He knew the place where Demming was leading him.

The special terminus allowed travelers to board trains set aside to convey them to Brookwood Cemetery. It was one of the largest cemeteries near London, designed to help diminish the overcrowding of London's older cemeteries. The land for Brookwood was spacious enough for thousands of plots, and Ben knew Amos Howe had been laid to rest in its grounds.

George had been too. Helen had been impressed with the philosophy behind its design and the fact that it had not been set aside exclusively for the rich or the poor.

After Demming's train departed, Ben bought a ticket for the next.

He knew where he'd find him. He'd been to Howe's grave once before to pay his own respects.

Though as the train wound its way toward Surrey, guilt gnawed at him. He crossed his arms, then loosened the knot of his tie, but nothing would ease the tension. He'd not visited George's grave since the burial, all in an attempt to avoid the guilt that assailed him now.

But emotions couldn't be willed away. Meeting Alexandra had shown him that. He couldn't deny what she evoked in him no matter how hard he tried, and he had no desire to try.

Even if he told himself he'd mastered stoicism at work, it was an illusion. He cared deeply about the victims he encountered in his work, about finding answers, solving cases.

And he couldn't bury the guilt he felt over George's death deep enough to save himself from facing it.

The irony wasn't lost on him that Jack Demming was leading him toward that reckoning because he was a faithful brother.

Exiting the train, he took in deep lungfuls of fresh air and rolled his shoulders. He could face this place again. And once this case was resolved, he'd face George again too.

Demming stood silently at his brother's grave, head bowed, his broad shoulders hunched.

The thief had come alone, and that was a boon for Ben, since he still had healing bruises from their last encounter. Still, he approached slowly, and the grass did an excellent job of masking his footsteps.

"Didn't think you'd follow me this far," Demming said when Ben was only a few steps away.

"When did you know?"

Demming turned back, a bemused look on his face. "Not as subtle as you think you are, Detective."

Ben glanced around, wondering if he'd walked straight into some snare the thief had set. But there were no men lurking behind the cemetery's trees.

"What do you want with me, Drake?" Demming rocked on his heels and cast another glance Ben's way. "Or did you come to pay your respects to my brother too?"

Ben approached until they were shoulder to shoulder, both staring down at Howe's modest marker.

"Do you know the man who killed your brother?"

Demming scoffed, gesturing at the ground. "Amos didn't even give you the man's name and look where 'e is."

"Don't you yearn to see him caught? For Amos's sake?"

Demming glared at him. "Not that simple. As you well know."

"You fear M that much?"

"I ain't a fool, whatever you think. Got minions everywhere, he does. And riches to spare. Bastard can buy anyone. Manipulate anyone. Want to know the maddest part?"

"I want to know his name." Ben resisted the urge to haul Demming back with him, throw him in a cell, and let him sweat awhile before doing his damnedest to get the name out of him.

"Devil of a man. Doesn't care if 'e succeeds. Blackmail. Theft. Corruption. It's all a game for 'im."

"So he wants us chasing our tails."

Demming grunted, but a smile began to inch up the edges of his mouth. "It's working, ain't it?"

Ben clenched his teeth and shot a glance over his shoulder. George's plot wasn't far away, and guilt warred with frustration inside his chest.

"Someone back there?" Demming didn't turn, but Ben sensed the tension in his stance.

"No, no one. I have family here too."

For the first time, Demming looked at him with something other than loathing and distrust.

"My brother," Ben said quietly.

"So you've been 'ere."

"Not in a long while." He looked at Demming directly. "Too long."

Demming dipped his head, considering.

Ben willed him to relent, to give him something. Anything.

"You've probably already met 'im."

"I beg your pardon?"

"Likes disguises, he does. Might 'ave already left you something that will tell you 'is name too." Demming turned, took a step closer. "A game, Drake," he whispered gruffly. "Never forget the rotter's playing a game." He raised a fist and Ben clenched his own hands, ready to defend himself.

Instead, Demming raised the fist to his mouth and seemed to be overcome. "Amos. Me. You. We're all just pieces for 'im to move about."

"Then help me stop him. Lead me to him. Give me anything."

The thief's eyes were bleak and glassy, as if the grief had come back sharp. "The devil's already circling. Sooner or later, 'e'll come to you."

THE BOY CAME INTO Princes a quarter of an hour before Allie would usually begin turning down the gaslights. Mr. Gibson was already busy with the day's-end tidying of his workshop.

"Are you Miss Prince, then?" the lad asked, his forehead bunched in concentration as if he'd had to search a crowd for her in the empty shop.

"I am indeed." Allie strode toward the boy, who rocked and shifted as he stood before her. He exuded a palpable energy, like a bird alighting for a moment but eager to take flight once again.

As soon as she drew near, the boy shoved a folded and sealed square of paper at her.

"Message from Detective Inspector Drake, miss."

Allie's pulse ticked up as she retrieved the folded paper. Was Ben hurt or in trouble?

The boy watched her with fierce intensity, and she realized he intended to wait until she'd read the note.

Allie unsealed the wax and found a short message that immediately put her mind at ease and brought a smile to her face.

Could you call around at Hanson Street this evening?

—Ben

"Any reply, miss?" At the boy's expectant look, she dug into the pocket of her skirt and pulled out a coin.

"No reply, but please take this for your trouble."

"Thank you, miss." He polished the coin on his lapel and slipped it into his pocket.

Allie expected him to run out the door to expend some of his pent-up energy, but he shocked her by lingering.

"Least it made you smile," he said, gesturing to the note. "Duke's messages often don't."

"Oh?" She'd have to ask Ben about his nickname. The sergeant at Scotland Yard had used it too. "Is the inspector very fierce?"

The boy immediately shook his head. "Not unless you've crossed the law, so see that ya don't." He gave her a cheeky wink and lifted his cap. "Good day to you, Miss Prince."

"And to you, good sir."

This time, he did fly. He was through the door and out of sight before she drew her next breath.

"Anything amiss?" Mr. Gibson had donned his coat and hat and approached the main store counter.

"Not at all." Allie closed her hand around Ben's message.

"A message from Inspector Drake?" He asked the question lightly, as if he wasn't sure of the answer, but she knew as well as he did that conversations in the front of the shop carried to the back.

"I'm going to visit him this evening." Allie watched for the older man's reaction.

In true Mr. Gibson style, he gave nothing away.

"I suppose you think me scandalous."

"How could I?" He took a few steps closer. "I was in love myself once, you know."

"We haven't declared—"

He lifted a hand to stop her, though Allie already felt heat seeping into her cheeks.

"I'm pleased for you, Miss Prince." He tutted and dipped his chin. "You know your own mind."

"It hasn't always felt that way." She'd been waiting for so long. Waiting to be included in her family's adventures. Waiting for her moment to shine.

"I believe it's always been true." He assessed her, but his gaze held warmth and kindness. "You need not live up to anything, you know. You're clever and spirited and must carve your own path."

Such a summation from a man who usually avoided emotion felt a bit like receiving an unexpected gift.

"Thank you, Mr. Gibson."

"Of course." He smiled and tipped his hat at her. "Now, I must be off. Good evening to you, Miss Prince."

He headed for the front door in his usual clipped gait, but he stopped at the threshold and turned back to her.

"Lord Holcroft's diamond will be finished on time. He asked for it to be delivered Monday. The chips alone will make for fine jewelry pieces."

"Wonderful."

"I'm glad to know he wasn't some ne'er-do-well."

Allie chuckled. "I'm very relieved too."

He nodded and then headed out into the chilly autumn evening. After dousing all the lights and checking that all the shop's most valuable items were locked away, Allie did the same.

She wanted to rush over to see Ben immediately, but she headed home first to wash and change into something finer than the serviceable black skirt and white shirt she'd worn to work.

A little over half an hour after leaving Princes, she stood on his doorstep.

She only knocked once before he opened the door and reached for her.

He took her hand and led her to the drawing room, and she was on the verge of asking if his sister was at home when he closed the door and wrapped her in his arms.

The kiss was the sweetest welcome she'd ever had in her life. His lips were warm and eager, and she clutched at his shirtfront, every bit as hungry for him.

He threaded his fingers in the hair at her nape, and a pin slipped free.

"Forgive me." He whispered the words against her lips and then bent to retrieve the fallen pin.

"Don't ever apologize for that sort of welcome." She opened her hand, and he laid the escaped pin in her palm. "I could get used to being greeted in that manner."

He smiled at that and watched her as she replaced the pin, his gaze roving over the features of her face as if he was memorizing the sight of her.

"I take it you're pleased to see me." No one had ever looked at her the way Ben did, as if she was as fascinating as a gem with endless facets.

"I am always pleased to see you, but I didn't even give you a chance to take off your coat." He moved behind her as he spoke, then reached around for the lapels of her coat.

Allie grasped his hands, savoring the feel of having his arms around her.

"Are you all right?" He tilted his head to look at her.

"Just enjoying the moment." She shrugged out of her coat and spun to face him. "Was your day as interesting as mine?"

His warm, welcoming smile didn't match the two carved lines between his brows.

"Oh. Something's troubling you." Allie reached up to stroke her finger across the lines. "What is it?"

"It's rather terrifying how easily you read me now." He cupped her cheek. "There's something I must do before I tell you about my day."

"What is it?"

He swept his thumb across her lower lip. "This."

As soon as the word was out, his lips met hers, and she clutched at his shoulder. The heat of his breath sent a warm trickle of pleasure all the way to her toes.

He took his time kissing her tonight, as if he was tasting, savoring. As if she were delicious, and he couldn't get enough. No one had ever touched her so intimately, so tenderly.

In his arms, she felt safe, wanted. Their connection wasn't something she'd been seeking, but it felt as if it was precisely what she needed.

"Tell me what's troubling you," she urged when he lifted his head and tucked a strand of hair behind her ear. "Then I'll tell you my news."

He drew her over to a chair by the fire. Then he lifted another cushioned chair to bring over, and she frowned.

"What is it?" he asked.

"Do we need two chairs?"

He grinned and set the second chair down. After sitting in the one by the fire, he lifted his hand to her. She took it and settled onto his lap.

"Much better," she said with a satisfied smile.

He chuckled.

Images came into her mind of a lifetime of evenings seated before the fire on his lap, both of them recounting the events of their day.

Though marriage hadn't been anything she'd ever yearned for, she quite liked the idea of such a future with him.

"Tell me what's causing these this evening." She ran her fingertip gently along the ridges between his brows again.

Ben took a breath. "There was an attempt on the Crown Jewels."

She gripped his shoulder hard. "And we didn't stop it." The guilt she felt shocked her. As if she'd failed in some way.

"No, sweetheart." He stroked a hand down her back. "There was only an attempt. Nothing was stolen. They weren't successful."

"And were they caught?"

Ben worked his jaw, and that was all the answer she needed.

"They were not. But I promise you they will be." Before M, he'd had a perfect record of solving every case assigned to him. He was determined to retain that record. M wouldn't elude him forever, and these would-be thieves would be caught too.

"I know you'll find them." She gripped his shoulder again. This time more tenderly.

He appreciated her faith in him, though he'd done little since they'd met to impress her with his record as a detective.

"Tell me your news," he urged her.

"Well, it's not unrelated, I suppose."

"Oh?"

"Lord Holcroft came into the shop again. This time I spoke to him." She looked pensive, as if recalling the exchange. "I no longer think he is the man I saw at Hawlston's. He came in to deliver his uncut diamond, and he was . . ."

"He was what?"

"Different than when he came before. Jovial and talkative. Kind. The more I spoke to him, the more I knew he was not the other man."

"Who we can now suspect may have been involved in an attempt on the Crown Jewels."

She clenched her fist where it lay against his chest. "I wish I could remember something to help you identify him. Or any of the other men who were with him."

"Fitz, the man I hired to monitor Hawlston's, will remain on the job for a few more days. Perhaps they'll return."

Allie thought it unlikely, and she suspected Ben did too.

"This is an official investigation now. We'll question all of the coffeehouse staff."

"Mrs. Cline won't be happy with that."

"Mmm." He grinned. "What I'm trying to say is that your lead may still prove crucial."

Allie would like the men in the shop to be found and questioned, at the very least, but most important was finding those responsible for the attempt on the Crown Jewels.

"Are you hungry?" Ben pulled her in a bit closer. "Mrs. Pratt will have dinner waiting."

She didn't want to leave this spot. Her hunger was for him. Nothing else. "Must we leave this room to eat?"

"No. We can have trays sent in."

She was being selfish. Perhaps he was hungry for something more substantial than snuggling by the fire.

"Not yet," she told him. "Kiss me first."

Ben trailed his fingers along the curve of her cheek, then slid his hand along the line of her throat. That touch melted her insides, and she considered whether they could make love right there in the chair.

"If I kiss you," he murmured, his eyes locked on hers, "I won't ever want to stop."

"Not ever?"

He bent and caught her lower lip between his teeth, then soothed the bite with a flick of his tongue.

"Not ever."

CHAPTER SIXTEEN

A̶LLIE DECIDED on taking a cab ride to Princes rather than the omnibus the next morning because she wanted to hold on to the peace she felt after spending another evening at Ben's.

The thieves had been thwarted in their attempt on the jewels, and Lord Holcroft was simply an amiable nobleman. She felt an odd contentedness that she realized she'd been yearning for. All her life, she'd been waiting for her moment, struggling to discover how she might make her mark on the world.

But her heart was feeling fuller now, and her hopes had nothing to do with finding treasure or earning a headline in the newspapers.

She alighted from the cab, paid the cabbie, and unlocked the shop's front door with an eagerness for what the day would bring, and even more, a yearning for the evening and more time with a certain detective inspector.

Normally, Grendel trotted out to greet her when she entered the shop. It was Gren's way of reminding Allie that she was ready for her breakfast before curling up on the settee in the back for the remainder of the day.

When the cat didn't appear, even after being called, Allie made her way into the darkened back room. She turned up the gaslight, and her heart jumped into her throat.

The back room looked as if a storm had blown through. Her books and papers were strewn across the floor. Every drawer in her desk and the nearby filing cabinet stood open, their contents rifled or tipped out. A few crates were broken too.

She rushed over to Mr. Gibson's workroom door and queasiness washed over her. The door was ajar, its lock bashed and mangled as if someone had taken a maul or a rock to it.

Inside, she found the safe intact but dented. A few years past, she'd installed a safe with a combination lock and she'd never been more grateful for her own foresight.

Her heart still raced, and her blood thrashed in her ears, but she drew in her first relieved breath.

Then fear seized her again.

"Grendel?" If any harm had come to that cat, she'd be heartbroken. And racked with guilt.

She should have seen to hiring a night watchman or invested in stronger locks.

"Grendel? Come on, lady." Allie bent to push aside books and papers and boxes, then got down on her knees to look under the settee. Grendel wasn't there.

Since nothing looked disturbed in the front of the shop, she assumed the door connecting them had remained closed during the attempted robbery. So she had to be in the back. Allie called to her in a soothing voice as she searched behind crates and under her desk.

Had she darted past when Allie opened the door?

She decided to make a quick search of the front of the shop too.

While she got on her hands and knees to check under cabinets and furnishings on display, the bell on the door chimed. She whipped up to see who'd entered, and a sigh of relief escaped when she saw the kindly face of Mr. Gibson.

Though when he spotted her, his pleasant expression crumbled.

"My goodness, Miss Prince, what's happened?" Mr. Gibson immediately made his way over and offered a hand to help her up. "Did you take a tumble?"

"No, I was looking for Grendel." Allie gestured toward the back room. "We've had a break-in, and I can't find her."

Saying it all aloud made tears well in her eyes. When one trickled down her cheek, she swiped at it with the back of her hand. This was no time to fall to pieces. Taking responsibility for running Princes meant that even the unexpected and the dreaded were hers to manage.

"Good heavens." Mr. Gibson had approached the threshold of the back room. "I suppose they've cracked the safe."

"No, that is the single bit of good news. They

didn't. And nothing up front looks to have been disturbed."

"It is my fault." His shoulders slumped, and he rolled his hands together nervously. "I've meant to make inquiries about hiring a night watchman but then got busy with the Holcroft diamond."

"It is *not* your fault. I should have seen to hiring someone. Though we may have lost nothing. Could you check your workroom?" She wasn't certain what pieces he had in progress and how much of it he had placed in the safe. All of it, she hoped.

"Of course."

"Oh, Grendel. Where have you got to?" Allie suspected the cat hid herself during the break-in, and unless the thieves left the alley door open, she wouldn't have darted out. She was a cat made for the indoors. She loved quiet, and a comfortable place to rest, and her meals delivered right on time.

"Perhaps some cream," Mr. Gibson called faintly from the back.

"Yes, of course." There was nothing the elderly feline liked more than milk or cream, though it no longer agreed with her and was only given as a very occasional treat. "I'll go fetch some from Hawlston's."

Allie was still trembling when she entered the busy cafe, but she tried not to let it show.

After Allie waited in a short queue, Mrs. Cline offered a greeting with her usual smile. "You're back to your early visits, Miss Prince."

"I'm afraid I'm not here for coffee this morning." Something in her voice gave her away.

"Oh no, dear, what's got you fretting?"

Allie swallowed and leaned in. "We had a break-in last night."

Mrs. Cline let out a gasp. As a business owner on the same street, this would be of special concern to the coffeehouse manager.

"Nothing was taken, at least as far as I can tell," Allie rushed to add. "But I can't find Grendel. She lives in the shop . . ." Worry for the gray ball of fluff welled up. "Could I buy a dish of cream?"

Mrs. Cline turned to one of the girls who helped behind the counter. "Hazel, fetch a bit of cream for Miss Prince."

A moment later, the young woman returned with a little filled glass bottle and set it on the counter.

Mrs. Cline slid it toward Allie. "Never you mind about the cost. Go and find your cat, miss."

"Thank you." Allie scooped up the bottle and headed back to Princes.

Another wave of dread washed over her when she could see Mr. Gibson pacing near the front door as she stepped inside.

"What is it?"

"A mystery, that's what it is." He looked as fretful as she'd ever seen him, his brows drawn in a single line and a patina of sweat glistening on his forehead. "I've searched through everything in my workroom. There were some small bits left out. A gold watch chain I've been working to repair. An ormolu clock I've fixed for Lord Corning."

"Oh no—"

"No, no, none of that was taken."

"Then what was?"

He shook his head and when he looked at her again, his eyes had gone bleak, almost haunted.

"I can't explain it, Miss Prince. The safe door seemed to be intact, so like you, I assumed it had not been cracked, only bashed a bit. But the door is indeed broken. Removed at some point, I'd say, but then put back in place to make it seem unbroken."

"What's missing?" Allie swallowed hard. They had valuable art, some porcelain that would fetch a pretty price at auction, but the most expensive items Princes carried were the gems and jewelry pieces.

"Lord Holcroft's diamond is missing as well as two smaller sapphires I was to set for Lady Dalrymple," he finally said, then lifted both hands to his head. "I thought the safe was secure. We purchased the best on the market."

Allie approached and dared to lay a hand gently on his arm. "I trusted that it was too. You're scrupulous and always have been."

"Why did they replace the door? And why didn't they take all the gems out of the safe?"

"I don't know."

"We should send for a constable." He lowered his hands and started for the front door. "I'll fetch a messenger."

Allie took the bottle of cream into the back room, found a teacup saucer, and poured a bit in.

Everything in her yearned to begin tidying the room, but she suspected the police would wish to see it as it was. She also didn't want to create so much noise that she put a nervous Grendel off from finally coming out. So she set the dish on the floor and headed back to the front of the shop.

Mr. Gibson was nowhere in sight, but she hoped he hadn't had to go far to find a messenger. There was a foot patrolman who came through at least once in the morning and afternoon, so they could speak to him if necessary.

She checked the locked money box under the counter. Though there was no evidence of ransacking among the displays, paranoia had overtaken her thoughts now, and she felt as if she should check everything twice.

A knock on the front door made her jump, and she turned to find a gentleman standing on the other side. He watched her with a questioning tilt to his brow.

Neither of them had put out the OPEN sign, but the door was unlocked, so Allie waved the stranger inside.

"Hello, miss," he said immediately, then removed his hat and clutched it in his gloved hands. "You don't know me—"

"No, I don't." Allie couldn't help the new distrustful tone in her voice. "Who are you?"

"Arthur Fitzroy, miss. I'm a colleague of Inspector Drake's, who I think you know." His eyes lightened a fraction, and he took another step forward. "I overheard you speaking to the proprietress next door, and I believe I may be of some assistance to you."

"Are you a detective too?"

"I am." He smiled as if to offer reassurance, though there was a bit of charm in it too. "Though a private one. I don't work for the Metropolitan Police."

"I see."

He lifted the hand still holding his hat and waved it to encompass the shop. "You've had a break-in?" After the question was out, he scanned the displays and crowded furnishings and walls dappled with art. He looked utterly confused.

"In the back of the shop. Not up here, or at least as far as I can tell."

Mr. Gibson returned at that moment, chafing his hands, and casting a wary gaze at Mr. Fitzroy. "Found a messenger. We should have a constable with us soon."

"This is Mr. Fitzroy," Allie explained. "He's a private detective and knows Inspector Drake."

Mr. Gibson's face seemed to lose some of its tension. "Have you told him about our mystery?"

"Not yet." Allie felt sick at the thought that they'd lost such valuable pieces. She'd have to speak to Lord Holcroft sooner rather than later. And Lady Dalrymple. Though judging by its size, Holcroft's diamond was likely ten times the value of her ladyship's sapphires.

"Do you mind if I have a look?" Mr. Fitzroy asked.

Allie debated for a moment, but Mr. Gibson appeared eager to agree. He'd already taken a step toward the back room and cast a glance at Fitzroy as if expecting him to follow.

"Let me go in first, gentlemen. I'm hoping our shop cat may have made an appearance."

Allie trod carefully as she approached the threshold, and she said a little prayer at almost the same moment that she saw the glint of feline eyes looking back at her.

"Hello, lady," Allie said softly, then turned a glance at Mr. Gibson and smiled. "It worked."

"The first good news of the day."

Grendel apparently wasn't pleased with chatter outside the door and crept under the settee again, though Allie could still see the glow of her golden eyes as she watched them.

Allie continued in with soft footsteps and bent to scoop up the cat while Mr. Fitzroy followed behind and surveyed the room.

"Have you assembled a list of all that was taken?"

Allie exchanged a glance with Mr. Gibson. "As far as we can tell, only three gems from our safe."

"They cracked the safe? That's impressive."

"The odd thing is that we found the safe closed when we arrived." Mr. Gibson gestured toward the cast-iron door.

"It's a heavy door. Could it have swung shut?" Mr. Fitzroy high-stepped over books and papers, careful where to land his feet, and made his way to the safe.

"I think it's very possible," Allie told him, "if

they hadn't damaged both hinges when they forced it open."

After a moment, the detective cast a look back at her. "That is odd, isn't it?"

"Speaking of odd, what do you say the odds are we'll recover the gems, Mr. Fitzroy?" asked Mr. Gibson.

Mr. Fitzroy whistled through his teeth and shot each of them a look that could only be construed as pitying.

"That's as I thought," Mr. Gibson said miserably. "Whatever we repay Holcroft and Lady Dalrymple shall come out of my wages." He shot Allie a steely look with that pronouncement.

He knew she'd never agree. "We have insurance for just this occasion, Mr. Gibson. In truth, we've been lucky. There hasn't been a theft at Princes for as long as I can remember."

Her reassurance didn't seem to make Mr. Gibson feel any better. Nor Allie, in truth. They both knew that the value of Holcroft's diamond would exceed what their insurance could cover.

He stared forlornly at his rummaged workroom and mumbled, "The constable will be here soon."

His words proved prophetic. Not five minutes later, a fresh-faced uniformed constable strode through the front door, and Mr. Fitzroy greeted him as if they were old friends.

In short order, Fitzroy had introduced Detective Constable Baker to each of them. Soon after, the young man had his notepad and pencil out and began making notes about the state of the back room.

The constable made the assumption that Mr. Gibson was the proprietor and directed all of his questions to him.

Allie still held Grendel in her arms. The cat had finally begun purring, but she seemed unnerved by the men's voices, so Allie carried her to the main shop counter and let her sit atop it.

Fitzroy followed her out.

"Thank you for coming to check on us, Mr. Fitzroy."

"You're most welcome, Miss Prince. You can find me next door in the mornings if I can ever be of more assistance." He deftly drew out a card from his waistcoat pocket as he spoke. "And I'll leave my card if you ever find yourself in need of a private inquiry agent."

Allie examined the man's card. "You're the one who's been watching the coffeehouse." She met his watchful gaze. "And I take it you've seen nothing of the men I overheard."

"You're the tip," he said quietly. "Of course you are." He laughed, but Allie wasn't sure why. "It all makes sense now. But no, I've seen no man with dark glasses and heard no word of a jewel theft."

"What do you mean that it all makes sense?"

He ducked his head as if suddenly hesitant to say more, though nothing about him struck her as a man given to hesitation. "Not sure Drake would want me to say."

"Well, now I'm more curious than ever."

Fitzroy chuckled. "He hired me with his own funds to test your tip. Not a common thing for a detective inspector at Scotland Yard to do."

"I see." Allie couldn't help but be pleased to know Ben had gone out of his way to investigate her story, even if via unconventional means. She only wished her tip and Fitz's efforts had prevented the attempt on the Crown Jewels.

"How did you become acquainted with Inspector Drake?"

Fitzroy lifted a finger as if to bid her to wait. Something outside the shop windows seemed to have caught his interest.

"Why don't we let him tell you himself?"

BEN DESCENDED FROM THE carriage and was through the front door of Princes in three strides. He could finally draw a deep breath again when he saw her.

Alexandra was there, behind the counter, looking wonderful and well and in one piece, and his heart began to settle into a normal patter.

"Ben," she said on an exhale.

"Drake," Fitz called at nearly the same time.

When Fitz registered her quiet exclamation, he shot Ben an arch look.

Ben ignored his friend and beelined for Alexandra.

"Are you all right?" It was the only thing he truly needed to know.

"I'm fine. Neither of us were here when the break-in occurred."

"Thank God for that." The anxious knot in his chest loosened a fraction.

"And the loss consisted of only three gems," Fitz told him.

"Three very expensive gems," Allie put in under her breath.

Ben was having trouble focusing on anything but Alexandra. He scanned her features, attempting to discern how she was truly feeling. To his surprise, she shifted her gaze to Fitz.

"I wouldn't say the loss was minimal, Mr. Fitzroy." She looked up at Ben again. "Lord Holcroft's diamond was taken along with some sapphires for another customer." She nibbled at her lower lip and cast a glance toward the back room. "That diamond was sizable. Twenty carats, perhaps."

Fitzroy sucked air through his teeth. "Didn't know that. I'm sorry, Miss Prince."

Ben reached out and placed a hand over hers, not caring what Fitzroy made of it.

When he turned back, Fitz was putting his hat back on and pulling his gloves from his pocket.

"Are you off?" Ben asked him.

"Not much more I can do here. You made good time, my friend, but Detective Constable Baker arrived before you. He's in the back with Gibson. He'll be able to fill you in."

Ben stepped toward him, and Fitz held out his hand, but Ben wasn't interested in leave-taking.

"I need to speak to Baker," he told him quietly. "Will you stay with her while I do?"

"Of course," Fitz told him, but his brows rose

as if the request perplexed him. "You think this is more than just a robbery?"

"I don't know, but I mean to find out."

"Are you two going to let me in on what you're whispering about?" Alexandra said, coming out from behind the counter and giving Grendel a re-assuring pat on the head as she did.

"This won't be my case, but I'm going to see if Baker will share what details he's gathered. Fitz will stay with you while I speak to him."

"I don't require a minder, Ben. I'm all right."

"Indulge me. It will only be a moment."

As he approached the back room, he heard her frustrated sigh and understood. He knew she wasn't a lady who'd tolerate such overprotective measures for long. From what he knew of them, her own family had treated her in such a manner, and he had no wish to cage or control her.

But after receiving Fitz's note about the break-in, the worst memories of his life had been reignited, and during the carriage ride to Princes, those fearful images played out in his mind. He'd known when his brother went missing that he'd met some dire end. No one had believed him. But his gut had told him so.

That same feeling roiled in his gut now. The sense that this break-in couldn't be put down to opportunistic robbery, or part of the usual cycle of crime statistics in Mayfair.

Demming's words played in his head. That they were all just chess pieces being moved about.

He sensed the hand moving them, manipulating, striking fear, creating chaos.

And he could not shake the sickening feeling that Alexandra had become a pawn because of her association with him.

That sickening feeling deepened when he entered the back room of Princes and saw that chaos had been wreaked on this part of her shop. She hadn't mentioned anything missing from her desk or shelves or inventory, and yet nearly every inch of the space had been ransacked.

"Sir, did someone send for you?" Detective Constable Baker looked understandably shocked to see him.

Mr. Gibson nodded in acknowledgment. "Inspector."

"Fitzroy informed me of the break-in," he told Baker. "I'm acquainted with Miss Prince." The young man's gaze flickered with surprise, but Ben decided to leave the explanation brief. "What have you discovered?"

Baker gestured toward Mr. Gibson's workroom. "As you see. An attack was made on the safe by force and yet it's curious since some items were left and others were taken. If they went to all the trouble to break the safe, why not take all of it?"

"A very good question."

"This is odd too." Baker picked up a teacup on Mr. Gibson's workshop table. He tipped the cup so that Ben could see what was inside. "These bits of paper were found inside the safe. Looks like a torn-up letter, but they contain no writing but a few random letters on some pieces."

Ben raised his hand, and Baker considered him a moment before handing over the teacup.

When he did, Ben strode to Gibson's work-bench and tipped the pieces out. Among them, he found what he feared he would. One torn piece contained an ornately written *M* in thick ink.

He swallowed back bile. "Take possession of these and have them photographed. I want a copy of those images when you do."

"Why, sir? I didn't realize this was your case."

Ben stared the young man down until Baker clenched his jaw and gave one sharp nod.

"This may pertain to a case I'm working on and any evidence you collect shall be shared with me. If you wish to question that, put those queries to Haverstock."

Helen was forever trying to teach him about chess gambits. Which reminded him that to catch a wily criminal, he often had to imagine their moves two or three steps ahead.

But it seemed he'd failed with M.

And now that failure had spread to touch Alexandra too.

Chapter Seventeen

Once Allie had found Grendel and Ben had come, she'd realized that they'd need to keep the shop shut for the day, if not for the remainder of the week. Though Mr. Gibson insisted on staying to help tidy the mess, Allie insisted just as vehemently that he head home after a couple of hours.

He looked exhausted, and she sensed that the strain was wearing on him too heavily.

Now, a few hours after his departure, she'd mostly put the back room to rights. But she hadn't worked alone. After speaking to Mr. Fitzroy and returning to Scotland Yard, Ben came back to the shop only an hour later, insisting that he'd secured permission to take the remainder of the day off to assist her.

They'd swept and dusted and refilled drawers that had been dumped for no apparent reason, and now there were only a few items that hadn't been put back where they belonged.

"I'm missing a fountain pen and a book," she told Ben, who'd set himself the task of hammering a nail into the broken side of a drawer.

"Maybe under the settee?"

Allie got down on her knees to look. "Clever man." She reached back and retrieved the pretty pen that had been a gift from her mother. "That just leaves the book."

"Do you know which one?"

"I do. One of the pirate histories. It was on top of the pile that usually sits at the edge of my desk." That gave her an idea, and she got up and walked over to look under the desk. Then she checked whether it might have gotten wedged between the desk and the wall. "Why would thieves take a handful of gems and one book when they'd managed to break a safe full of loose stones and finished jewelry pieces?"

"I don't know, but I'll let Baker know about the missing book. And be sure to tell him of anything else you notice that's amiss over the coming days." Ben wouldn't meet her eyes. He kept his focus on the drawer, and then he approached to slide it into place in her desk. "That looks right, doesn't it?"

"It's looks as good as new. Thank you." Allie reached up to stroke her fingers along the line of his jaw.

He caught her hand before she could withdraw it and laid a heated kiss against her palm.

They'd been together for hours and barely touched each other, and Allie had longed to reach for him. To soak in the comfort of his embrace. Now she stepped closer and wrapped her arms around his middle. She was immediately soothed by the strong, towering warmth of his body.

He wrapped her in a tender embrace and kissed the top of her head.

Allie closed her eyes. "I'm warning you. I could happily stay here for a good long while," she told him in a voice raspy with exhaustion.

Rather than chuckle, as she expected him to, she felt his body tense and looked up at him.

"Is something wrong?"

His answer was a kiss. Though it was a quick one, a mere tantalizing taste. Not at all the way he usually kissed her.

"How long will you keep the shop closed?" His eyes had darkened to a stormy green. "The remainder of the week at least, I'm assuming."

"Yes, I think that's likely." Allie cast a glance toward the broken safe in Mr. Gibson's workshop. "I believe the insurance agent will wish to see the safe and perhaps do his own examination before we can see to any repairs. Though I'm hoping to replace it with something better."

"Hoping?"

"The cost of reimbursing Holcroft for the loss of his diamond will be . . ." A flutter of panic seized her and the next breath she drew was a sharp inhale. "We'll have to see what his valuation of the stone is. But it will be steep."

He dipped his head, and she could hear the grinding sound as he clenched his teeth. She felt that tension in the muscles of his arms as he held her.

"Ben, please tell me what you're thinking."

"While the shop is closed, I'm assuming you'll

remain at home." He reached up to cradle her cheek in his palm. "I'm going to ask a constable to stand watch over Manchester Square."

Allie pulled back, her hands on his shirtfront. "Why? A theft from the shop doesn't mean I'm in any danger at home."

"I have reason to believe the theft is connected to . . ." He hesitated, weighing his next words as he kept his gaze locked on hers. "Other crimes. All of them engineered by the same man."

"Engineered?"

"He keeps his hands clean. Stays in the shadows." Ben dipped his head and swallowed hard. "But he has a network of minions who he pays to do his bidding."

Allie shivered. "You fear what he'll do next?"

"Of course. Especially now that it's touched you." He drew her a bit closer. "If anything happened to you . . ." He stopped and shook his head. "I will not allow anything to happen to you, so please remain at home and know that a constable will always be keeping watch."

She felt his determination, and she believed he'd go to any length to keep her safe.

"I'm not entirely defenseless, you know. I have a basic understanding of how to use every weapon we carry in the shop—pistols, swords, knives. Mama insisted." If they were going to handle antique weapons or display them for customers, she believed they should be familiar with their use. Papa had relished teaching Allie and her siblings while also delivering a history lesson about each piece.

"It won't come to that, but promise me, Alexandra. You'll stay at home for the next few days."

Allie pushed gently at his chest before stepping out of his embrace. She began pacing. "I'm not sure I like the idea of being caged up at home."

"Only for a few days."

"You'll catch him in that time?"

"I have to." His jaw was so tight now that she was shocked he could speak. The more he said, the more tension seemed to rise in him until he was like a coiled spring. She had the sense that he wished he could leave her now and begin the hunt.

Then realization dawned, and the pain of it nearly stole all the air in her lungs.

"I won't see you while I'm to remain at home, will I?"

He shoved a hand through his hair and then faced her. His expression had become that same cool mask he'd worn the day they met. "It's safest for you if we remain apart."

Allie was momentarily dumbstruck. The day was turning out to be one of the worst of her life, and she still didn't understand why.

"There's a great deal you're not saying. Perhaps you think you're protecting me, but I won't be left behind and left out of things anymore." She approached but kept her arms crossed.

If she reached for him, or if he touched her, she feared tears would come. She didn't want to be clouded by emotion at this moment. She wanted to understand what he was wrestling with.

For a moment, his unyielding expression softened. He was no longer the formidable Inspector Drake. He was Ben, who she'd come to care for— No, it was more than that. Ben, who she'd come to love.

"Do you not understand that if I could take you away from the city, I would? Believe me, Alexandra, there's nothing I want more. To take us both off to some seaside village. I dream about that."

"Then let us go," she said impulsively. Though as soon as the words were out, trepidation and guilt rushed in. Leaving the shop at such a crucial time was not ideal. Yet she couldn't imagine anything sweeter than a few days alone with Ben, just the two of them.

"I cannot," he told her with biting finality. "I will not. There's a man somewhere in this city planning his next act of mayhem, and I must catch him."

He was back to the man she'd met at Scotland Yard—fierce and grim-faced.

Allie hugged her arms around herself, feeling further from him than she had since that first day.

"He's been toying with me for months."

"Toying with you?"

"This is a game to him, Alexandra. One of his men said we're like chess pieces to be moved about." His eyes had gone stark, his mouth tight. "And now he's dared to cause you harm."

"I still don't understand. Why do you think the theft is connected?"

"Because the theft makes no sense and because he left a calling card of sorts. Scraps of paper with an initial that I believe indicates his name. Or perhaps his rank." He disheveled more hair, then reached up as if to tug at his necktie, apparently forgetting that he'd shed it an hour ago. "I've already said too much."

In two steps, he was in front of her again. He touched her hesitantly, carefully, a hand against her arm. Not holding her but creating a point of contact that somehow instantly warmed her insides.

"Now do you understand why I must be single-minded in this? I've underestimated him, and I cannot do that again." He ducked his head to catch her gaze. "So will you promise me? I cannot be distracted. I need to know you're safe."

Allie drew in a long breath and sighed. "I'm to have lunch with Jo this week."

"Can she not come to you?"

"Perhaps."

She drew her lower lip between her teeth and considered all that she'd planned to do in the next few days.

"I must speak to the two customers whose gems were stolen. Lady Dalrymple and Lord Holcroft. He's expecting his cut gems to be delivered on Monday."

"Could you write to them?"

Allie arched a brow. "Their valuables were stolen while in our possession. They deserve more than a letter."

"Can they both wait until next week?"

"I'm not sure they can." Holcroft was the most pressing case. She doubted word of the break-in would spread to him, but she wanted to alert him well before his expected delivery date. "I can speak to Mr. Gibson. Perhaps he can make a visit to both customers."

It didn't sit well with her. She was responsible for Princes, and losing customers' property wasn't a matter to be dealt with lightly.

Ben stroked his hand along her arm, attempting to soothe or perhaps persuade her.

"Let's get you home," he said quietly.

Allie bit her lip and then dared to ask, "Will you stay with me tonight?"

He closed his eyes. "I shouldn't, but I hope you know how much I wish I could."

It was just what she'd been afraid he'd say.

"But you will see me home yourself?"

He glanced toward the front of Princes, and it struck her then that he hadn't even planned to take her home. No doubt, a constable was outside already, waiting to begin his watch over her.

She could also tell that it cost him something—the thought of parting from her tonight. For days.

"I'll see you home." He held out his hand.

When she laced her fingers through his, Allie couldn't help but wonder how long it would be until she could touch him again.

THE NEXT MORNING, BEN summoned two of his most promising detective constables to his office.

If he was going to catch M in the next few days—and every minute the man was free to wreak havoc seemed like too much—he needed to divide the investigatory load.

He emphasized the discretion needed for the case and also made clear to each man that late hours and extra diligence would be demanded of them. Each was ambitious and hardworking, and both had readily agreed.

With the two new cases he'd begun reassigned and reports collected from the detectives he'd had making inquiries that might help lead him to M, he sat down with Gates and Riley for the focused hunt he planned for the coming days.

On his office wall, he'd pinned facts he knew and also cordoned off a section for hypotheses about M that he'd not yet been able to prove, such as the suspicion that he may be a noble or military man with a grudge against the royals.

"Gates, get to the bottom of the Bedford Square address. Others have made inquiries that led nowhere. Track down the previous owner. A leasing agent. Someone had to have conducted the sale of the property at some point. Speak to neighbors in the square too."

"I'll see to it immediately, sir."

"Riley, you're going back over everything collected so far. With special attention to the pieces of paper." Ben glanced at the photograph of the newspaper clipping found at the jeweler's. "I know it's tedious, but it's the details that matter most. Somewhere, there's a thread that will lead us to him."

The young detective didn't seem a bit daunted by the pile of documents in front of him.

"One file seems to be missing, sir." Riley ran his finger down a page of notes he'd made. "The last case you worked?"

"I still need to clear it with Haverstock, but a good deal of what's on the board emerged in that case." The chances of Haverstock allowing the two detective constables access to the details of the attempted blackmail of the prince of England were slim, but Ben intended to make a persuasive argument. Connecting the cases would make the whole picture clearer. The two young detectives only knew that they were seeking an unnamed mastermind known as M who was likely behind the attempt on the Crown Jewels and the break-in at Princes of London.

"And the list of Demming's associates, sir?"

"Leave them to me," Ben told Riley.

Both young detectives exchanged a look.

"Do you really think any of them will name this puppet master pulling their strings, Duke?" Gates asked.

Riley followed up. "They've protected him thus far. And they have the example of what happened to Amos Howe to dissuade them."

"Demming is angry," Ben told them. "He may still be in M's pocket, but he wants vengeance for his brother. A single detail dropped in a drunken rant could be the key we need."

"Understood." Riley tapped a pencil on the table. "Maybe the best strategy is getting Demming drunk and talkative."

"Agreed." Ben nodded. "Or one of his allies."

Ben was on the verge of closing the meeting when a knock sounded at his office door. "Come in."

Ransome stuck his head in, his eyes widening at the sight of the assembled detectives. "Haverstock wants to see you, Duke."

Ben didn't have to ask when he was expected. When Haverstock summoned you, an immediate response was required.

"On my way."

Once Ransome withdrew, Ben confirmed with each detective that they knew their next steps. "I want a report at the end of each day on your progress. This case is confidential and urgent."

Both men offered a nod of understanding, and Ben left them to proceed.

Two minutes later, he was outside Haverstock's office and rapped twice before the chief bid him to enter.

Haverstock didn't make him wait to be addressed this time.

He stood behind his desk, arms crossed, and stared Ben down. His white brows were drawn so tight, they formed a single bushy line, and the skin above his whiskers had taken on a ruddy hue.

The last time he'd seen Haverstock so unsettled had been in Wellingdon's drawing room when Alexandra wouldn't be cowed by him.

"Sir?"

"Brief me on your recent . . ." He hissed the last word and seemed to take a moment to collect himself. "Activities."

"I've assembled a small team to continue the investigation into M's whereabouts and identity."

"Those men have not been cleared to attend to Special Branch matters, and you know that."

"I have not given them access to any delicate case files, but I'd like to."

"I'm sure you would." Haverstock attempted a semblance of a smile. "If this case is too much for you—"

"It is not, sir."

"But suddenly you've called in reinforcements." Haverstock tipped his chin up as if attempting to look down his nose at Ben. Of course, it failed entirely since the man was several inches shorter. "I hope this has nothing to do with a break-in at an antique shop in Mayfair and your dalliance with its proprietor."

Ben held his breath a moment. It was the only way to stifle the urge to offer a scathing reply.

"The cases are connected," he finally bit out. "And it's an escalation in—"

"An escalation because your mistress has been inconvenienced?"

"She's not my mistress." Now Ben was the one hissing, and he was certain his own cheeks were flushed. His blood was boiling in his veins, and he wasn't far from the compulsion to toss the man out his own window.

"Then you've proposed to the girl, have you? Does she know your history?" Haverstock's brows arched, one after the other, as if he was relishing these questions most of all. Questions that had nothing to do with his professional abilities and everything to do with what Haverstock thought was his trump card—his knowledge of Ben's father.

"That, sir, is none of your business."

"Ah." He uncrossed his arms and strode the two steps to his desk, lifting an envelope from the top. "Someone has decided to make it my business."

Ben noted that there was no return address on the envelope and no address for Haverstock either, as if it had been hand delivered.

The envelope was flat, but the glee in Haverstock's eyes told him whatever was inside was as toxic as an adder's bite.

Ben reached inside and slid out two photographs, and bile rushed into his throat. He swallowed it back, fighting the scarlet at the edge of his vision. He willed his hand to hold the photographs steady.

They were grainy, one a bit blurred, but he remembered the moment they were taken.

He remembered every moment he'd spent with Alexandra.

One was of them standing on the pavement together in front of Princes. The day after they'd met. He hadn't even kissed her yet, but he had already wanted to. The next was of them on his doorstep, in those early morning hours after a night of bliss in her arms.

He resisted lifting his gaze to Haverstock's, not because he felt an ounce of the guilt or shame the old bastard clearly wished to stoke. But because he was an adversary now, and the worst part was that he likely always had been, and Ben had been too ignorant to see it.

"I cannot keep you on this case, Drake." Haverstock swung his hand toward the images in Ben's hand. "You've been compromised."

"No." Officially, Haverstock's decisions trumped Ben's, but he would pursue this case unofficially if he had to.

"Unless you've ended matters with Miss Prince, you are compromised and in a position of authority on a case in which you have a personal interest."

Ben bit down so hard, the coppery taste of his own blood filled his mouth.

"Have you put the lady aside or not?"

"I have." Haverstock had no right to any detail regarding his relationship with Alexandra, but Ben would tell the wily old bastard what he wished to hear.

"And yet you spent hours at her shop yesterday rather than attending to your duties here."

"There was a break-in—"

"And Detective Constable Baker was on hand to see to that."

"As I said . . ." Ben did finally lift his gaze and

looked at the chief directly. If he had any currency to use with the man, if there was a shred of allegiance left between them, he meant to leverage every speck of it. "The cases are connected, and I won't be removed."

Haverstock rocked back on his heels, almost looking amused by Ben's vehemence. Usually, that preceded a moment when he intended to revel in his own power.

"You may continue on the case if—" Haverstock lifted a finger and somehow stretched an inch taller. "*If* you set aside Miss Prince and give your entire focus to it."

Set aside Miss Prince. It's what his own logic had dictated as soon as he saw that scrap of paper with the letter *M* on it in her safe. M intended to strike fear in him, and judging by the photographs, he wanted him off the case.

But logic was no longer his lodestar.

Somehow, Alexandra had excavated his heart, and his love for her had made it louder than whatever logic he'd leaned on before.

He no longer had any illusions about Haverstock, and so the man deserved no access to his innermost thoughts. He would play by his rules. For now.

"It's already done."

"It had better be. If you fail and those photographs are exposed, what shall I say to the superintendent?"

"I won't fail." He couldn't. Not because of any bloody promotion, but because of Alexandra. M had dared to bring harm to her shop, and if Ben thought too long about other ways the madman could harm her, he wouldn't be able to concentrate long enough to do his job.

"See that you don't."

CHAPTER EIGHTEEN

Bʏ ᴛʜᴇ afternoon of her first day of confinement at home, Allie had started a book and put it down, finished off a knitting project, and, with Lottie's help, rearranged much of her wardrobe for no reason other than to keep herself distracted.

But once she sat down to take a cup of tea at midday, all she could think about was Ben.

When he'd deposited her at her doorstep the previous night, there'd been a wildness in his eyes that had nothing to do with desire for her. Indeed, he seemed eager to part from her for the first time since they'd met.

He'd looked like a desperate man, and she'd wanted nothing more than to soothe him. And yet she'd known it wasn't what he wanted. He wanted that wild, desperate drive to fill him up so that he could catch the man who'd robbed her shop and attempted to steal the Crown Jewels.

She also understood that he thought he could keep her safe if he stayed away, and if she stayed locked inside her house. Yet it was only the first day of her forced isolation, and she was finding it impossible to settle.

During the week, she was at Princes. That's how it had been for years. That was a part of her life that gave her satisfaction and a sense of purpose. And though she'd sent a note to Mr. Gibson, letting him know that she'd decided to close the shop for the rest of the week, she knew him too well to believe he'd stay away.

Though they couldn't open the shop without an undamaged and trustworthy safe to store valuables in, he was forever working on half a dozen repair or restoration projects, and she knew he'd find plenty to do without the interruption of customers.

She wanted to be there too.

Though, if she kept to her calendar, she wouldn't be there this afternoon anyway. She'd planned to take the afternoon off to spend a few hours with Jo, who had an idea for a holiday charity event that would combine their book club and bicycle members and any guests they wished to invite.

Jo insisted she'd need Allie's organizational skills to pull it off.

Allie had Lottie take a message to the Wellingdon household first thing to let Jo know she was to remain at home, but she'd yet to receive a reply.

Allie found Lottie standing in the foyer, staring out the long rectangular window glass near the front door. She turned when she heard Allie's approach and smiled.

"Any word from Lady Josephine?"

"Afraid not, miss. Just collected the post if you wish to see that." Lottie picked up a small pile from the hall table and handed it to Allie.

"I'm meant to be at Jo's in three quarters of an hour." Allie tapped her fingers against the little pile of letters. "Is the constable out there?"

"There's two of them. One's in the square across the way. The other walks by now and then. Perhaps he's watching the back of the house."

This was nonsense. Ben was worried for her safety. She understood that, but being confined to her house when she had a business to see to? It was maddening.

Allie strode to the front door, squinting at the greenery in the square across the way. "He's the one on the bench?"

"Sometimes he sits on the bench. Sometimes he strolls around the square." Lottie lingered behind her. "Will you be going to Lady Josephine's, miss?"

"What if she's on her way here?"

"Wouldn't she have let you know?"

Ben would be furious if she disregarded what he'd asked of her when it hadn't even been a single full day of confinement yet.

Confinement. Memories rushed in. Being confined to bed because her fever was high, and she was too exhausted to be anywhere else. Confined to her room so that she didn't get Eve or Dom sick. And staying behind while they all went off on grand adventures—that felt like a kind of confinement too.

So it was no wonder this single day of staying at home when she wished to be elsewhere, doing things, being useful, was such an enormous struggle.

But there was a man watching out front and one monitoring the back garden. Unless she wanted to abscond like a criminal breaking out of prison, she'd have to be candid about her plans.

"Why couldn't he come with me to Jo's?" Allie shot a look over her shoulder at Lottie.

Lottie shrugged. "Can't imagine why he couldn't. We could have the carriage brought around." The Prince family carriage was rarely put to use. It was old and too ostentatious, but it was roomy and the perfect vehicle to carry Allie and one of her watchful constables to Jo's.

"I'll go up and change." Allie felt lighter the moment she'd decided, at least as long as she could keep herself from considering Ben's reaction if he got word of her escape.

"Would you speak to the constable, Lottie?"

"Of course, miss." Her eyes brightened. She was always pleased to be part of one of Allie's impulsive ventures.

Allie rushed upstairs to dress before she could talk herself out of her plan.

Fifteen minutes later, she'd changed into a gown fit for visiting Lord Wellingdon's household and decided not to fuss with her hair. As far as she knew, this luncheon was only to include the two of them and a good deal of dreaming of plans.

She slipped on her gloves as she descended the stairs and smiled when she saw Lottie waiting eagerly at the bottom.

"His name is Constable Collier and he's quite

amiable." She swallowed and frowned. "Though he does not think Inspector Drake will be pleased with this change."

"It's only a couple of hours, and I'll be watched over, which is what's most important to Be— Inspector Drake." Allie glanced out the front window and noted that the family carriage had already been brought around. "Besides, Inspector Drake needn't know."

"Of course he needn't." Lottie handed Allie her hat and helped her into her overcoat. "See you in a bit, miss."

"Back soon, Lottie."

Constable Collier was already waiting near the carriage. He was blond and handsome and Allie understood why Lottie had been watching at the window.

He helped her inside, but they exchanged few pleasantries on the short ride over to Jo's. The young man kept a watchful gaze outside the carriage windows, almost as if he expected them to be set upon and overtaken by highwaymen.

She wondered if she should be more frightened. Ben had only spoken of the threat he feared in the vaguest terms. Mayhem, he'd said. The criminal he sought was planning his next act of mayhem.

"Is the threat imminent, Constable?"

He looked at her as if stunned by her obliviousness. "If Inspector Drake says to keep watch, then I suspect it must be."

Allie had the distinct feeling that Ben hadn't

told the young man much more than he'd told her, though she hoped he had. Certainly, Collier needed to know what he was looking for.

When they arrived at Wellingdon House, Allie and the constable parted ways. He stood and assessed the townhouse, looked both ways on the street where it sat, and then positioned himself in a landscaped area across the way.

"You came!" Jo greeted Allie with all her usual enthusiasm. "Did you receive my reply? I'm afraid I got it off quite late."

"I didn't, but that's all right. I'm here now, though I had to bring the constable." Allie hoped Lady Wellingdon wouldn't notice or hear about the matter at all. It would only serve to reinforce her opinion of Allie.

"Where is he?" Jo tipped her head to look behind Allie as if the constable might be hidden at her back.

"He's positioned himself in the square."

"I'm sorry, my dear. I know you value your independence." Jo hooked her arm around Allie's. "Come with me to the drawing room. I've commandeered the space for our planning session, and it also affords us some privacy."

Once they were inside the room, Jo closed the panel doors behind them.

"I do want to plan the charity dinner, but I also want to hear more about what's caused Inspector Drake to demand you stay at home. Under guard." Jo took up her usual spot on the elegant settee and patted the space next to her.

Allie sat next to her friend and was shocked when she felt the sting of tears welling up.

The part she'd avoided thinking about all day was what weighed on her mind now. The fear. The question that had kept her up late until exhaustion had overtaken her.

"I don't know if I'll ever see him again."

Jo scooted a bit closer and offered Allie a pristine folded handkerchief from her pocket.

"I don't understand, my dear. Inspector Drake?"

"The way we parted from each other last night. I'm not certain. But I know he will let this case consume him."

"The theft at Princes." Jo reached out and clasped Allie's hand. "When I saw that in your note, it broke my heart. I dare say you and Mr. Gibson are devastated."

"It could have been worse. No one was harmed. But the whole thing was odd. Only a couple of gems taken from a safe full of them and bits of a torn letter found."

"Torn letter?" Jo jerked back as if it was the oddest thing she'd ever heard.

"It's a clue, isn't it?" It had been nagging at the corner of her mind, but she'd been concerned about Grendel and putting the back room to rights, and Detective Constable Baker had collected them before she'd even had a look.

"Is it?"

"What else would it be?" Allie shot up from the settee and began pacing. "Those pieces must mean something. Something significant." Allie pressed a hand to her mouth, trying to recall everything Ben had said. "Ben said a piece contained an initial that he believed indicated the thief's name. Or his rank."

Jo watched her, looking entirely befuddled.

"I'd like to see those pieces. The detective constable who came to take a report carried them away."

"Well, Inspector Drake will see to that, surely." Jo tipped her head as if to catch Allie's gaze. "You cannot solve the case for him, Allie."

"But perhaps I could help."

Jo scoffed but smiled at the same time. "You would make a fine detective, actually. A lady driven by her instincts. Curious. Organized."

"Impulsive." Allie didn't know if Jo was teasing her, but throwing out Dom's most common criticism seemed apropos.

"I am serious," Jo insisted. "Though I doubt Inspector Drake wants you involved in this at all, seeing as he's insisted that you remain cloistered at home."

Jo glanced down at the spot on the settee Allie had vacated. "Now, come and tell me why you think this means you'll never see the man again."

A knock sounded at the drawing room door, and Jo let out a little groan of frustration. "Olivia is having a fitting, but Mama promised I wasn't needed," she whispered.

With a little sigh of resignation, she sat up straight and turned toward the panel doors. "Come in."

Their butler, Mr. Best, opened the door. "Gentleman to see Miss Prince, my lady."

Allie and Jo exchanged a wide-eyed glance.

"From Scotland Yard, my lady," Best added with his usual even-toned gravitas.

Jo bit her lower lip to stifle a smile. "Is he tall, dark, and wearing a thunderous expression, Best?"

"That is an accurate description, my lady."

Allie didn't know whether to hide behind the furniture or rush out the door to greet him. Her heart was thudding, and she couldn't hold back a smile, despite knowing she was about to receive one of his signature glowers.

"Show him in," Jo said.

Then he was there. Filling the door frame. He wasn't wearing a glower. Exhaustion had darkened the skin beneath his eyes, and he definitely hadn't shaved, but he still looked marvelous.

"Lady Josephine, may I speak to Miss Prince alone?"

Allie couldn't take her eyes off Ben, but she felt Jo's gaze on her, insistent and questioning.

"It's all right, Jo."

"Only a few minutes, Inspector, and you mustn't be angry with her. She came to help me."

"Thank you, Lady Josephine." He flicked one glance at Jo as she departed.

"I suspect," Allie told him, "that you are angry whether Jo wishes you to be or not."

ALL THE WAY ON the carriage ride over, anger had simmered in his gut. He'd banged on the vehicle's wall, urging the cabbie to go faster. He'd argued with her in his head. Stubborn. Willful. Exasperating woman.

But now that she was in front of him, now that he could take a few steps and touch her, he let go of all of it.

She looked lovely. This room was full of light and all of it seemed drawn to her. Sunlight gilded the slope of her cheek, reddened the loose strand of hair that curled beside her ear. And her eyes were the brightest violet-blue he'd ever seen.

"You're silent," she said quietly. "Is that good or bad?"

Silence seemed best because what he needed to say and what he yearned to say were waging a war. A battle between his head and his heart. He was torn between a job he'd once thought meant everything to him, and a woman who had come along to prove him wrong.

Alexandra approached tentatively, but she drew close enough for him to catch her scent. A mix of flowers and beeswax and the coffee she was addicted to.

"Ben, I'd rather have you shout at me than this."

"I'm not going to shout." Perhaps he'd learned something in this after all. "I shouted at someone I cared for once, someone who was willful, and it didn't end well."

"You mean George?"

"Yes." Those memories were always ready to fill his mind if he let them, but he'd gotten good at pushing them away.

"Seems your life is full of willful people."

"It is, but I don't mind. Willful people make things happen. I admire tenacity."

"Am I tenacious?"

"How can you doubt it? You survived illnesses and being left on your own, and you turned that independence into a role that you seem to love."

"What happened to George?"

Ben felt something in him shuttering, a door coming down hard to push that story back. He couldn't get lost in the past any more than he could get lost in his feelings for her.

"Now isn't the time, Alexandra."

"Please, Ben. It haunts you, and I want to know why." She took a single step closer. Her tone had softened, and the pleading note in her voice pushed open the closed door in his mind.

In some strange way, he needed her to know. Maybe it would help her understand what he'd come to do.

"My brother was wayward. He grew up angry, resenting how our mother neglected us, that our father had abandoned us."

She didn't react to that.

"He joined a gang who spent their time at the docks, stealing, bullying, causing trouble." Ben swallowed. The argument they'd had rang in his ears as if it was echoing off the walls of the Wellingdons' luxurious drawing room. "I confronted him about his behavior. Demanded that he break ties with the gang, that he amend his ways."

Ben's throat began to tighten, as if his body was

trying to keep the rest in. Because the rest was the deepest pain he'd ever known. "He chose the gang. Refused to speak to me or Helen. And then he chose to steal from the gang." He swallowed against bile at the memories. "They killed him. Threw him in the Thames."

Allie said nothing but reached for him. She gripped his hand, then his arm, and then she fitted herself against him, wrapping her arms around him. The sweetness of her warmth, the soothing stroke of her hand down his back, nearly brought him to his knees.

Moments later, he realized he'd embraced her too, pulling her in so tightly that he could feel her heartbeat against his own chest.

He forced himself to loosen his hold. "I didn't come to talk about George," he rasped against her hair.

"So why have you come?" Allie tilted her head up to search his eyes.

"The second constable I assigned to guard your home sent word that you'd departed." He was grateful she'd at least had the sense to take Collier with her.

At those words, she stepped out of his embrace, though she kept a hand on his arm.

"I will not stay in that house and be idle, Ben." The words burst out in a fierce, unwavering tone, but then she swallowed hard.

"You've never stayed put anytime I've asked you to, so this wasn't a complete surprise." He felt a smile tugging at his lips but fought it back.

What he'd come to do required resolve. He could not be distracted by her loveliness, or even how he adored that she forever disregarded his dictates.

He had to put this to an end. Not because of bloody Haverstock and his manipulation, but because it was best for her. If she knew what he'd seen, the things he'd done . . .

She seemed to sense his resolve hardening, and pulled away from him entirely, crossing her arms and pacing along the contours of the Wellingdons' expensive rug.

"Let us compromise, Ben. I must be able to take care of matters at the shop. To visit my friend. Constable Collier came with me, as I'm sure you saw. Is that not protection enough?"

"That seems a fair compromise."

Midstep, she paused and spun to face him. "It is?"

"Yes. I know it's not reasonable to keep you from your work or your friends." He shook his head, recalling the fear and anger that had overtaken him last night. If he'd been able to lay hands on M, he would have destroyed the man.

"Thank you." She rushed toward him again, slid her arms around his middle, and he wrapped one arm around her.

God, how easy it would be to lose himself in her sweetness. But he couldn't. Not now. Not until M was found and imprisoned. Not ever if he truly wished the best for her.

"Alexandra," he managed to get out, his voice raw and rough.

She'd laid her head against his chest, and he could feel something in him rending apart.

He didn't press a kiss to her hair as he wished to. Didn't pull her closer or wrap her fully in his embrace.

And when she registered the stiffness with which he held her, she looked up.

"You haven't come to shout at me," she said on a hoarse whisper. "You've come to end this."

"You deserve better, Alexandra." Those were the words he'd repeated to himself on the cab ride. He murmured them under his breath, singed them into his brain. His damned heart could go on bleeding, but his head knew this was right.

She *did* deserve better than what he could offer.

Alexandra pushed his arm away and stepped past him. This time, she didn't pace. She walked toward the veranda door and looked out on the garden.

One glance back at him and she pushed the French doors open, heading out onto the sunlit stones.

She didn't stop there. He knew exactly where she was going.

When he followed her and found her behind the wall of the hedgerow, she wasn't pacing this time. She stood waiting for him, and she looked just as bewitching in the garden when it was drenched in sunlight as she had under the glow of the moon.

"Tell me here, where you kissed me, that you feel nothing for me," she demanded.

"I feel a great deal for you." He swallowed

against the next words, knowing he shouldn't let them loose. "You have my heart, such as it is."

She unclasped her crossed arms and reached for him.

He couldn't stop himself any more than he could stop his next breath. And as soon as he was in her arms, all his logic and resolve fled. He kissed her cheek, nipped at the edge of her ear. Only when he felt a pin hit his hand did he realize he'd slid his fingers into her hair.

Alexandra arched into him, lifted onto her toes, and seamed her body with his. He happily took her weight, and then her kiss, and the taste of her drew him under.

She gave him everything he craved, her warmth, her passion, her wonderful willful heart, and God, how he wished he could give her everything in return.

He turned so that her back was against the hedge, and she immediately hiked one knee up toward his hip.

"I imagined this the night you kissed me," she said as he trailed kisses down her neck.

"Me too, love," he told her before licking at the base of her throat. "Me too."

Her skirt was as complicated as a puzzle box, layers and flounces, and then petticoats with layers too. But as soon as his fingertips met hot bare flesh at the top of her stockings, it was all worth it. He wanted to drop to his knees and taste her. He wanted to rip past her drawers and dip his fingers into her heat.

But when he felt her fingers fumbling with the buttons at the fly of his trousers, he reached down to stop her. Dipping his head, he pressed his forehead gently to hers.

"We can't," he told her on a ragged exhale. "Not here. Not like this."

"Don't you dare tell me I deserve better."

"But you do."

With a little growl of frustration, she pivoted away from him. "Why do you get to decide that?"

"Because I know myself." He'd been someone else, or thought he could be, for a few idyllic days, but he couldn't be that man and catch a criminal like M.

"You deserve better than a man who becomes so obsessed with his work that he doesn't eat or sleep for days. One who, at those times, can't be bothered with kindnesses or basic niceties to the people around him."

She dipped her head, and he suspected she was debating between a dozen retorts whizzing through her clever mind.

"There are days when Helen and I don't even speak to each other. Each of us is so wrapped up in our work. It would be hard for anyone to live with."

"I become consumed with work too," she said with irritated vehemence. "My research. The shop. I don't know what to do with myself when I'm not at Princes."

She was a lady who yearned to be useful, to help, and he quite loved that about her.

"You deserve better. You always have. Better than being a child confined to bed with illnesses, subjected to the whims of a foolish doctor. Better than being left behind while your siblings went off on adventures without you."

"I made it through all of that just fine." She squared her shoulders, edged up her chin. That defiance had helped her make it through those years, and he so admired her for it.

"Of course you did, because you're strong. Willful. And you thrive on independence now. If you choose to let someone into your life, they should give themselves to you fully."

"And you can't? You won't?"

Everything in him wanted to tell her he could. That he'd give anything, do anything, to have her, to love and champion and support her. Whatever the status of his rusted-over heart, it was hers.

He was the problem. He'd made himself singularly focused over the last decade. Taken the most challenging cases. Done whatever Haverstock asked of him.

"I do not believe the world is a hopeful place like you do. I wake from nightmares of what I've seen and done for this job. I become consumed with it. Lost in it."

She stepped closer, laid a hand on his arm. A gentle, warm, grounding touch. "Then perhaps you need someone to pull you back. Someone to love you through that."

"And if you came to resent the effort of pulling me back from the abyss? I would lose you."

Ben was grateful she didn't rush in with a rebuttal. He could see her imagining that sort of life, that sort of responsibility.

"Perhaps you could find a balance," she said quietly, though he could see in her eyes that she wasn't certain he could.

"Cases like this turn me into something no one could live with—cold, hard, unfeeling. You saw it in me last night. Impatience and desperation to put things right."

"I did, and it scared me a little."

Bless her for being so thoroughly honest. He'd adored that from the moment he met her.

"I need to be that man now. Single-minded. Utterly focused. It will take nothing less to find this puppeteer."

"And I am a distraction."

"The greatest of my life. But there's more." He reached into his pocket. "He's been watching me."

She took the two images, curious and eager, and he saw the moment her expression turned to one of horror.

"And me, apparently."

"I believe the break-in at your shop is linked to these photographs. They were delivered to Haverstock this morning."

"For what purpose?"

"To prove that I am unfit to continue on the case because of my connection with you."

Alexandra pressed a hand to her throat. "I never meant for this to affect your career—"

"No, no, that's not my concern." The shock of

how much he'd changed in a little over a week struck him. "I want to solve this. Imprison him so that he can cause no more harm."

"This man is more than a thief, isn't he?"

Ben dipped his head. "He is. He's responsible for one murder that I know of, but I *will* catch him."

"Relentless." She looked into his eyes, her gaze full of tenderness, but searching too. "That's what one of your men called you."

Turning her head, she took in the neat rows of hedges and carefully tended flower beds of the Wellingdons' garden. When she looked at him again, the resolve he saw made his chest ache.

But he'd wanted this. He'd come to end this, but he hated it all the same.

"I suppose this is goodbye, Inspector Drake."

Ben reached for her hand, and she didn't immediately yield to his touch. She was a woman of resolve, and he adored her strength.

"Be safe, Alexandra." He bent to place a kiss on the back of her hand. "Keep Collier with you until this is finished. Please."

She said nothing. The odds of her heeding him weren't high.

So all he could do was catch M. And he would if it took his last breath.

CHAPTER NINETEEN

ALLIE WASN'T given to sleeping in late.

Perhaps because, as a child, she'd spent far too much time in bed. Now she was always eager to be up early. With the dawn in the spring and summer and just before first light now that the months were inching toward winter.

The day after her visit to Jo's, after those moments in the garden with Ben, Allie lay in bed, waiting for dawn to rouse her. But the weather was as gloomy as her mood. Rain pattered against the window and storm clouds hid the sun.

Lottie had come in to clean the grate and open her curtains, but Allie had sent her away. She knew the reprieve was only temporary, and sure enough, as her mantel clock ticked over to eight, a soft rap sounded at her bedroom door.

"Come in, Lottie."

"Are you quite all right, miss? Should I call for Dr. Allen?"

"I'm not ill, Lottie."

The girl approached the bed and stood as if trying to assess her.

Allie lay with her back to her, but it felt rude. When she turned over, Lottie let out a little gasp.

"Oh, miss. Heartsick, are you, then?"

Allie swiped at tear. "I'll get up. Will you choose a dress for me?"

"Of course." Lottie seemed thrilled to have a task to accomplish and soon had a pretty robin's-egg blue gown laid out, along with matching earbobs.

Allie yearned to feel as bright and vibrant as the gown Lottie helped her get into a quarter of an hour later.

"Shall I fetch you a tray for breakfast?"

"No, I shall come down." She met the girl's eyes in the mirror. "I don't wish to wallow."

Lottie gave her a soft, dimpled smile. "No, miss. That's not your style at all."

A few minutes later, Allie kept her word and went down to eat the breakfast the staff had prepared for her. She usually sat near a window in the morning room when she was the only family member at home, but the weather was so gray that she opted for a spot at the long dining table.

Lottie walked by more than she usually would.

Allie appreciated her concern and wished there wasn't cause for it.

"The post has come," Lottie announced when she entered the dining room ten minutes later.

She usually left it on the table in the foyer or brought it up to the desk in Allie's bedroom, but Allie understood that Lottie was kindly attempting to offer her a productive distraction.

So she scooped up the post and headed to the drawing room. A few pieces were invitations for Eve, one was a suspiciously perfumed letter for Dom, and one large envelope was addressed to her.

The return address listed their insurance company, Lloyd's of London. She'd begun the claims process by sending a note on the day of the break-in and returning a form the next day.

Allie pressed a hand to her middle and sent up a prayer before opening the envelope.

Their coverage would only provide five hundred pounds, which would not be enough to cover the loss of the diamond.

She pressed a hand to her mouth, willing her breakfast to stay down.

What on earth were they going to do?

She had to see Holcroft immediately, inform him of the loss, and determine his valuation of the stone.

A knock at the front door made her heart leap into her throat. Her foolish, hopeful heart.

It wouldn't be Ben, though that was the first thought when she heard the sound.

Lottie stepped into the room. "Lady Josephine Wellingdon to see you, miss."

Jo hadn't waited and stood behind Lottie, already pulling off her gloves. She wore an eager smile. Nothing at all like the forced one Allie returned.

"Thank you, Lottie."

Jo swept in and closed the door behind her with a soft snick.

"You look better than I expected you to," she said as she sat in the chair catty-corner to the settee Allie sat on.

"Do I? I suspect I feel precisely as you expected though."

Jo abandoned the chair and slumped down onto the settee next to her. "Oh, my dear. Do you want to cry?"

"No," Allie told her honestly. "I've cried enough."

"Quite right too."

Allie loved that Jo was prepared to support her, whatever her mood.

"Thank you for coming."

"Of course." She reached out and patted Allie's cheek. "Now, what's all this, then?" Jo tipped her head to scan the papers in her lap. "Oh dear. This is about the break-in, isn't it? Look at your poor safe."

Allie hadn't noticed that there were photographs included in the envelope. And underneath the letter, she also found a document marked "duplicate." It was Detective Constable Baker's report on the theft.

She pulled out the photographs and held them out so Jo could see too.

"Does anything seem odd to you?"

Jo narrowed her eyes and studied the image. "Other than the safe being broken into and still filled with jewelry?"

"Yes, other than that."

Jo squinted again. "No."

"How about those bits of paper?" Allie handed

the photographs over to Jo and went to the secretaire that Eve used. In the first drawer, she found what she sought and came back to the settee.

With the little gold filigree magnifying glass, she tried to make out what was written on the pieces of paper in one of the photographs.

"Do you have your little notebook?"

"Of course." Jo was in the habit of carrying far too many things in her skirt pockets, but she was almost never without a tiny notepad in a pretty etched metal case with a little dangling pencil attached by a chain.

"Write these letters down."

Jo dutifully extracted her notepad, flicked it open, and positioned the tiny pencil above a pristine page.

"I see a *D* and an *M*." Allie adjusted the magnifying glass. "What's that, do you think?"

Jo took another look. "A clock face. It appears to be an advertisement for a clock or a watch."

Allie frowned. "Why would that be in the safe?"

"Isn't Mr. Gibson a repairer of clocks and watches?" Jo mused. "Perhaps it's from some magazine about watch repair."

"I think the letters must mean something," Allie insisted.

"I suppose they do, but you cannot solve this case for him." Jo laid a hand on Allie's. "I know you wish to help. But let's do something diverting. Something that will make you feel better."

Allie managed not to blurt that what would truly satisfy her would be assisting to bring the case to a successful end. Somewhere, in the most wistful corner of her heart, she hoped that if the case were at an end, life would go back to the few perfect days she'd had with Ben.

Jo chafed her hand. "Tell me what would cheer you."

"I'd like to go to Princes," she admitted. "I know it's only been a couple of days, but I feel that I should be there. I miss it."

"Then Princes it is." Jo smiled and stood, pulling Allie along with her. "Let me take you in my carriage." She cast a glance toward the front window. "We can make room for that handsome constable too."

Allie groaned. She'd almost forgotten about Collier.

"You needn't accompany me if you have other engagements."

"Nonsense. I have none but to cheer you. Though there is some Christmas shopping I need to do on Bond Street, so I'll stay out of your way for a bit."

"Thank you." The prospect of returning to the shop did make Allie's bruised heart feel a tiny bit lighter.

BEN LOATHED THE TASTE of whiskey.

It reminded him of the man his mother had taken up with, and that man's rages and fists. It reminded him of how volatile George became after a glass or two.

He'd never seen it do any good. It made men boisterous and often violent.

But last night he'd craved it, and he'd recalled that Helen kept a bottle for medicinal purposes and poured himself a glass. Now, somehow, yesterday had merged into today, and the bottle was nearly empty.

He understood why others found solace in it.

It sheared the edges off pain and blurred reason. And memory. The first glass had filled his mind with a kind of idealistic warmth. He could almost believe that the world was a good place.

The second glass allowed him to think that he could make amends with Alexandra, and then make a life with her. It wouldn't matter where he'd come from, and she'd disregard his darkness. She'd love him despite all that. And he'd love her for all the magnificent things she was.

He'd cheer her as she wrote lady pirate books, and he'd spend hours with her poring over marriage and death and birth certificates if she wished it. They'd take the journeys she'd never been able to as a child.

In a whiskey haze, anything felt possible. But hours had passed since his last glass, and his logical mind had punched through his liquor-tinged dreams to remind him that life wasn't that kind.

At a rustle against the front door, he had the wild thought that it might be Alexandra. Not entirely sober, apparently.

But soon he recognized his sister's footsteps. He winced at her reaction when she saw the state of him and realized that he'd downed her whiskey.

"I see we're back to late nights." Helen walked

in with her usual briskness, discarding her coat and already planning the next activity, despite having worked a ridiculously long day.

But when she drew near him, she stopped and let out a little gasp.

She stomped closer and swept up his empty glass.

"Good God, Ben. It's ten in the morning."

"I started last evening if that eases your mind."

"It does not. Have you slept at all?"

He was still wearing his clothes from the previous day. "I don't think so." He squinted up at her. She'd turned up the gaslights, and they were suddenly a menace. "Did you?"

"I slept late yesterday. It was an overnight round. If you were compos mentis, you'd remember that." She let out a weary sigh and bent to look in his eyes. "You never drink. What's wrong?"

She took the glass and bottle from him, but there wasn't much alcohol remaining in either. After setting them aside, she sat down in front of him and took his face in her hands.

"Ben, what's happened? Is it Miss Prince? Has something happened to her?"

"Miss Prince?" Calling her that reminded him of the day they'd met. The spark of a lady, Helen had called her.

"Yes. Goodness, are you still completely ad-dled? Shall I throw cold water on you?"

Too many questions. *She* was the truly relent-less Drake. Not him.

"I'd appreciate it if you didn't," he told her, his voice gravelly. "I don't think it would fix anything."

"Well, it might get you to talk some sense to me, and I need to know what's wrong." Helen was rarely shaken. In years of nursing, she'd seen loss and terrible injuries and illnesses and remained stalwart, but he could hear the tinge of real worry in her voice, and he felt like a royal ass for causing it.

"I've never seen you like this before," she told him in a low voice. "And to be honest, it's a bit frightening. Benedict, what has happened?"

He stood and found his head weighed a thousand pounds and every muscle in his body fought him. How long had he been slumped in a straight-backed chair?

"The problem is what hasn't happened," he told Helen. "I should have caught him by now. And Miss Prince is safe and well. Or at least she will be if she keeps her distance from me."

"What exactly does that mean?"

"I'm not good for her. You know that as well as I do."

Helen stood. All the tenderness and worry he'd seen a moment ago turned to distaste. "I will not give credence to your drunken self-loathing."

Ben approached her, and she winced. He knew he looked a fright and no doubt smelled like a whiskey barrel. But he had to make her understand. He'd convinced himself. He could convince her too.

"You've met her. She's full of energy and vibrancy. And hope. And I'm none of those things."

Helen began tidying. She could never remain

still for long. "That's not true. You do have hope, or you wouldn't do the work you do."

Ben scoffed. "Helen, you're describing yourself."

She walked out of the room, and he thought perhaps that was her answer, but she returned soon after with a damp rag and began wiping down the table he'd made his home for the last several hours.

"People without hope don't become detectives. They don't become doctors or nurses. We do these things because we have hope that we can make things better."

"I can make the world better by finding him. By stopping him."

"And by walking away from Miss Prince." She tipped a look over her shoulder at him. "You know, there's nothing less appealing than a man playing martyr."

"That's not what I'm doing."

Helen proceeded to dust the mantel, which she well knew Mrs. Pratt had likely attended to this week. "You know it's what you're doing. Or at least you would know without whiskey."

Suddenly, she spun to face him. Anger fueled her now. He could feel it.

"I cannot believe this is the vice you choose, knowing our history with it."

"Maybe it's the vice I turn to *because* I do know our history."

"Benedict, you cannot solve this case if you're drunk."

He dragged a hand across the thick stubble on his face. "That is a good point."

"So this is because you've cut yourself off from Miss Prince, is it?"

"It was the right thing to do."

She rolled her eyes. He hadn't seen Helen roll her eyes since she was ten years old. "And why are you so bent on believing you'll lead that lady to destruction?"

The warm alcohol haze had entirely worn off now, and exhaustion swept in, but this answer was easiest.

"Because I have nothing to offer. I work all hours of the night. I deal with the most vile of creatures. And at the end of the day, what do I have left?" He spread his arms, lifted his hands. "Does she not deserve more than this?"

Helen assessed him grimly. "*This* is not what you're usually like at the end of the day. You're not a man prone to feeling sorry for himself on your best days."

He closed his eyes. This battle had been fought and won. He didn't have the strength to fight it out with Helen too.

"You do love her, don't you?"

The question came softly and hurt all the more for her tender tone.

His logic dredged up a reply. "I've known her little more than a week."

"And what does that matter? Love is not measured in length of acquaintance."

Ben opened his eyes again. The room spun a bit, but then came into focus.

Helen wore a fierce expression. "You should get some sleep."

He glanced at the table where he'd scribbled a few notes about the case before succumbing to whiskey's siren call.

"I have work to do."

"Sleep first or you won't be fit for work."

Ben felt a smile crack the tired lines of his face. "You'll make a fine doctor one day."

"Yes, I know I will. And may I boss you about a bit more?"

A rusty chuckle burst out of him. "You wouldn't be you unless you did."

"I shall take that as a compliment." She sniffed imperiously, then closed the distance between them. "Heed me, brother. I say this from my heart, and you know that's rare."

He stilled and drew in a long breath.

"Because of Miss Prince, I have seen you happy. Lighter. More yourself than you have been in years. She brings you joy, and I suspect you do the same for her."

"I don't know if that's true."

"You weren't always this grim-faced man, Ben. You are also kind and caring and generous."

"I need to solve this case." That was all that mattered. Especially when he wasn't certain he was any of those things anymore.

"Sleep. Then think on what I've said when the whiskey is out of your system and the case is solved." She reached out to pat him once on the center of his chest. "And don't forget to consult your heart in these matters, not just your very prodigious mind."

Ben knew she was right, but he couldn't consult his heart. Not yet.

"I'll try for a few winks," he told her. "Thank you, Helen."

She waved him off, apparently done with the moments of tenderhearted advice. "I'll thank you to stop drinking my medicinal whiskey."

Chapter Twenty

Allie strode through the front door of Princes and smiled at the bell's familiar chime.

For a moment, she simply stood and soaked it all in. The scent of old wood and aged book binding. Beeswax-polished shelves. The dark, enticing aroma of coffee.

As she ventured further into the shop, she danced her fingers over furniture pieces and fabrics. Velvet upholstery, intricate tapestries, the delicate edge of a silk fan.

The shop felt more like home than the expensive townhouse her father had purchased a few years before his death. Or even the upstairs rooms, most of which had been converted to storage space and Dom's bachelor domain.

She felt useful at Princes. The most useful. Running the shop had fallen to her by default, but it gave her a purpose, even if it would never be as impressive to anyone as Dom's and Eve's accomplishments.

"Well, hello. I hoped it was you." Mr. Gibson emerged from the back room wearing a smile.

"This place hasn't been the same without you, Miss Prince."

Allie was pleased to see him too. "I've missed you, Mr. Gibson."

"And I you, Miss Prince." He ducked his head as if embarrassed by their mutual exuberance. "I have something to show you."

When he scurried into the back room, she felt her first niggle of apprehension, but he soon emerged again with a small stack of papers.

He approached and spread them out on the main counter, and she could see that they were advertisements for various safes and vaults.

"I thought you'd want to have a look at these. Your decision will, of course, be the final say, but I think these two seem quite promising." He pointed to the two on top. "They're the most updated devices. And the manufacturer of this one even claims that they guarantee their safes to be theft-proof."

Allie perused the advertisements, noting the various claims and guarantees. She glanced at Mr. Gibson. "I wonder how many of these guarantees are legally binding."

He chuckled softly. "As do I. Advertisers are bold nowadays."

"They are indeed." She agreed with him about the two that he liked the best, and she was already leaning toward the one that seemed a bit more spacious than their current safe. They needed the extra space and had for some time. "This one, I think."

Mr. Gibson smiled. "We're in accord, and I will see to ordering it straightaway if you approve."

"I do. We must have it in order to reopen." She dug in her bag before he could depart. "I noticed in the photographs the police took that there are bits of what appears to be a clock advertisement." She handed him the photograph. "Is this from a magazine of yours?"

He scanned the image with a quizzical frown. "No, not at all."

"The bits of paper. You'd never seen them?"

"No." He tipped his head as he assessed her. "What do you think they mean?"

"I wish I knew."

"Well, as I told the young detective, those pieces were not in the safe the night before. A true mystery."

"One that I suppose Inspector . . ." She couldn't bring herself to say his name. She was being ridiculous, but it caught in her throat.

Mr. Gibson seemed to sense her hesitation and finished the thought for her. "Inspector Drake will suss it all out, I'm sure."

"I'm sure he will," she agreed. Then a thought struck. She went behind the counter and pulled out the top drawer.

Lord Holcroft's calling card was hard to miss with its bright crimson-red paper. She lifted it out and tucked it into her coat pocket.

"My goal today is to go and speak to Lord Holcroft about his lost stone. We need to know his valuation and then we can determine how to recompense him."

"I take it Inspector Drake expressed no hope of recovering the gems?"

"I don't think we can rely on that." Allie had rarely heard of stolen jewels being recovered. They were simply too easy to recut or place in new settings and resell. "We can hope, of course. And I'll say as much to Lord Holcroft, but it will be a matter of whether he's willing to wait for the resolution of the case."

Mr. Gibson looked pensive. "If I'd lost a gem so valuable, I'm not sure I would be willing to." He chafed his hands as if ready to set himself a task. "Right, then if you're going to Holcroft, I should visit Lady Dalrymple. Divide and conquer, so to speak."

Allie smiled. "Yes, though in this case, it's divide and smooth over. Which I'm not always good at."

"You'll do well, Miss Prince. I have every faith in you."

"I truly appreciate that you do."

Allie hadn't yet taken off her coat, so she slid her gloves on and prepared to depart.

"Oh, just so you know, Constable Collier has been assigned to accompany me, so you may notice him lurking outside at times. At least until the case has been resolved."

Mr. Gibson craned his neck to catch a glimpse of the young man who stood on the pavement outside.

"And Lady Josephine will stop by after she's

finished Christmas shopping. If I haven't returned, will you ask her to wait?"

"Of course, miss. Good luck with Lord Holcroft."

Trepidation about the meeting had already begun to steal a bit of her pleasure at being back at Princes.

"Thank you. I suspect I'll need it."

DEMMING WAS PROVING AS wily as a fox. Every time Ben thought he had a solid lead on where to find the man, he went to ground and disappeared.

So Ben focused on the other avenues of investigation. Via a partial watermark, the stationery in the Princes safe had been linked to a stationer not far from the shop itself. Ben had a constable go there to retrieve a list of all those who'd purchased the particular bond and shade of paper in the last year. It had arrived in his office an hour ago, and it contained five M names.

He considered calling on each of them until Riley rushed into his office.

"Sir, I've found what you've been looking for."

Ben knew he didn't mean M himself, but he flicked his hand to bid the young man to come forward and explain himself.

He immediately pulled a folded document from his pocket.

"The previous constable was onto the wrong house agent. This is the right one. He says the Bedford Square property isn't let. It was sold three years ago, along with two other properties on the same square to the same man."

"One man bought three London townhouses all in one go? What's his name?" Ben stuck out his hand, impatient to see the document.

Riley handed the crumpled sheet over, and Ben realized it was just the young man's rather haphazardly written notes. He didn't like straight lines, apparently, and words streaked across the page at various angles.

"What's the man's name, Riley?"

"As you see there, sir. Lord Thomas Holcroft."

Ben dug in his pocket for a key, twisted it in the lock of his desk drawer, and pulled out his revolver from the dark recesses where he kept it unloaded and secured. He scooped up a box of bullets and shoved both in his pocket.

"Go. Take three constables, or as many as you can get. Surround the houses on Bedford Square, but don't approach." He shot the young man a hard look. "Do you hear me? Don't approach until you hear my signal."

"Yes, sir." Riley stood ready, anxious.

"Now, Riley."

Ben nearly overtook the young man as they both strode quickly from his office.

Ten minutes later, Ben had hailed a cab headed for Princes, his heart in his throat. He bridled his imagination and pulled the reins tight.

Monday. She'd said Holcroft expected his diamond on Monday.

Now he only hoped she'd gone to the shop today. He had to stop her.

If that bastard laid a finger on her—

"Faster!" he shouted up when the cab slowed, snagged by midday traffic.

The vehicle was small, and the cabbie was an expert at maneuvering London's clogged thoroughfares. He pulled alongside a growler and then shot past it. Only a moment later, they tilted wildly around a corner and were in the throngs near Bond Street.

When the cab slowed, Ben considered jumping out and sprinting on foot the rest of the way.

Miraculously, the cabbie found a path through and turned them onto Moulton Street. Ben tossed up twice the fare and darted through the front door of Princes.

Lady Josephine startled in the chair where she'd been reading, dropping her book onto her lap.

"Goodness, Inspector. You gave me quite a fright."

"Forgive me. Where's Alexandra?"

"She's on an errand." She glanced at the row of antique clocks. "I'm expecting her at any moment."

"She's gone to see Lord Holcroft about his diamond, Inspector." Mr. Gibson emerged from the back of the shop, his brows peaked high in concern. "Is anything amiss, Inspector?"

"Yes, Gibson, it is." Ben strode forward. "Do you know the address she went to?"

Gibson gestured toward the front counter. "He'd left his card, but she may have taken it. Grosvenor Square. Number eight, I believe."

Ben rushed back out into the street, eating up the pavement as he sought a cab.

One edged toward the curb to collect him, and he shouted up the address.

Nausea threatened as they made their way out of the busy shopping district, up Brook Street, toward one of London's most fashionable squares. The distance was no more than a leisurely walk, and every time the carriage slowed, he wished he had headed out on foot.

When he spotted her, he banged the wall of the carriage to stop and jumped out. She walked along the pavement, safe and unharmed.

"Alexandra."

She turned immediately, shock, a bit of tenderness, and then irritation flickering over her face in succession.

"What do you want, Inspector?"

He was next to her in a heartbeat, and he forced himself not to reach for her.

"I need you to listen to me."

She lifted a brow in reply. "I'm here to take care of a business matter. What is it?"

Suddenly, he couldn't think. Couldn't get his tongue to form words. She had not yet gone to number eight, and his heart flip-flopped in his chest at that excellent realization, but he needed a strategy, and quickly.

"I'll accompany you."

"What? Why? This has nothing to do with you, Inspector." She darted a gaze toward the green in the center of the square. "And I already have a shadow."

Constable Collier sat on a wrought iron bench, giving Ben a quizzical look.

"You know how to use a revolver, yes?" He reached into his pocket, considering whether to urge her to take it into the meeting with Holcroft.

"I . . ." She huffed in frustration. "I have held one, fired one. A long time ago. Why?"

"Do you have a roomy pocket in that skirt?"

"I don't. Why? I wouldn't want a revolver even if I had enormous pockets."

Ben moved closer, and she took a single step back.

"The man you've come to meet isn't Holcroft. Or at least, he's not the kindly aristocrat you think he is."

"How do you know?"

"Too much to explain. But he either works for M or . . ." The other possibility made his hand tremble against the revolver in his pocket. "Or he *is* M."

Her mouth fell open. She snapped it shut. Then she set her jaw, and he could see the gears of her mind churning.

"If we go in together, there will be no subtlety to it, and he might do something drastic." She glanced down the row of townhouses. "Let me go in and draw him out."

"No." He wanted her with him or away from this square entirely.

She sighed wearily. "It's like with Grendel. I had to lure her with a bit of cream. I'll see if I can draw him out of the house. Let me try." She licked her lips as if assessing the risk. "You and Collier will be close if anything goes awry."

"If I see you step into that house, I'm coming in after you."

"Good," she said in a breathy whisper. "If he's what you say he is, I don't relish being alone with that man."

Ben took up a spot behind a tree, approaching as if he were merely a gentleman on a midday stroll.

Collier watched him from several feet away.

Ben scanned the area and gestured for the constable to proceed up the street, out of view of the front windows of number eight.

Allie shot one glance back at him before stepping up and lifting the door knocker.

Minutes ticked by, then she tried again.

An elderly lady in a mobcap opened to her a moment later.

"Hello, miss."

"Hello, I'm here to see Lord Holcroft."

"Who?" The gray-haired lady sounded genuinely confused.

"Lord Thomas Holcroft. I have his card." Allie dug in her pocket and looked down at a crimson rectangle much like the one she'd brought to Ben. She stared down at the card in surprise, then rubbed her fingers together. "Does he not reside here?" she asked the woman.

"I've never heard that name in my life, and I've served the Denbys some fifteen years."

Ben heard a man's voice echo behind the woman but couldn't make out what he was saying.

"Oh, Lord Denby. This young lady is seeking a Lord Holcroft and believes he lives here."

The man strode forward, and the housekeeper receded.

"Is this some cruel joke?" He stuck his head out and scanned the square. "Who sent you?"

"Forgive me, Lord Denby. No joke is intended. I was given a card with this address on it by a man I believed to be Lord Holcroft."

"Well, he's never lived here, and he does not live anymore at all."

Allie glanced back toward Ben. "I beg your pardon, my lord. You knew him?"

"Barely. He was a child. A friend of my son's. They both died. A boating accident."

Allie dipped her head before looking up at the man again. "I'm very sorry, Lord Denby, and I hope you'll forgive the misunderstanding."

The man harrumphed and unceremoniously shut the door in her face.

Allie turned, descended the steps, and stood on the pavement looking bereft. Ben strode out of the park and drew her away from the Denby townhouse.

"What's going on?" she asked him. She didn't seem angry or even truly confused. She looked sad, and he yearned to comfort her.

"We're still in the game, Alexandra, and I don't

know all the answers. But I do know where to look next." He dared to reach for her hand and was glad she let him. "Go back to Princes with Collier. I need to know you're safe. It feels as if I'm close. This could be over tonight."

"I want to go with you."

"Out of the question."

She planted a hand on her hip. "If this is a chess game, then he's made me one of the players too. Sent a man into my shop, or perhaps disguised himself. All to trick me. To draw me here. He expected a delivery today. He knew I'd go to this address." Raising her hands in exasperation, she demanded, "What is his plan?"

"I do not know. All the more reason that I want your involvement to end now."

"I could be a lure."

Ben laughed because she confounded him. Drove him mad.

"You use cream to catch a cat. Cheese to draw a mouse." She was warming to her argument and her eyes began to sparkle. "And sometimes in chess, you dangle your queen to draw the opponent out."

"I'm not dangling you anywhere."

"Because I'm a woman."

Ben took her arms into his hands. His self-control was frayed by exhaustion and the effects of whiskey, and she would not hear him.

"Because I love you, Alexandra. And I cannot see any harm done to you."

Tears welled in her eyes, and he pulled her into

his arms. She tucked her cheek against his chest, and he didn't even care that the feather on her fancy little hat tickled his chin.

He didn't care about anything but keeping her safe.

"I love you too," she murmured. Then she tipped her head up. "That's why I'm coming with you."

HE'D LOST HIS MIND. It was really the only explanation. He'd lost his heart to her and now he'd lost his mind, as well.

As the carriage wheeled toward Bedford Square, she sat beside him, bristling with energy. Eagerness.

God help him.

He knew he was a fool for allowing this. Derelict in his duty too. Christ, he'd left the man he had personally selected to guard her behind and ordered Collier to make his own way to Bedford Square since a hansom couldn't contain all of them.

The only thing tethering him was the feel of her hand against his knee.

"There will be constables there already, though I've directed them to hold back. None of them will have approached the houses yet. Though I trust that they've surveilled them and determined exits."

Ben groaned at the memory of his last visit to Bedford Square. "He's fooled me with this gambit once before. I went in the back of the house while he was escaping out the front."

"You agree to my plan?"

"Frankly, love, I hate your plan." He wanted her away from all this madness. "But it may work," he conceded.

Turning to her, he reached up and cupped her cheek. "But if it does not work, you are to depart with one of the constables. Understood?"

She pressed her lips together, then nibbled her lower one.

"Alexandra. Do not ignore me this time. We try it your way, and then we try it mine." He reached up with his other hand, cradling her head. "Promise me."

"I promise."

It was the first time she'd ever agreed to do as he asked of her, and he hoped she intended to keep her word.

"Try that house first." Ben pointed to the vacant one he'd searched last month. Back when he'd thought it was M's only house in the square.

As directed, the carriage made a trip around the square and then stopped near the house in question.

Alexandra alighted and strode straight up to the front door.

Ben watched from the shadows of the carriage. While she tried knocking, he scanned the square and spotted a few of his constables. One walked the green at a leisurely pace. Another was tucked into a passage near M's side-by-side houses.

To his shock, someone opened the door to Alexandra.

Ben didn't recognize the man, but judging by the way he was dressed, he suspected it was one of Demming's men.

"Must 'ave the wrong 'ouse," the man grumbled.

His accent confirmed Ben's suspicions.

Alexandra turned and headed back out onto the pavement. She was careful not to look his way or to take note of any of the plainclothes men positioned around the square.

She strode toward the green and Ben expected her to approach and speak to him, but she veered off the other way instead.

He gritted his teeth.

An old man stood, cane in hand, waiting while his fluffy white dog sniffed at the grass.

"Excuse me, sir," Alexandra called to him. "I'm looking for Lord Holcroft's home and seem to have been given the wrong address."

The old man cupped a hand around his ear. "Beg pardon, lady?"

Alexandra stepped closer. Ben considered how long it would take him to sprint to where the two of them stood. Everyone seemed like a threat to him now. Even decrepit old men.

"Holcroft," she repeated.

The old man mumbled something that Ben couldn't hear, then lifted his cane to point at one of the houses he knew to be owned, at least on paper, by Lord Holcroft.

Alexandra nodded and then turned to make her way toward the townhouse on the other side of the square. She climbed two steps and knocked using a golden knocker in the center of the house's red door.

Ben began a walk around the square, intending to position himself closer. He shot a look at one of his men and gestured with his chin toward the house in question. Out of the corner of his eye, he saw another of his men head around into the mews behind the house.

A tall oak would provide perfect cover and keep him in good aiming distance. He made his way toward the tree and heard a door open.

Alexandra stood talking to someone, but on this side of the street with thick tree cover, he couldn't make out the person in the shadows.

He darted toward the trunk of the tree, and once he was concealed, he cast a glance around it to see if she'd succeeded in drawing someone out the front door, as had been their plan.

Panic clawed its way up his throat.

The red door had shut, and Alexandra was no-where to be seen.

CHAPTER TWENTY-ONE

I_T WASN'T_ until she was standing next to him that she knew the old man was familiar. At first, she had been drawn in, thinking he might be an unassuming resident of the square. It was the dog that had put her mind at ease.

And he'd kept up the facade well. Even feigned being hard of hearing to draw her closer.

Close enough that Ben and the others surrounding the square wouldn't hear their exchange.

He was the man who'd come into her shop— the talkative, amiable version of Holcroft.

"There are sharpshooters on high, positioned on four houses in the square," he'd whispered. "All pointed at your detective inspector."

Her body had threatened to betray her then. She'd frozen when she should have run. Lost her voice the one time she should have blurted something useful.

Now she was glad she hadn't.

However the elusive M had led Ben to believe this was where M could be found, the criminal mastermind had done it well. She and Ben were creatures in a fishbowl, and she believed the claim of sharpshooters was more than a boast. High ground was the best position from which to strike.

"Go and knock at number two and go inside." The man—actor, criminal, conspirator, whatever he was—smiled. "Go now, little bird. A cage has been prepared for you."

Allie did as she was bid because she could not bear to be the cause of harm to Ben.

They may be dreadful thieves, but she'd felt menace from the man who'd given her instructions. For one who feigned amiability well, he wore chilling coldness better.

The man inside the door was brawny and had gripped her arm so hard, her fingers began to go numb.

He'd led her through an elegantly appointed townhouse. Then he'd suddenly clapped his beefy hand over her eyes and shoved her into another room, then another, and finally released her.

Her prison was blue. A cool, muted blue box of a room with no wainscoting or friezes or gilding— none of the touches that one would usually find in a fine London townhouse.

She'd paced at first, searching the blank, un-adorned walls for any kind of opening. The door she'd been pushed through had no inner handle and blended with the wall almost seamlessly.

A bit later, she shed her coat and gloves and hat and considered removing her boots, since the heel of her boot was probably the closest thing to a hammer on her person. She could strike someone hard if necessary. Or chip away at these bloody walls if it came to that.

After a while, she slumped onto the polished wood floor. But she couldn't stay still for long and began pacing again.

"I picked this room for you because it matches your eyes. Don't you think?"

Allie spun toward the voice, but there was no else in the room.

Then she saw it. A grate painted over in the far wall. He was using some mechanism to transfer his voice through it.

"Why are you doing this?"

Laughter filled the room, high-pitched and without a hint of true mirth. "It amuses me. Is that not enough?"

"But you're not very good at any of it." Allie wondered if she'd regret her boldness, but for a man who didn't have the courage to show himself, she felt it was warranted. "You failed to steal the regalia and only stole back a diamond that is apparently your own."

"You forgot the blackmail, or didn't your lover tell you about that? I suppose the prince's sins are too much for your delicate ears."

"He didn't tell me. Did you fail at that too?"

"Failure matters not. I didn't need Bertie's blackmail payment or to place the stolen Imperial Crown on my head to succeed. I struck fear into his heart. Caused the old dragon on the throne a bit of embarrassment. That is success, Miss

Prince." The man's shout echoed in the room. "Chaos is its own reward, Miss Prince."

"Is it?" Perhaps if she could keep him talking, she could give Ben and the constables in the square time to unfold their own plan. And she was certain Ben had one.

"To those who feel safe, pompous, and untouchable in their wealth and power, nothing is as dangerous as chaos. My family was disgraced and stripped of its power. Should the queen and her offspring not at least feel a bit of fear?"

"You hate them."

The only reply was snide laughter. "Hate is too simple. It is a complicated loathing."

Allie heard the faint echo of other men's voices beyond the walls of the room.

"Loathing doesn't seem very rewarding if you never achieve your ends."

From the grate, she heard rustling and then a long, irritated sigh. "But I have achieved every end I wished for. I thought you clever, but it seems I was mistaken. And I might say the same for your detective."

"Then why not leave us alone and find someone clever to torment?"

Laughter came again, booming around the room. So loud Allie reached up to cover her ears.

All she could think about was Ben. She knew he'd try to get into the house, that he wouldn't stop until he got to her, but she feared what he might face. Beyond the behemoth at the door, she suspected there were more men guarding this madman.

She lifted her hands from her ears. The laughter had stopped, but she could hear the spine-chilling sound of breathing through the grate.

What did he have planned for them that would evoke such maniacal laughter?

Walking toward the wall furthest from the grate, she slid down to the floor, her legs splayed in front of her. She should have taken Ben's revolver. Or kept a knife in her boot. Eve probably kept a knife in her boot. Dom surely did.

Tipping her head back against the wall, she closed her eyes.

Shouting beyond the wall caused her to flick her eyes open again. She turned, pressing her ear to the wall, and her heartbeat rioted.

Ben's voice. He was shouting, and then she heard the thud of footsteps and the crash of furniture.

She closed her eyes again, feigning fatigue, and listened intently.

A sound came that she hadn't heard in years, and tears welled in her eyes. Someone had fired a gun, and soon after a chorus of shouting ensued. Maddeningly, she could not make out anything clearly. It was as if the walls were stuffed with cotton wool.

She glared at the grate in the wall, unsure whether the madman could see her or only speak to her through some mechanism, the way some servants' quarters in the wealthiest households had speaking tubes connected to their masters' suites.

If any harm came to Ben, she'd claw through the wall to get the cowardly phantom of a man.

NOT ONLY WAS THE pain sharp, but it was hot too. As if all the blood in his body had rushed to the spot.

The bullet caught his arm near his bicep. But he still had use of it, and his fingers worked fine too. As soon as he'd gotten out of his overcoat and suit jacket, it became clear that the bullet had grazed him.

His own bullet had done much worse.

They'd fired almost simultaneously, and M's man went down with a resounding thud. Once Ben had kicked the man's pistol away, he'd been unable to rouse him.

Though he had no time for it now, guilt sat waiting on his shoulders for him. He hadn't meant to take a life, only to capture one man.

His constables had three other men in shackles, but they insisted the man Ben shot was the one who'd taken Alexandra to one of the rooms. He'd been questioning and threatening them for the last ten minutes while trying to staunch his blood with a bit of torn shirt from his other arm.

"Try the blue room," one finally mumbled.

"Where's that?"

"Hidden inside that room." He stared across from Ben at what looked to be a ballroom.

Ben strode inside and realized that the room

was an illusion. Mirrors lined the walls to make it seem larger, but it was truncated, and there was a door between two mirrors. So flat and unadorned that it blended into the rest of the wall. But a gold latch glinted and caught his eye.

Twisting it, he pushed in and thanked Christ he'd found her.

She shot to her feet, looking scared and confused, and she ran into his arms.

Ben caught her with his uninjured arm and pulled her out of the room.

"Wait," she said, sliding her hands down his arms.

When he winced, she pulled back, and her eyes shot wide when she spotted the blood.

"It's nothing," he told her. "A scratch."

"Did he shoot you?"

When she started to turn back to the room, Ben wrapped a hand around her wrist to stop her.

"No," she whispered. "Look." She pointed high on the far wall, but he saw nothing.

"Tip your head. You'll see a painted grate." She turned back to face him. "He spoke to me through it," she whispered. "He's back there, beyond that wall."

Ben led her out and slid the door almost shut behind him.

He gestured to one of his men guarding the three they'd shackled.

"Come with me out back and you'll take position behind the house to the right of this one. Send Wainwright and anyone he wants to take post out front," he told his man quietly. "He's in that house, and I'm going to flush him out."

Alexandra moved past Ben.

"Where are you going?"

"He will have heard all of this," she shout-whispered. "He'll already have fled."

"No carriage will have left this square, nor the mews behind, without us hearing," Constable Eddings told her.

"Then he's on foot." She pulled away from him, lifted her skirt, and broke into a run toward the front door.

"There," she shouted, pointing to a tall man in a long dark coat with a black beard and dark glasses.

Ben lifted his revolver from his pocket and approached the man, who was walking as if he was on an afternoon stroll. "Stop. Police."

The man jerked to a stop and whirled toward him with a smile. "Good afternoon, Inspector."

Allie placed a hand on his uninjured arm and whispered, "I don't think it's M. It's not the one who got me into the house."

"How do you know?" Ben asked her, never taking his eyes from the man.

"Because this is the man I overheard at Hawlston's and saw in the alley."

The tall man nodded at her, as if acknowledging her claim, but said nothing.

"I'm still taking him in." Ben lifted a pair of shackles from his other pocket.

Allie took them and attached them to the man's outstretched wrists.

M's confederate was being far too bloody accommodating.

Soon, Ben saw why. A man emerged from one of the other M properties wearing the same disguise. Then another in the same disguise, though far shorter, strode out of a house he didn't know had any connection to M at all.

Collier, who had apparently made his way to Bedford Square after all, approached one of the men. That one wasn't nearly as accommodating and put up a boisterous resistance to Collier's questioning. Another constable apprehended one of M's other disguised men.

"Always a bloody game."

"I'll speak to them all." Alexandra seemed shockingly unfazed by the madness. "I'll know his voice."

"Collect all three of them," Ben shouted, his voice echoing off the buildings in the squares. "I still need to search that house," he told her. "Stay with Collier or one of the other men. Never go off alone."

"You mean like you are right now."

He bent to kiss her cheek, and then left her. He had to. He had to find M and put an end to his games.

As he climbed the two stairs toward the townhouse's facade, it reminded him too much of his first time in Bedford Square. The afternoon was waning toward dusk, but there were no lights on in any of the windows. No curtains on most of them either.

He feared it was another shell of a house. Another blind alley. Another trick.

Then he caught a flash of movement out of the corner of his eye. An old man emerged from a house two doors down. Not one of the M properties. He wore a dark wool coat with a bright white fur collar. Enormous gold-rimmed glasses obscured his eyes.

"Too much hubbub in this square if you ask me," he said in an affronted aristocratic voice. "What are you all gadding about for?" He waved his cane. "Shouting and rushing and carrying on."

"We're seeking a criminal, sir."

The man grumbled and harrumphed and then hobbled down his steps, leaning heavily on his cane. At the pavement, he turned toward Ben.

"I do hope you find him."

Ben twisted the latch on the townhouse door, prepared to force it, but it gave way.

A madman criminal in an unlocked townhouse.

And that was the moment he knew. He cast a gaze at the old man hobbling unsteadily down the pavement. And his gut told him he'd just been taken for a fool again.

Ben approached the old man quickly but managed to keep himself from breaking into a run.

Not for the first time, he wished he could move with more stealth, that his boots hit the pavement more quietly. But if the old man was M, he'd not yet given up his ruse. He hobbled slowly, steadily down the pavement.

"Hold there, old man." He lifted his revolver and pulled back the hammer. "I'd like to speak to you. Don't you think it's about time we met face-to-face?"

Ben heard a click, and then the hunched old man rose to his full height and spun to face him. He held the walking stick at the height of Ben's chest, and there was no mistaking the hollow barrel of the cane, nor the little trigger that M had slipped his index finger around.

Ben had heard of cane guns, but he'd never been at the wrong end of one.

"There's only one bullet," M said. "But you're ever so close. I can't miss, can I?"

Ben held his revolver steady. "This square is crawling with Met policemen. You won't get far."

"Farther than you, Inspector." His voice had flattened to a singsong tone. Not unlike a petulant child. "Shall we step back a few paces?" he said in mock seriousness. "Do it like an old-fashioned duel?"

The sky was darkening as they spoke, but in his periphery, Ben noticed movement in the green. He prayed it was one of his men, or preferably several, maneuvering to create a cordon around M.

"Yes," Ben told him, "let's do it like a duel."

The madman smiled underneath his bushy mustache and stepped backward, his cane-pistol still trained on Ben. Ben took one step back, and the movement in his periphery shot forward.

A moment later, an object sailed through the air toward them. Toward M. The mastermind caught sight of it late and swung wildly with his cane in an attempt to deflect it.

Ben rushed him, pushing the cane from his hand and using the full force of his body to tumble the smaller man to the ground.

M let out a high-pitched scream, then he squirmed and squealed, kicking and flailing like an animal caught in a trap.

Alexandra rushed up a moment later, her gait uneven. Then she bent and picked up the object that had thwacked M's head before Ben tackled him.

It was her boot.

She smiled and winked at Ben when he looked up at her.

"Constable," she shouted, "we need your shackles."

To his shock, M's arms slackened and he stopped kicking. Ben braced his hands on the ground and lifted some of his weight off the man, thinking perhaps he'd lost consciousness.

But then he saw M's chest heave as he began weeping.

Ben tugged at the mustache and beard, which both peeled off readily. Then he plucked the glasses away and stared in shock.

He was young. Not much older than twenty.

Ben stared up at Alexandra. "I'm not sure it's him."

"Stand him up," she told him.

Ben heaved the weeping young man to his feet and turned him so that the constable who'd approached could clap him in shackles.

Alexandra drew closer. Too close for Ben's comfort.

"Keep your distance."

"I'm not frightened of him, but I do have a question." She looked up at the young man, who stood several heads above her. "Do you still think chaos is its own reward?"

The young man sniffed, straightened up tall, squared his fur-covered shoulders, and looked down at her with a smirk. Not a tear in sight. "I struck fear in their hearts, Miss Prince, and that pleases me. And I did enjoy meddling with you and your detective."

Sickening laughter burst out of him.

"It's him," Alexandra said decisively before turning back to face Ben. "Do you still have doubts that he's your M?"

"Soon the world will know my name," the man whispered as if to himself.

Ben felt disgust for the young man, but now a bit of pity too. There was madness in his eyes, a wild sort of instability he'd rarely seen in even the cruelest criminals. It chilled his blood that one so young could be so lost to his own hateful machinations.

"Get a wagon to carry them all back to the Yard," he told the constable, who still stood awaiting orders.

"Already here, Duke." The man nudged his

chin toward M. "Just waiting to add him to the lot."

"Once he's there, I want double watch on him."

"He knows I'm a slippery one," M said in a grating singsong voice as the constable led him away.

Ben turned to Alexandra and shook his head in wonder. "Saved by a boot."

She laughed, and he did too.

"Technically, I didn't save you."

"I beg to differ. Take it from the man who had a pistol pointed at his heart."

"It's just a cane, isn't it?" She walked over, bent, and retrieved it. When she examined it further, she gasped. "How clever it is."

"Not as clever as a boot as deterrent."

She smiled proudly. "It was awfully good timing on my part."

"Undeniably so." Ben reached for her hand.

She clasped his eagerly, and something flickered to life in his chest.

"Deserves a write-up in the London newspapers, if you ask me. The *Illustrated Police News*, perhaps."

"Don't tease me." She squeezed his hand.

Ben wanted to kiss her. He'd never wanted anything more. But the night wasn't over yet.

"There will be a great deal to do over the next few days."

"I understand." She watched as the police wagon pulled out of the square and headed toward Scotland Yard. "Will you come and see me when it's all done? If only to visit?"

"I will. I promise I will." Hope kindled inside him. Just an ember, but he wanted to stoke it.

"That's enough, then," she said with quiet resolve.

But Ben still believed she deserved so much more.

CHAPTER TWENTY-TWO

One week later

THE FOURTH Saturday of the month dawned bright, with blue skies and just the right nip of autumn chill in the air. Trees still held on to some color, but gold and red and orange decorated the ground too and crunched delightfully under the wheels of Allie's bicycle as she rode to Hyde Park.

In her wicker basket, she carried a flannel-covered jug of Hawlston's coffee, and she knew Jo would have come in the family carriage with her bicycle lashed to the back so that she could bring a picnic basket full of warm hand pies and a jug of tea for those who preferred it.

Jo waved in welcome as she rode up, and most of the rest of their bicycle club was already present. Most had leaned their bicycles against trees while they sipped steaming cups of tea.

"Thank goodness," Agnes Russell called. "She's finally here with the coffee."

"We are pleased to see you too, Allie. Coffee or no coffee," Marion Russell retorted. She was ever the sweet counterpart to her rather acerbic cousin.

Though Allie enjoyed both ladies because they were both passionate about bicycling.

October was sometimes their last group ride of the season, since the weather could take a turn by the end of November, so all of them were in high spirits with such fair weather for a day out of doors.

"We still need to have our meeting about the charity dinner," Jo said when she approached to hand Allie a cup from those she'd brought.

"We do. Our first try got a bit . . . derailed."

Jo leaned in. "Never mind about that. We have time."

Allie didn't like thinking about that day because the feelings all rushed back. Jo seemed to understand that and did her best to avoid the topic or any mention of Benedict Drake.

Once everyone had a refill of tea or a fresh cup of coffee, Agnes offered up their usual toast.

"To sisterhood, to mobility, to independence."

Everyone raised their drink to their club's motto.

Together, the group of seven ladies laughed and chatted and caught up as they hadn't done since their last meeting in September. Once the jugs of warm refreshment were empty, the Wellingdons' footman collected all the cups, and everyone began bundling up to prepare for their ride.

From Hyde Park, they usually wound down toward the Natural History Museum and around Chelsea, then up through Kensington and back into the park. Occasionally, they went east toward Mayfair and would also pass by Princes if the area wasn't too crowded with shoppers.

"I think we'll take our southerly route today," Jo announced. "Oh goodness. Shelton, I almost forgot the books."

The footman hadn't forgotten, apparently; he stood nearby with a box teeming with the American bicycling book she'd shown to Allie.

"Before we head off, I'd like to gift each of you a copy of this book I thought perhaps we could read as a group over the winter months."

"Always trying to turn us into a book club, Lady Jo," Agnes put in archly.

"You've found me out, Agnes." Jo winked at her. "I'm a wily book club mastermind."

After the books had been distributed, each lady took a moment to flip through theirs. Then most placed it in the basket or saddle bags attached to their bicycle.

Allie noticed that a couple of ladies had drawn together in gossipy whispers, and they kept darting looks toward the park entrance nearest the Albert Memorial.

She turned back to get a look at what had so caught their interest, and her heart did a little jig inside her chest.

Benedict Drake strode toward them with a bunch of flowers—dark, velvet-petaled violets—in his hand.

She blinked, not quite believing the evidence of her eyes.

He wore no hat, no gloves, but he looked remarkably dashing in an ink-black suit, a wind-swept overcoat, and an emerald-green waistcoat.

She hadn't heard from him in days. Not even a note. And she'd seen nothing in the papers about the arrest of the man he'd called M or the resolution of the case that had consumed so much of his energy.

When tidying at home, she'd discovered something about the calling card Holcroft had given her. Lottie had come to her distraught. While brushing Allie's overcoat clean, she'd discovered a stain in the satin lining of her pocket.

A crimson stain.

It had come off the calling card, and when Allie had fully washed it away, it revealed a name. Mortimer Denby. Those bits of paper—the M and the D and clock to indicate *time*—finally made sense. She'd sent a note to Ben immediately, and it had been two days with no word.

Her hopeful heart still told her that now that the case was over, they could be together. But he hadn't come. She'd begun to give up on the idea that he would.

So to see him now, striding toward them in a magnificent display of masculine appeal, made her a little giddy.

"Oh bother, who is that?" Agnes groused. "Does he know this is a ladies-only bicycle club?"

"I don't think we can prevent men from walking through Hyde Park entirely, Agnes." Marion shot her cousin an amused look.

"He's not here for us," Jo said softly.

Jo was right, of course. His gaze was entirely fixed on Allie.

As he drew closer, she felt as if she might leap out of her skin. Anticipation and yearning and hope filled her so quickly that she felt a bit dizzy.

"I'm sorry I didn't reply to your note, but thank you for it," he said as soon as he was close. He stopped a few steps away from her, giving her room to come to him. "I'd gotten his name out of him. The son of that poor man in Grosvenor Square, who thought he'd died five years ago."

"You have enough to keep him from hurting anyone else?"

"I do. But I thought telling you in a note wouldn't suffice. Besides, I have more to say and wanted to come in person."

"Does he not see that we are conducting a meeting?" Agnes said in a not-at-all-quiet tone.

For the first time, Ben skimmed his gaze over the gathering. "I ask your patience and forgiveness, ladies. I need to speak to Miss Prince."

"Is it important?" Agnes asked with rude frankness.

"Quite important."

She emitted a long, weary sigh. "Very well, then."

Allie couldn't help but chuckle. "It's not you," she whispered to him. "She's like that with everyone."

"It's all right," he told her with a smile. "I won't be deterred today."

He looked down as if just recalling he clutched a bundle of violets. "These are for you."

"I'd hoped." Allie took them, drew in their rich scent, and smiled. "But what is the occasion?"

He swallowed hard, his gaze fixed on hers. "First, an apology. I was . . ." He bent his head, then lifted it, his eyes bright. "Wrong. And I'm sorry. I gave in to fear. I let it rule me. Even my hunger for advancement was driven by fear. Of not measuring up. Not making up for what happened to George."

Allie's eyes welled with tears, but she refused to let them fall until he'd finished.

"But even in that wrongness," he said more quietly, "I knew the truth. That you mattered most. That meeting you was the most important moment of my life."

"Oh, Ben—"

"There's more," he said with a delicious grin that made her heart thud against her ribs. "I like how you changed me. I like all the ways you defied me and were honest and impulsive and turned my single-minded world upside down."

He reached into the upper pocket of his overcoat and hesitated. One brow winged up, and he glanced over her head at the assembled ladies.

Silently, he was asking her permission to make a scene.

Allie smiled in reply.

With two fingers, he dug deeper and soon emerged with a small, perfect box.

"Alexandra Prince, I would like to request a lifetime's worth of you turning my life upside down." He took a step closer, crunching across fallen leaves.

Then he lowered himself to one knee and opened the box. "Will you marry me?"

Inside sat a lovely gold ring with a single round diamond surrounded by polished green stones.

"Are those what I think they are?"

"You said green amber is rare, but Mr. Gibson managed to find a stone to cut into all the tiny ones."

"So you two have been conspiring."

He chuckled. "A bit."

"What's your answer, Miss Prince?" Agnes barked. "We're a quarter of an hour late al—"

"Hush," several of the ladies crowed in unison.

"Take your time, Allie," Jo offered in a kind, soft voice.

"Marriage is a trap for women," Agnes grumbled, "so she should take all the time she needs."

"Agnes!" Marion Russell hissed. "Really?"

Allie kept her eyes on Ben while the ladies murmured behind her.

"It won't be a prison," he said quietly. "I know you value your independence, and I won't take it from you."

"I'll keep running the shop."

"Of course you will."

"And you'll stay on at Scotland Yard?" Allie couldn't forget that he'd used the job as a rationale for putting his feelings for her aside.

"I'm considering my options." There wasn't an ounce of regret in his tone. In fact, he sounded downright hopeful. "Private inquiry agent might suit me better."

"Maybe it would." She didn't like much of what she'd heard of Sir Felix Haverstock or his hold over Ben.

"So will you, Alexandra?"

"Yes."

He stood and pulled her into an embrace, pulled her right off her feet, and she didn't mind a bit.

"With all my heart, yes," she whispered against his neck.

"With all my heart too," he murmured in her ear.

TWO DAYS LATER, AN hour before Allie and Mr. Gibson were preparing to close up for the day, a coach pulled up to the curb in front of the shop.

Dom and Eve had sent a telegram the day before, but Allie wasn't certain when to expect them.

It took several minutes for the coachmen to take down all of their luggage, and Allie came out to offer to help carry the pile in.

Eve embraced her immediately. "It's so good to see you."

Allie smiled and gave her sister a squeeze. "You too."

"You'll be glad you didn't come on this one. Every single thing that could go wrong did, at least in terms of our travel arrangements."

"Not *everything* went wrong," Dom announced as he approached with a polished wooden box that he carried as gently as if he was balancing an infant in his arms. "We found this." He lifted it out to Allie. "Will you carry it in while we get the bags?" He pointed as soon as he'd handed the box off. "And be careful."

"Of course." She imagined what treasure might be nestled inside as she brought it back into the shop and set it gently on the counter.

They always brought the scent of fresh air and trampled grass and freshly turned earth with them when they came back from an expedition, or so it seemed to Allie.

And this time, they both seemed brimming with eagerness to show her what they found.

Dom shucked his coat, casually draping it over one of a pair of eighteenth-century chairs. Eve was still unraveling her scarf when she shot him an exasperated look.

"Well, come on and show her."

He strode to the counter dramatically, and then stepped behind it.

With his usual flair for the theatrical, he flicked the metal clasp on the box and lifted its lid open inch by inch.

Allie stepped closer to peer inside.

A beautiful strip of stamped gold, not much longer than the length of her index finger, glinted in the gaslights' glow.

Indeed, its shine seemed to make the whole box glow as if it was indeed some hallowed object.

"Do you recognize that styling?" Eve prompted.

"Anglo-Saxon?"

She beamed with pride. "Anglo-Saxon indeed. Not the Viking hoard Dom expected."

Dom doffed an invisible hat at Eve. "This is

your find, and I've already acknowledged it a half dozen times."

"Yes, but I wanted you to do it in front of Allie for good measure."

They both laughed.

"And there's more. So much more," Eve enthused. "We're going to assemble a full crew and return for a complete excavation. This is a ship's burial and the things we've already found, Allie, you can't imagine."

"I'm going to write to Van Arsdale and get you on the crew, Allie," Dom vowed.

Allie looked at each of them in turn, happy for them but without an ounce of eagerness to leave London, or the shop, or her fiancé.

"Actually, I'm content here," she told them. "I don't want to join the crew."

Dom blinked in disbelief. Eve tipped her head in confusion.

"If you're certain," Eve said slowly. "Whatever you prefer, of course."

"I prefer to manage the shop."

Dom shrugged. "Well, that's settled, then." He yawned and ran a hand through his hair. "God, I'm exhausted. And starving."

"Well, I should imagine you are." Mr. Gibson was dressed for departing, but Allie knew he'd overheard her siblings' arrival and would come up to greet them first.

"Gibson," Dom said with true warmth, "aren't you a sight for sore eyes." He walked over and shook Mr. Gibson's hand vigorously.

"Thank you," Eve said, "both of you, for watching over the shop."

Allie exchanged a glance with Mr. Gibson.

"Did anything happen while we were away?" Dom asked with mild interest. He scanned his gaze around the shop. "Everything looks much the same, so I'm assuming it was business as usual."

Allie pressed her lips together and Mr. Gibson's bushy gray brows danced on his forehead.

"There are a few things to report," Allie told them as evenly as she could manage.

"Oh?" Eve looked intrigued.

"To start, we have a new and much-improved safe."

Eve and Dom exchanged a look.

"Why?" Dom asked, his brows dipping now. "That must have been quite an expense."

"Luckily, we keep up our insurance payments and Lloyd's of London covered the replacement due to theft."

"What?" Eve gasped.

"Theft of what?" Dom asked, already striding toward the back room.

"That is a rather complicated story," Mr. Gibson told him. "But do let me show you the new safe."

"I want to see too," Eve said, and then followed them both to Mr. Gibson's workroom.

Allie waited in the front, planting herself near the windows and looking out for any sign of Ben. Each time a hansom slowed, she expected him to dash out.

Finally, one pulled right into the spot that Eve and Dom's coach had recently vacated, and he stepped down. He spotted her and gave her a wolfish smile.

A moment later, he was through the door and in her arms.

His greeting kisses were dizzying and delicious. This time he pulled her nearly off her toes, sweeping his tongue into her mouth to deepen the kiss.

When he turned with her, his boot heel caught the edge of one of Dom's bags.

Ben looked down and settled her gently onto her feet. "They're back."

"They are." Allie still kept hold of him, one hand on his chest, the other resting on his injured arm.

"And you're certain you want to spring this on them first thing?"

"We're happy and we should share it." She stroked her hand along the hard muscles of his arm. "They'll be happy for us too."

"Excuse me," Dom all but shouted from the back room. He was using his overprotective brother voice. "Who are you?"

Allie laughed as she turned to face her brother, and Dom looked at her as if she'd lost her wits.

"Dom, Eve, this is Detective Inspector Benedict Drake."

"For a little while longer," Ben whispered so only she could hear.

Allie glanced back at him, and he smiled. After they'd talked the matter through, and he'd pondered on his own, he'd decided to tender his notice to Scotland Yard and open his own detective agency.

Mr. Fitzroy was trying to lure him to his own agency, but Ben liked the idea of independence. And Allie couldn't have agreed more.

"Is he here about the theft?" Eve queried as she stepped out of the back with Mr. Gibson.

"He was here about the theft actually. And about a strange conversation I overheard at Hawlston's."

"And then to find you before you went to the house of a madman," Ben said quietly.

"Would someone like to tell me what the hell is going on?" Dom strode to the center of the room and glared at Ben.

"We had an adventurous couple of weeks," Allie told them with not a small amount of pleasure. "Then he asked me to marry him, and I said yes."

Ben drew closer and curled his hand around her waist.

Dom stood slack-jawed, darting his gaze from Allie to Ben and back again.

Eve stood with one hand over her mouth and then moved past Dom to give Allie a hug. She offered Ben a smile too.

"May I offer a pre-wedding welcome to the Prince family, Detective Inspector?" she said.

"Ben will do just fine." He reached out his hand to shake hers.

Dom's jaw was clenched and he was frozen in the contemplative mode that led either to acceptance or to him railing against fate.

Finally, some of the tension in his body eased and he approached to offer Ben his hand.

"This is highly irregular, but I welcome you too." Dom turned a disgruntled look Allie's way. "I take it we'll get further explanation at some point."

"Perhaps we can all go out to dinner, and we'll tell you the whole complicated story," Allie offered.

"We should," Eve agreed. "In fact, if Dom and I get washed and changed, we could try for this evening."

Dom murmured in agreement.

"Will you join us, Mr. Gibson?" Allie asked. "You're part of the family too."

"I'd be delighted."

Ben shifted from behind her and took up the spot Dom had vacated in the center of the room.

"Before anyone departs, I thought you'd all like to have a look at this." He dug in his pocket and pulled out a folded and neatly clipped rectangle of newspaper. "I'm assuming you haven't seen today's *Illustrated Police News*?"

Allie shook her head, disbelieving, and reached for the clipping.

Unfolding the paper carefully, she gulped and laughed at the same time.

"Is this real?"

"As you see. It's very real indeed."

The article featured sketches of her and Ben and a rather extreme caricature of Mortimer Denby. The title read *Lady Shop Owner Helps Nab Jewel Thief.*

Eve and Dom and Mr. Gibson crowded in for a look too.

Dom lifted his gaze to Allie's with a sort of awestruck pride. "It seems your days while we were gone weren't humdrum at all."

"Goodness," Eve said as she skimmed the article. "You hit him with your boot?"

"Saved by that bloody boot." Ben chuckled, and Allie pushed at his chest playfully. "We should pin this," he told her, "in the back."

"We most definitely should," Eve agreed. In fact, she took the page right out of Allie's fingers and marched straight back to do it.

"Thank you," Allie told Ben, turning to twine her arms around his neck. "For understanding how much that would mean to me."

"Thank you for marching into my office." He glanced up to see that Mr. Gibson and Dom were distracted and gave her a quick kiss. "And for saving me."

"With the boot," she teased.

"From my fear and stubborn foolishness. Here with you is exactly where I'm meant to be."

"And where you'll stay?"

"Always."

EPILOGUE

$\mathcal{A}$LLIE WOKE with a start, and it took her a moment to realize where she was.

Then she felt the soothing warmth of her husband's body against hers and smiled. Now she remembered. She'd settled onto his lap an hour ago after discovering that you can indeed make love in a carriage.

Ben stroked his fingers down her cheek and offered her a sleepy smile in return.

"Was it a good nap?" he asked, his voice deep and husky as if he'd nodded off for a bit too.

"It was," Allie told him as she shifted onto the carriage bench next to him. Every inch of her body that had been pressed against his was deliciously warm, and she was tempted to snuggle in closer and doze off again. "But we should arrive soon, if the weather holds, and I want to remember as much as I can."

Allie was determined to imprint this trip upon her mind and detail it as thoroughly as she could in writing. Though she didn't know if she'd ever print her travel journals—and she hoped there would be many more—she'd decided when they'd set off from London that she'd record her impressions the way her mother used to during her journeys with Father.

County Mayo was such a lush, vibrant green it took her breath away, and tonight they would be arriving in Newport, near Rockfleet Castle, purportedly the principal stronghold of lady pirate Grace O'Malley. Allie couldn't wait for her first sight of what remained of the fifteenth-century structure.

She noticed Ben had set aside his journal too.

"What were you writing?" She glanced down at the brown leather-bound volume. "Or sketching?"

He'd only revealed his sketches to her recently, claiming they weren't quite up to snuff. But they were, and Allie loved seeing what he found interesting enough to capture with his pencil. He'd explained that he came by whatever skill he possessed via his work as a detective, since he'd often sketch out what he saw at crime scenes. His style was loose but vivid, as he'd trained himself to capture his subject quickly.

"May I see?" she asked, reaching out to tap her fingers against the journal.

He scooped the volume up for her and flipped to the page he'd been working on.

Allie leaned in, expecting to see the Irish countryside—a thicket of trees, fluffy sheep, or even the windswept clouds. Instead, she found studies of her. Half a dozen profiles of her sleeping, but he'd managed to capture something unique in each of them. The way the light caught the slope of her cheek and cast the rest of her face in shadow. A slight smile on her lips as if she'd been dreaming of something pleasing. The pinched lines between her brows when a dream turned troubling. He noted her every freckle and beauty mark as if he was drawing a map.

Ben had captured her in much more detail than his usual drawings.

"How did you manage all this with me practically in your lap?" she asked in an awestruck whisper.

"I'm a very determined man." He winked and smiled, a full-bodied one that crinkled the skin by his eyes and made a dimple appear in his cheek.

The carriage began to climb what felt like a rather sizable hill and Allie clutched at Ben's lapel to keep herself steady. One discovery she'd made about travel was that hours of jostling in a carriage did not make her stomach very happy—especially now.

"I've got you," Ben reassured her, and wrapped his arm a bit more tightly around her.

"Perhaps our next journey should be on a boat," she told him with a chuckle.

He shot her a dubious glance. "Seasickness is quite unforgiving, or so I understand."

The prospect did not sound appealing.

"But at least we'd be on the sea with plenty of fresh air."

"I'm game if you are, wife." He pressed a kiss to her forehead and then let out a concerned hum.

"You are quite warm, love. If you're feeling unwell, we can ask the driver to stop for a bit."

She'd noticed that she ran hotter of late, especially when queasiness overcame her.

"I'm all right. We should arrive soon and then we can walk or rest or do whatever we please."

He used his free arm to reach for a flask of brewed tea that had long gone cold but that had proved oddly soothing to her stomach. She took a few sips and then drew in a few deep breaths. Which caused the oddest stitch in her middle.

Ben noticed her distress—he noticed everything where her needs and well-being were concerned.

"Tell me what's wrong."

Allie looked into his green eyes, so full of tenderness, love, and concern, and though it was not the moment she'd hoped for, she could not hold back anymore. She wanted to share everything with him. Always.

"I'm not ill, Ben."

He frowned and then let out a relieved sigh. "Well, thank God for that, love, but you seem ill at ease. Is it just the confines of the carriage?" He lifted her hand that still lay against his lapel and kissed her fingers. "Is it just being trapped in here with me for hours on end?"

Allie laughed and swept her fingers along his stubbled jaw. "Don't be silly. I love being with you anywhere we are, and you're so busy of late that it feels quite decadent to get you all to myself."

His private detection services were in high demand, and he relished the autonomy to handle cases on his own without the machinations of someone like Haverstock above him.

"Then what is it, Alexandra?" His voice held a note of concern that she immediately wanted to soothe.

Nibbling her lower lip, she clasped his hand and lowered it to her belly.

"I suppose it's not entirely accurate to say I have you all to myself," she told him, capturing his gaze to see if he'd read her meaning. "If one wishes to be thoroughly accurate."

He dropped his gaze to her stomach, then arched one brow, followed quickly by the other.

"Are you saying . . . ?" He swallowed hard and his brow furrowed even as his mouth began to curve in a smile. "A child?"

"Yes." Allie couldn't help beaming. She'd waited weeks to speak to Helen about her suspicions, and they'd only been confirmed two days before beginning their trip.

She'd planned to tell him over their first dinner on the west coast of Ireland, but now she wondered why she'd waited at all. The joy should be shared.

But the longer she smiled, she couldn't help but notice that Ben's had already begun to falter. A flutter of fear skittered through her.

"You are happy to hear the news, aren't you?"

He reached for her then, and Allie went into his arms. He buried his face against her neck and left a trail of kisses along her neck, behind her ear, against her hair.

"I am happy, love."

But Allie could hear the hitch in his voice. She arched back to meet his gaze.

"Then why do you sound so worried, Ben?"

Rather than answer, he cast his gaze out the window a moment, his brow still furrowed.

In the six months since their marriage, Allie had come to realize that he was a pensive man at times. His brand of cleverness required time to mull, assemble clues and sometimes his thoughts, before he was ready to explain an idea or a conclusion he'd come to.

Allie strove for patience in those moments, and even now when she so desperately wished to know what he felt about the news that their family of two would soon grow.

"I never knew my father," he finally said, turning a pained look her way. "And the men who took up with my mother never came close to earning the title."

Everything in her yearned to rush in with reassurances, but she could see that there was more he wished to say. She squeezed his hand but said nothing as she waited.

"What if I don't know how to be a good father?"

"You do," Allie told him with utter certainty. "You know how to love, to protect, to guide. You have loved and supported me, believed in me, as no one in my life ever has. Do the same for our child and they will flourish." She kissed his cheek, nuzzled the soft stubble along his jaw.

Ben turned his head and captured her lips in a

gentle kiss. "You will be a magnificent mother, Alexandra."

She laid a hand across her belly again. "It feels fitting that they're coming with us on our first journey." A lump welled up in her throat and she swallowed it down. "I never want our child to feel as if they've been left behind."

"We'll take them with us on our travels whenever we can," Ben assured her.

"They'll know they're accepted by us and encouraged no matter what endeavor they wish to pursue."

Ben let out a grumble of protest. "If they wish to pursue a life of crime, my encouragement may have its limits."

Laughter burst from Allie and she pushed playfully at her husband's chest. Then she stilled, realizing he may have meant the quip quite seriously. Perhaps he was thinking of his brother and how he had fallen in with a dangerous lot.

Ben ducked his head to catch her gaze. "Sweetheart, I do not truly fear our child will have criminal inclinations."

"Nor do I." Now it was Allie's turn to fall into pensive musings. "When I think of our future and our child, my only thought is that we'll love each other through all of it. The joy and the challenges."

Ben didn't answer in words. He bent his head and kissed her, a tender yet dizzying exploration that made Allie breathless. Then he bent to touch his forehead to hers.

"I am a better man for finding you, and that is how I know all will be well for our child. When we're together, everything feels right. I love you."

"I love you." It did feel right. From the moment she'd walked into his office, she'd felt a draw, an undeniable spark. And now she felt a sense of belonging she'd begun to doubt she'd ever feel.

The carriage swung and dipped and then began to slow. They both looked out the window to watch their approach toward the village where they'd spend the night.

She'd made it all the way to Ireland, finally, but what felt even better was being in her husband's arms and going on this journey—and that they'd take all future journeys—together.

ACKNOWLEDGMENTS

THANK YOU to my editor, Allie, for your patience and feedback on a book that has gone through a longer process than I ever expected it to. Your guidance helped me so much. And thanks to Jill, my agent, who always responds swiftly and is willing to step in to help. I'm lucky to have worked with both of you on this one.

Discover more swoon-worthy books from Christy Carlyle and Avon Books

Love on Holiday

The Duke's Den

Romancing the Rules

Accidental Heirs

DISCOVER GREAT AUTHORS, EXCLUSIVE OFFERS, AND MORE AT HC.COM